KATIE EVERSON wanted to be an acrobat, but that's not what happened. She grew up in Milton Keynes and has lived in London and Sydney, but is now back where it all began, the pull of home tugging her full circle. After side-lining acrobatics, she became a bookseller and realized all she wanted to do was make books. When characters began to talk among themselves in her head, she knew it was time to put finger to keyboard and write.

When Katie is not writing or being a professional design nerd in the publishing industry, she can be found enjoying big ol' family dinners with her parents, four older siblings and a multitude of nieces and nephews.

Follow Katie on Twitter **@ksleverson** and visit her at **www.katieeverson.co.uk**

DROP

KATIE EVERSON

This is a work of fiction. Names, characters, places and incidents are either the product of the author's imagination or, if real, used fictitiously. All statements, activities, stunts, descriptions, information and material of any other kind contained herein are included for entertainment purposes only and should not be relied on for accuracy or replicated, as they may result in injury.

First published in Great Britain 2015 by Walker Books Ltd
87 Vauxhall Walk, London SE11 5HJ

2 4 6 8 10 9 7 5 3 1

This book has been typeset in Bembo

Printed and bound in Great Britain by Clays Ltd, St Ives plc

British Library Cataloguing in Publication Data:
a catalogue record for this book is available from the British Library

ISBN 978-1-4063-5627-4

www.walker.co.uk

For Juliet

PROLOGUE

I've got no soul. I had one once but, like losing your virginity, losing your soul is easy to do. *Oops!* There it goes. Like misplacing your keys. An annoying but unremarkable event. I remember the moment, the smell of sweat. I can picture the cubicle door with its lipstick graffiti hearts and eyeliner drawings. I can feel my bare legs sticking to the stained floor, tacky from spilled beer and *godknowswhat.*

Losing your soul is easy to do. One too many vodkas. One too many pills.

Or maybe it happens over a series of moments. A bad choice. A dream. A kiss.

Like getting laid for the first time, it's never how you picture it.

PART 1

CHAPTER 1

Right now I'm having a schiz-out. I feel like a giant slice of death that's been reheated in the microwave. It's OK. I'm used to it. But, fuck, I miss feeling human. How did it get this way? When did it start? Christ, I don't even know. How's it going to end?

I'm so cold all the time. I find comfort in hidden places. The places no one knows I go. Like when brushing my teeth rhythmically. Balancing on the long side of the bath. Counting. One, two, brush, step. *Stalk the knife-edge.* It's no more than a sole's width. With perfectly pointed toes and stretched calves, my left leg extended in front, absolutely no arch, I tap the surface lightly with my big toe. A slow-motion can-can dentistry dance. Turn, walk, tap for four minutes exactly. Repeat as necessary. I own the bath, brush, beam. In that moment, I feel a little warmer.

I smoke. That helps. Speeding up death makes me feel more alive. Good health is just the slowest way to die. Smoke heats my lungs up. Makes me notice them. I think of my lungs as great oak trees and cigarettes as the obnoxious kid with a stick, flailing wildly in the branches, sending birds shooting out in every direction. *Hmmm-haaaa*, breathe in, breathe out. Dying feels good.

I like it when the delicate particles of dead ember reject the ashtray and go fluttering, flying up like tiny ghosts of dead butterflies. Beautiful. Yeah, I like to provoke my lungs, get them to fight back. People work the same way. BOOM! Like a firecracker, you can set people off so easily.

Oh yes. And a bit of white powder, a couple of pills, whatever. I do that now and then.

CHAPTER 2

I wasn't always like this. I know what you're thinking: druggie, junkie, wreckhead, trashbag. But I'm not sticking needles in my arm or sleeping on the streets, or stealing to feed the habit. I'm not one of *those*. I'm just a normal sort of girl really, a bit shy, a bit sad, and there are little things that make me feel better for a while.

A year ago I moved to London with my dad. My mum came too, but you wouldn't know it. She's never at home. In fact, she's the whole reason we moved here. Her career, her promotion, her success, *her* life. I'd say I'm the least successful of her projects. Everything she does is a project to be managed, and evaluated. Ask her, "On a scale of one to ten, how satisfied are you with your daughter?" and she'll say "one – not very," I'm sure. But hey, she gets *nul points* from me for parenting skills. OK, maybe that's harsh but I just wish she'd chill out. And if she did maybe she would be around more.

I've moved house loads of times before, but this is different. This new place will become old, will become home.

Mum isn't chasing any more; she caught the butterfly. This is it, her dream job. The man-hours, late nights in the office paid off; the payrise and title are hers: Science Correspondent for London's biggest newspaper. Sometimes she even gets on the news. It sounds kind of flash, but I piece together my idea of Mum's lifestyle from the news and what I overhear when she gets home, usually around one a.m. She writes some seriously weird shit. "Evidence for dark matter in high-energy gamma rays", "Is graphene really a wonder-material?", "Trees over 100 metres tall cannot grow leaves", "Swiss cheese plants experience stress". She's up and out the door again by seven a.m. Kisses her coffee cup goodbye more than me or Dad in the mornings. So it's like *Happy Days* around my house. Absentee mum: check. No Weetabix: check. Happy-fucking-days.

Moving day is a rare day off for Mum. Day off from work, that is, not from being an uptight cow.

"Carla! What *are* you doing? Can you please show some initiative and put the boxes marked 'office' in the *office*?"

"There's no room in the *office*."

"Then make room," she snarls. *Ugh*.

I start to unpack colour-coded lever-arch files rammed with papers. PRESS RELEASES, STRATEGIES, JOURNALS, ATLAS, CERN, ENVIRONMENT, PHYSICS. So dull. ENVIRONMENT decides to tsunami over the desk.

Mum shakes her head. Exhales. Sighs.

I prickle, but silently slide the papers back into place.

She gets the bulgy fire eyes. "Not there! That goes in the filing cabinet," she huffs, pulling a yellow file labelled

DEVELOPMENT from my hands, clenching her teeth so her cheekbones protrude and her temples contract.

"Oh … OK, sorry, I didn't know." It feels like she's always angry. She finally has what she's always wanted, but it's still not enough. Even in high-flying careerville, her paradise island, she still carries her suitcase of misery.

Mum puts down a pile of books. "Sorry, Carla. I don't mean to take it out on you. Moving house, new job. It's all a bit stressful."

Dad appears in the doorway. "Tea, girls?"

"If you put '*G* and' in front of it. Can you put a wedge of lime in, and put the glass in the freezer for ten minutes first? I hate a warm glass," Mum says. "Please, love? Thanks." Her iPhone dings. Dad is tall and stately, with small, round, bluish-grey eyes resting on high, plump cheeks, pearls in an oyster. Kind eyes. His eyebrows momentarily arch and he resembles a scared owl. But it's OK; the scared-owl look is Dad's general expression for discontent, upset, frustration … even for the times he finds his own lame jokes amusing.

Mum hangs up her call.

"Kate, love, I haven't got to the kitchen boxes yet," Dad says. "Just got tea bags in my pocket. Caffeine contingency."

He's a practical man.

"Rob, I need a proper drink. Could you please just do this one thing for me? I'm exhausted."

"Sorry, love. The gin is under an avalanche of crap and I'm not digging for it." His eyebrows peak mid-forehead.

"I'll get it myself." She launches through the office door, towards the kitchen. I hear the shuffle of boxes, a clatter of china, the screech of packing tape, then the clink of glass against glass. She returns to the doorway, the bottle of Gordon's a green glass pendulum swinging from her right hand, her face brick-red with stress. She throws a glance at Dad as if to say, "There, was that so hard?" Dad looks blank, avoiding the conflict. She returns to the kitchen. Dad's so calm. Aside from those gravity-defying eyebrows, that is. He can be stern, and I'm sure he gets angry, but he has compromise down to a *T*, including letting Mum get on with *it*. *It* being her irrational outbursts and general anger-management issues. Maybe he thinks that sparing me a prolonged parental argument is for the best. Five-minute huff? Hour-long shouting match? Weigh it up. Mostly he's a calming influence on Mum.

He follows her to the kitchen. "Why not put your feet up for half an hour? Carla and I will unpack the office," he says. "I just set the telly up. That dancing programme will be on soon."

He's the master of diplomacy. People say opposites attract. In the case of Kate and Rob Carroll, that's true. Mum is overtly outraged all the time. I would say Dad is "inraged". Quietly brewing his anger, then letting it out in late-night hushed tones when they think I'm asleep. They've always been like this. She shouts and pouts, Dad discusses and compromises. Maybe not everyone's idea of love but it seems to work for them.

He loves me though, my dad. I know he does. My earliest memory is of him and me. I'm watching the little winged seeds tumble from the sycamore tree in the front garden of the house-eight-houses-ago – we lived there until I was ten.

Twirling like ballerinas, the seeds dance to the ground.

Below the tree is a wild strawberry patch. The strawberries taste sour, but I don't mind. I shovel a handful into my mouth and my face bunches up as if I've bitten right into a lemon. The tips of my fingers are stained pink with juices. My daddy is high in the tree, trimming branches. I bet he can see all the way to Grandma's house from up there.

He shakes the branches and lots of tiny pairs of wings come dancing down. So pretty. *Butterflies, lots of little butterflies,* I think to myself. He climbs down and cups my face in his hands, like he really, really loves me. His skin is calloused and rough from working hard, but I don't mind. He unhooks a sycamore seed from my hair. He smells like camping trips.

"Hey, angel, do you know what we're doing today?" I shake my head excitedly. This means we're doing something fun. Daddy smiles and the skin around his eyes crinkles up. He looks funny with the sun lighting up all those little cracks and creases. Birds have been marching on his face. "We're going ice skating. I'm going to teach you. That'll be fun, won't it?"

I love my dad.

I love that memory.

I guess I'm kind of nervous about being in the Big Smoke. Our new house, complete with sash windows and ornate door knocker, may be slap bang in the middle of a neat, leafy street, but if you walk down the road, past the park, you're in another world.

From our new pad you can walk ten minutes in one

direction and get the best eggs Benedict of your life and drink unpronounceable teas from vintage cups and saucers in a quirky cafe with a ceiling full of chandeliers; or browse independent shops that seem like gift shops in some upper-class theme park called Poshland. You can buy candles and antique furniture and weird art and be, like, totally chic or whatever. *Or* walk ten minutes in the opposite direction and possibly be stabbed forty times in the neck. I had *literally* seen it on TV the week before we moved. "Following news of the fatal stabbing of a teenager in Peckham, the thirteenth knife-related death in South London this year, *Newsnight* asks: Is London knife crime out of control?"

But machetes, daggers, samurai swords and blunt-but-deadly bread knives aside, there are things I feel *much* more apprehensive about:

1. being invisible at my new school
2. being so very vanilla that I have nothing to recommend myself to others, which means 1. is practically a write-off
3. by some miracle, attracting friends into orbit around my person, but spectacularly failing to keep them there.

I've never really bothered with mates and social standings before. There was always an expiry date on them, with Mum on contract; a year here, six months there. We might as well have been Travellers, or living on army bases. My world was constantly changing. But now? Now I'm putting down roots and have all of London and the whole of sixth form to cram my entire filmic aspirations into: friends, popularity, grades, the *good life* as defined by a lifetime of watching John Hughes films and *Clueless* on repeat.

I'm freaking Molly Ringwald in *Pretty in Pink* and it's my time to shine.

CHAPTER 3

Just as a mirror reflects only what's in front of it, what you get out of life depends on what you put in. Before leaving home on my first day at Thorncroft School, I stand in front of the mirror. I see my bed's reflection, the corner of my desk and a pale wash of sky framed by the sash window. I don't see myself. I am the invisible girl. But I'm tired of being unseen. I'm going to change, to fit in for once and be popular. I'm going to be somebody. I just hope that no one sees through me.

I'm psyching myself up on the way to school, breathing deeply, then blowing out all the air and hopefully my nerves with it. I traverse tree-lined streets past rows of yellow-brick houses with immaculate white-painted window surrounds and small but perfectly manicured front gardens, then I cross the park. In daylight it's a picture-perfect green haven and, if you find the right spot far from the road noise where the trees are tall enough to block the skyline, you feel you're anywhere but in a city. At night it's a completely different story, with shadows stalking you and the trees whispering. I follow the curve of the river and hit Sandringham Avenue, darting past dog shit and bus stops, under a dodgy railway bridge sheltering drunks, cider cans and used condoms, until shops appear. There's Ali's Foodstore, the doctors', pharmacy, off-licence and chippy. Thorncroft School, biggest of all the buildings, sits head of the table, yellow brick with window frames painted in a jarring cobalt-blue gloss.

I collect my timetable from the school office. Mrs Vernon, the receptionist, directs me to the form room. Inevitably I get lost in the maze of corridors and end up in the sports hall before a Year 11 girl takes me to A2.

My stomach feels weird and fluttery, like a deflating balloon. The first day at a new school is always the worst, as if some law makes it illegal for new kids to slip into the system unnoticed. *Oh God, oh God, oh God. Please don't notice me.* It's the same every time I move schools. But this time, it's permanent, real-life-staying-put-till-end-of-sixth-form-finishing-your-exams-time-to-make-friends-stationary schooling. The blood drains from my face. My innards turn inside out. Carla Carroll: late, shy and licensed to hurl.

I knock on the form-room door. Through the glass – you know that glass with wire mesh like graph paper? – I see a man in brown loafers crouching on the wipe-clean vinyl floor. Shards of glass and spilled water glint under the energy-saving fluorescent lights. He tilts his head towards the knock, which was evidently not inaudible, as I'd hoped. I wish I was somewhere else – anywhere – a beach, the park, at home, under that tree with my dad twirling butterflies down to me.

The door opens. My chest wheezes involuntarily as the

balloon empties. Thirty pairs of eyes fix on me. *Shit.*

Mr Brown Shoes waves me into the room. "Come in, er, Carla, is it?" he asks. I manage an affirmative grunt. "Welcome. Take a seat. We've got a slight spillage to attend to and then we'll get cracking with proper introductions."

I want to die. Instead I mumble, "OK, um, yeah," and sit down at the table with the fewest people, by the window.

My eyes flit around the room, unable to focus. Everyone is looking at me, all perched on metal-framed stools with seats of moulded off-white acrylic the colour of an overcast sky. I try to ignore the visual dissection I'm receiving. *Newbie. Geek. Ugly. Rabbit. In. Headlights.*

I focus on Mr Brown Shoes. He's swarthy, taller than average, but not a skyscraper, more a multi-storey car park; olive-skinned with cocoa-dark hair tousled into thick, messy curls. Fittingly flamboyant for a secondary school art teacher. Kimonos and earrings and you're looking at local college teacher/failed artist, but unkempt locks, that's fine. There's something perfect about him. I don't mean like *that.* There's just something calming about him, magnetic, pleasing. He seems balanced.

He glides over to where I'm sitting. He's wearing a forgettable sky-blue shirt and jeans, but has a brilliant scent that conjures vivid images of Marrakesh – pulsing sun, bustle, life and spices.

"I'm Mr Havelock. Head of Year 12. These inattentive monkeys are your new form group," he says.

"Hey, Ted, we're not monkeys! I'm a tiger, mate." A boy jumps off a stool and claws with his hands. *"Raaaaaa!"* He launches at me. I panic. I push him and he backs off. "Easy, tiger!" The boy cocks an eyebrow. "Already trying to rip my clothes off. I like that."

The whole class laughs. I die inside.

Mr Havelock glares at the boy, his cheeks flooded with red. "Back to your seat, you cocky fool."

"Only trying to make the new girl feel comfortable, Mr H. You know, calm her nerves, make her laugh."

I glance at my attacker. He's unbelievably handsome. Easily the most beautiful boy I've ever seen. Eyes like coffee beans, long dark lashes flicking against milky skin. High cheekbones and a smooth jaw like lathe-turned wood, sculpted to perfection. He's wearing skinny jeans, their low-slung waistline exposing his boxers. A spike protrudes from his left earlobe and a ring circles his bottom lip. All is forgiven…

Still, I wish I was anywhere but here, away from these glaring eyes.

"Does she look like she's laughing?" Mr Havelock smiles, tight-lipped. "Get on with your work, Mr Masterson."

"You all right, Carla?" he asks.

Yeah, apart from wanting to curl up and hide in the ventilation system for the rest of the day, I'm great.

"Mmmm," I mumble. My brain calculates the quickest exit route. Options include:

1. window on left
2. form-room door
3. fire escape at back of room
4. spontaneously combust.

Unfortunately, it isn't over. Six hours of classes remain: double Biology, Chemistry, English Lit, Psychology and Art: my AS-level subjects.

I'm good at school. I've got my head around Dadaism and I can describe cognitive dissonance. I'm not a total geek or anything, I get stuff wrong and I find coursework a pain in the arse like anyone else. I just try to do my best. Usually that means getting into the top achievers, upper sets, fast-track classes.

I guess I can be hard on myself sometimes. *It's-not good-enough-don't-you-want-to-achieve-something?* rings in my head for days if I don't put the effort in.

I try to keep to myself, silently clock-watch my way to three fifteen. But despite the nerves, I *need* someone to take an interest in me, say something vaguely friendly. I suppose unless I emanate some signs of life I'm bound to be ignored. *Hello, I'm here, I'm new, I'm nervous. Somebody speak to me. I'm not weird, honest.* Regrettably, the words just swim in circles around my head.

Art is the last lesson before lunch, back in my form room, A2, my timetable tells me. I sit in the same seat as at the start of this hideous day. I swear, everyone thinks I'm mute. Or a mutant. Or both. I challenge myself to string at least *one* sentence together by the end of the lesson.

We're studying sculpture, which I'm excited about. Art's a subject I actually enjoy. Ideas bubble inside me, bursting to get out. Whether drawing, painting, writing or, I hope, after this course, sculpting, I seem to do it well. Art's an outlet, a way of expressing myself. I sound like a hippy. Whatever.

Most of the class have already started their sculptures. The girl to my right has designed a brooch in the shape of two birds facing each other, fiery-looking, enamelled in orange. The guy to my left is making a horse from old cogs and washers.

Pointless and hideous. I like the brooch. I hate the horse. I already know what I'm going to make. My favourite insect, animal, living creature: a butterfly. They're so beautiful.

I draw a few sketches and make a list of materials and equipment.

The girl with the brooch design taps my sketchbook.

"That's lovely." She smiles warmly. "I wish I could draw like that."

"Thanks. It's an *Ornithoptera alexandrae* – Queen Alexandra's Birdwing. Their wings are like patchwork." Finally. Someone has made contact with me, the alien. I come in peace!

"I'm Lauren," the girl says.

"Carla."

Lauren has jet-black hair pulled back into a knotty blob and green eyes that shine, unaided by make-up. She pulls out a tin of Vaseline and coats her lips. I notice she doesn't wear rings, or any jewellery, not even studs in her ears. She's unintimidating, safe. My shyness subsides and I gear up to compliment her brooch, but stop, distracted by a low hum of voices from the next table. I twirl my pencil like a baton between my fingers.

"Yeah, mate," the beautiful boy says, "that's what I'm talking about! It was a massive night. We didn't get home till eight a.m."

"Ha ha! You must have been dead for, like, a week after that."

"Slinky was totally on form."

I turn my head to get a better look at them.

"You should have seen the VJ set-up! It was huge. The

screen was almost on the ceiling, sitting on scaffold."

Mr Havelock must have caught me staring, because he darts over to the boys.

"Finn! Do you mind? I'm trying to teach a class." His face darkens. *Finn, his name is Finn.*

"Sorry, Ted. Won't happen again." Finn looks genuinely sorry. Then he smiles widely.

"Come on. You're seventeen. Act it." Havelock's look of irritation fades. "Get on with your work."

I wonder what Finn and the other boy were talking about. Sounds pretty cool, whatever it was.

Lunchtime arrives. At least I've strung together one sentence. I'm not a total outcast, a mute mutant; a lonely, newbie freak. Success!

I swear, even with a whole scout troop on an orienteering trip to help me, I'd have difficulty finding my way around this place. It's like the bloody Bermuda Triangle for new students. I might never escape. Searching for the sixth-form common room takes half my lunch break.

Eventually I find it. There's a kitchen in one corner; a couple of guys perch on the worktop, playing with their phones. The walls are lined with hard, low blue chairs, inhumane hybrids – half seat, half torture device. They look poised to snap closed like a Venus flytrap if you sit on them. There are two long tables in the middle of the room, with safer, if not more comfortable, benches.

I see Lauren and a friend at a table, eating lunch. She waves me over and I gratefully accept. No one wants to be a loner at lunchtime.

"Hey," I say and sit in the space opposite her, next to the other girl.

"This is Sienna," Lauren says, "our resident spelunking enthusiast."

Sienna has a thick copper fringe, cut severely just above her eyes, and skin like porcelain.

"Spelunking?" I ask.

"She likes to crawl about in dingy caves."

"I want to be a speleologist." Sienna looks at me through a curtain of hair. "Study cave systems. In Austria there's a giant cave filled with ice sculptures made when the snow above thawed, drained into the cave and refroze. It's amazing."

"It sounds, um, cold. Cool, I mean." I can't get the right words out.

"Sienna spends so much time in the dark, she's lost the genes for skin pigmentation. That's why she's so white!"

"I'm Irish!" Sienna turns to me. "So where are you from?" There's a question.

"All over the place. More recently, Nottingham. But I've lived in Bath, Cardiff, Cheltenham..."

"Are you in witness protection or something?"

"My family just moves around a lot."

"I bet you have to say that."

I shrug. But then I realize I have a real chance to make friends here and I'm screwing it up.

"We're fugitives. On the run. My dad stole Simon Cowell's helicopter for a joke. Took it for a joyride."

Lauren raises an eyebrow and takes a bite of cheese sandwich. I fiddle with the frayed straps of my bag, then take out a chicken roll wrapped in foil. Dad made it from last night's leftovers. I munch away.

Sienna laughs. "It all makes sense now."

Lauren finishes her sandwich and starts on an apple.

I whip out my timetable, hoping my new acquaintances will be in the same lessons. "I know you take Art, Lauren, but do either of you take these other classes?" I ask, spreading the crumpled piece of A4 on the table.

"Let's see." Lauren studies the paper. "I take Biology."

Sienna perks up. "Me too, and Chemistry. You've basically found the Science geeks."

"What am I in for?"

"With us? A thrill ride of cellular organization, anaerobic respiration, inherited variation and the occasional trip to the cinema."

Lauren ignores Sienna. "Miss Tillsman, the Biology teacher, is all right. A bit loopy. She has a serious mascara goop problem. Always in the right eye. It can be hard to concentrate with that thing just sitting there like a baby slug."

"We mark the goop on a scale of one to five," Sienna says. "One: Minor goop; Two: Goopus Maximus; Three: Goopasaurus Rex; Four: 'Is it a bird, is it a plane?'; Five: 'That thing is so huge, how can she even see us? It looks like the bloody Death Star.'"

"It freaks me out. I'm so OCD I just want to stick my finger right in there and scratch it out." Lauren shudders.

"That's disgusting," Sienna says.

"Look forward to it," I say.

The common-room door flies open. A group of guys and girls walks in. They sit on the other table, their feet on the benches. Finn tosses a helmet in his hands.

"So, enlighten me," I say to Lauren. "Who are they?"

"That's Finn Masterson. Nice guy. The local fittie. Slight problem with authority. Greg White, hockey captain. Georgia Presco with the mess of curls and scary red talons. She's a model in her spare time. Goes out with Greg. Her parents won eight million on the Lotto last year! She didn't fancy going to a posh school and leaving Greg, so she's still here."

"And that's Violet Brody with the shiny shampoo-ad hair that's been known to blind people if it catches the light," Sienna says, pointing to a girl who looks like she's stepped right out of an American Apparel commercial. She embodies cool. Tall, sleek, chic, shining eyes… And cheekbones. I mean, I know everyone has them, but hers are set some magic way that makes her face a perfect shape.

"They say her hair's woven from a unicorn's mane," Sienna chips in, leaning closer, "and sprayed with real diamonds."

Lauren rolls her eyes. "She's basically the queen bee. The guys fall over themselves to impress her."

"Didn't Jay Fletcher write her that song in Year 10? And sing it at the talent show?" Sienna asks.

"Ohmygod, that was classic."

"How did it go again?"

Lauren straightens up and strums air guitar, closing her eyes to exaggerate the emotion:

"Violet, you're so beautiful,
A man could get violent,
With passion, not fists, I'm not like that.
If I couldn't have you,

I'd take a vow of silence.

Oh, Violet, be mine,

We can shine together for ever in the twilight."

Sienna descends into hysterics. "And the whole crowd started chanting, 'Take the vow of silence!'"

"She's popular, then?"

Lauren shrugs. "I guess. So, that's Fat Mike, self-explanatory." She continues the lesson, Cool Kids 101. "The tall one's James 'Slinky' Tyler. He smokes a lot of weed."

"Why do they call him Slinky?"

"Because he's always looking round corners. Like a Slinky goes down steps. Paranoid on account of the fact he smokes so much. Plus he's really tall. And that's Isaac, Finn's older brother. He's in year 13. The strong, silent type. They're impossibly cool. If you like that sort of thing."

The curly-haired girl accidentally drops her folder on the floor. Finn hops off the table and retrieves it. She thanks him.

"I'm going to the shop. Anyone want anything?" Finn asks the room. There's a chorus of mumbled negatives.

"You'll be late for class," Isaac tells his brother.

"Yes, I will," Finn replies.

I've been to enough schools to know that when you start, you pick a group and you stay there. I never really bothered to stray from my social sub-group, the Brainy Plain Girls, two-thirds of the way down the pecking order. Of course, the categories differ depending on location and there's some overlap, but it normally goes something like this:

Beautiful People

Impossibly Cool Hipsters

Sports Freaks
Geek Chic
Emos
Brainy Plain Girls
IT Crowd
Oral Hygiene Deficients.

I feel like this new school, my final-ever school, is in some ways a last-ditch attempt to climb that ladder.

There's nothing wrong with mid-range social standing, not at all, but, I guess, I'd really like to have my time in the sun.

Finn, Isaac, Violet, Georgia, Greg: they're all magnetic, *alive* with this *energy*. There's a charisma about them that I long to have. I want to be in on their secrets and jokes; to tell a story and have them rapt, tipping back their heads, roaring with laughter; for them to link arms with me in the corridor and think, *Wow, that Carla is really* someone.

It's time for change. It's time to twirl around in that phone box and exit as all-singing, all-dancing Super Carla.

Is hanging around with the Brainy Plain Girls going to get me where I want to be? Probably not… But I need the friends. And they *are* nice… Maybe I'm not worthy of the top spot anyway. One of the Beautiful People? It's just a fantasy; a deluded, last-third-of-the-ladder fantasy. This is where I'm meant to be, and I ought to be thankful I've made human contact at all.

The bell rings. I shove my timetable and the half-eaten chicken roll into my bag.

"Come on," says Sienna. "I'll show you to the Chemistry lab."

CHAPTER 4

At my last school I could get lost in a sea of blue shirts. Thorncroft sixth-formers don't wear uniform and stand out like shark fins in that sea. I feel like a minnow, a flicker of colour, tiny but just visible. These sharks will eat me alive. I want to be accepted, popular. If I'm going to be here a while, I have to *be* somebody. I have to become a shark.

"OK, listen up, people!" booms Mr Paluk, the Chemistry teacher. "This demonstration involves electrolyzing water, and the explosive recombination of hydrogen and oxygen. Goggles on!"

The lab door bursts open. A figure appears, all beaming smile and confidence and oh-so-late. Paluk rolls his eyes, obviously used to this behaviour. Finn perches at the front in the only free space, the seat next to me. He throws me a grin. My self-awareness sky-rockets. Still, I can't help but smile back. He's here, sitting next to me, breathing the same air...

The whole class moves to retrieve goggles from the box on our bench.

The Girl With the Blinding Hair touches his shoulder and he turns to face her.

"Be my partner, Finn? Marcus said he'd swap." Violet runs her fingers through her uber-straight, dark cherry locks.

"I have a partner, Vi. I'll catch you in History."

He picked *me* over *her*?

Violet shrugs, takes a pair of goggles and heads back to her seat.

"Looks like we're lab buddies," he says.

"I guess so," I say, mentally cramming joy into my jeans pocket so it doesn't spill out as a crazy three-foot grin across my face.

Finn oozes confidence. I could learn a thing or two from him. Finn Masterson: Master of Ease. I'm wound tighter than a spring.

Mr Paluk turns to the whiteboard and draws up a list of the equipment and chemicals we need next to a diagram of the apparatus.

I watch Finn set up the experiment. He seems eager and like he knows what he's doing. Behold: behind his cocky exterior beats the heart of a scientist. Swoon.

He holds out a rubber bung to me.

"Can you thread the platinum wire through this, please?"

I take the silver string and poke it through. I glance up at the diagram, grab some plastic tubing and put it into place.

"Hey, sorry if I scared you with the tiger thing this morning. I can be an idiot sometimes. Just tell me to shove off if I get lairy."

"It's OK," I say. "First day. Wasn't expecting to be pounced on."

"Yeah, pouncing is usually a day three or four thing." He smiles.

He rolls up his sleeves, exposing strong, muscular arms. The skin is scraped from his elbows, which look red and sore. He pours a solution of hydrated sodium sulphate into a glass jar.

"You like Chemistry?" I enquire.

"Don't I seem the type?" he asks, batting his chocolate lashes. I'm starting to think he's the one with the legendary looks, not Violet Brody. He's like Thor or Hercules or I don't know, Robert Downey Jr in *Iron Man*. Gorgeous.

"*Are* you the type?" I ask, sarcastically.

"Oh, she strikes me in the chest!" Finn fakes an arrow with a piece of plastic tubing and thrusts it at his torso. "I like many things, Carla."

He remembered my name.

He peeks at me through his not-so-cool goggles and I realize that while he still looks stunning, I probably look like Deirdre Barlow from *Corrie*.

"Yeah, I like Chemistry. It's something I get. Surprised?"

"No, just sketching your character."

"You can sketch me any time." He winks, then stares at me for what seems an eternity.

"Are you going to put the bung in?"

"Excuse me?" I feel a flush creeping up my neck and across my cheeks.

"In the jar. Are you going to put the bung in or just stand there holding it? I don't think this experiment is going to work without it."

"Oh, I thought... Never mind." I put the stopper in the top of the jar.

"Press it hard. We've got to make it gas-tight."

I search deep in my armoury of social skills, which, as it happens, isn't that deep, for something to say. The only subject I can think of is school.

"How about Art? You like it as much as Chemistry?"

"Not exactly. It's not that I don't *like* it. Basically, I thought it would be a doss. I was wrong though. It's hard work."

I connect the wires to a power pack. Soon bubbles start to appear in the solution around the wires.

"Beaker." Finn holds out his hand expectantly, like a surgeon waiting for a scalpel. He smiles so widely, so openly. It's infectious. I smile back and pass the beaker. He pours in some water.

"Washing-up liquid."

I hand him the bottle. He adds a squirt to the water.

"Tube." I put the other end of the plastic tube into the beaker.

"Careful, this is a tricky manoeuvre." He mock-wipes sweat from his brow while, being this close to him, I *actually* start to sweat. It's my first day. My heart has grown three sizes bigger and will soon pound right out of my chest.

Gas starts to bubble in the beaker. While he's watching it, my eyes develop minds of their own and start to roam across his torso, his neck, his thick hair.

"Now comes the fun part. Bunsen burner on," he says, throwing me a glance so full of warmth and charm I feel I've been lit from the inside and can be seen glowing from space.

"Check."

"Spatula."

"Coming at ya." I smile, then inwardly groan at saying such a dorkish thing.

Finn scoops some bubbles onto the spatula, holds it in the Bunsen flame and, CRACK! They explode with a bang.

"This is why I like Chemistry, tiger."

CHAPTER 5

I stand outside the lab, paralyzed from the waist down. Panic. Everyone has disappeared to their next lessons. The bell's about to ring, but I have no idea where to find the English room. There's a map on the wall and I'm frantically trying to find E3. I glance from my timetable to the map and back again.

"Where are you supposed to be?" Finn puts a hand on my shoulder.

I point to my timetable. "E3. It doesn't seem to be on here."

"That's because it's *not* on there. You know what? This map is old. E3's in the new wing." He traces a finger over an oblong shape. His watch catches the light. Looks expensive. "This part of the building was demolished, like, six months ago. Come on, I'll show you where E3 is."

"It's like this school is conspiring to make things as difficult as possible for new students. Invisible rooms. Identical corridors. Non-existent buildings."

"Yeah, they don't make it easy."

"Won't you be late for your lesson?" I ask.

"Mr Wilkinson will live. Come on. It's this way."

"Is that your thing? Late for everything?"

"One whole morning and she has me all figured out!" Finn shrugs. "Let's just say, I run to my own schedule."

I follow him along the corridor and through a set of cobalt-blue doors.

"Thanks," I say. "I was starting to get the fear."

"It's lucky I'm never on time for anything then. It means I can go around being the hero, saving girls from perilous situations like facing the wrath of" – he glances at my timetable – "Mr Rochester." Finn smiles an easy smile. "So how come you're only just joining the year?"

"My mum changed jobs. We moved from Nottingham on Saturday."

"You don't sound very northern," he says.

"We weren't there long. Less than a year. I was born in Southampton, but we moved around a lot. What about you?"

"London. Born and bred. OK, I'm from Watford originally. But close enough. So if you need a guide, maybe I could show you what magical delights London can offer? Teach you some Cockney. Although I'd have to learn it myself first. And I promise I won't pounce on you."

We walk through a maze of blue corridors and although I should be making a mental map for later, I find myself distracted by Finn, tucking my hair behind my ear one too many times, smiling coyly, attempting to make jokes and cringing inside at every word that falls from my mouth.

"Thanks. I could do with some help fitting in." *Cringe.*

"I think you'll fit in just fine." *Smile.*

"Here we are." Finn puts his hand on the small of my back and guides me through some more blue doors, "I Adam and Eve it's up the apple and pears, and to the right," he says in an appalling East End accent. "Be careful, Mr Rochester can be a pain in the bottle and glass."

"I thought you didn't know Cockney."

"That's the best I've got to offer."

"Well, Tom Hanks."

"Huh?"

"Thanks. Tom Hanks. Rhyming slang for thanks."

"Right. If you say so. See you later, tiger."

When I get home, Dad is stacking boxes in the garage.

"Look what I found." He pulls out a canvas with a purple flower painted on, another with a boat on a choppy sea, then an underwater scene with a seahorse.

"Oh, here's a good one." A penguin and a rabbit frolicking on a hillside.

"I never was that great with geography."

"Pity penguins aren't native to England. You used to take commissions, you know. Tenner a canvas. Rather enterprising at seven years old."

"How much would you pay now? I could do with some new jeans and maybe an iPad."

"You'll be lucky! As it happens, I already own several masterpieces. So, sorry, no iPad today. How was your first day?"

"I survived."

"I should hope so."

I tell Dad about my teachers and Lauren and Sienna. He seems satisfied that the transition to school number eight has been relatively painless.

"I thought we could have baked potatoes and salad for tea."

"Great."

I don't bother asking where Mum is. It'll be the same old story. She'll probably pop up on the news later, reporting some story about a newly discovered subatomic do-hickey or a goat that's given birth to a duck or something.

Later, Dad and I sit down to tea together. Ravenous after the not-so-filling half-roll I had for lunch, I eat it in, like, five seconds flat, then crash out on my bed, exhausted.

CHAPTER 6

My first week draws to a close. Finn and Havelock have locked horns a few times. Nothing major. Seems to me Finn's just the chatty type. With a slight timekeeping issue. Mostly Havelock ignores him. Maybe he's given up on him. But I think he just plain likes him. Maybe Finn has won him over.

It must be kind of empowering to get one up on a teacher. We're sixteen and seventeen after all. Sixteen is almost fully fledged, one-hundred-per-cent adult. We're able to make our own decisions and do whatever we want. Get *B*s instead of *A*s. Score sixty-five percent rather than seventy-five.

Not me. I pile so much pressure on myself to achieve. I always have.

I envy Finn. He seems free. I'd like to be assertive like him.

By Thursday, I'm accepted into the seventy-five-per-cent-or-more club, with Lauren and Sienna, a small urban family of three. Actually they are pretty interesting. Lauren is down-to-earth and intelligent. Sienna is really driven. I like them a lot.

But I keep thinking I want something more. I feel drawn to Finn and his crowd like Juliet to Romeo, spaghetti to meatballs. Here I am, ready to make potentially lifelong friends, vocal talents permitting. I bloody well want to be cool for once. Not uber-popular, just stylish, interesting … not afraid to be myself… Only, I'm not quite sure who "myself" is.

At lunch on Friday, Lauren invites me to watch the hockey game that evening. Hockey is big at Thorncroft and there's a match against Chainey Lane, another school in the borough. I'm chuffed to be asked. I feel there's a real possibility of a friendship lasting longer than six months. Bonus. But while I'm glad to be making friends, something twists in me when we arrive together pitch-side. Doubt creeps around my middle and tightens. I feel *terrible.* Lauren is just the sort of mate I ought to be making, but…

Finn's crowd stands on the sidelines, watching Greg thrash his hockey stick about on the AstroTurf. Violet drapes an arm around Finn's shoulder. He's more interested in the game. And me, apparently. I catch him glancing my way more than once.

I don't know why I'm getting this attention. I'm not complaining, quite the opposite, but it puts me on edge. I'm torn between two worlds. Lauren could be a great friend, so why do I want to jump ship and swim as fast as I can to Finn's island? It's more than a physical attraction, it's his confidence, knowing that people accept and respect you…

Greg expertly weaves the ball through the opposing players. There are some violent tackles.

Lauren's phone rings. She answers it, then wanders away from the pitch in order to hear better.

I open my sketchbook and begin to draw. I work quickly, doing loads of rough drawings, trying to capture the sense of movement. Then I start sketching Finn. His long legs, his T-shirt clinging tightly to his torso, the scratches on his arms. I notice another graze on the side of his high cheekbone.

"What are you drawing?"

Lauren leans in to see what I'm doing and I instantly snap the book shut.

"Nothing." She shoots me an "if you say so" look. "Honestly, it's nothing. Just the hockey players."

Greg rushes past us, as if on skates.

"He's really fast," I say. The other players can't match his pace. It's easy to see why he's captain. I open my book again and continue sketching, filling in shadows, totally engrossed.

"Carla." Lauren nudges me on the arm.

"What?" I look up.

"When I said you could draw me any time, I wasn't serious," Finn says, a twinkle in his eye. He taps the page. "This is really good."

I'm mute, crushed with embarrassment. I open and close my mouth like a gormless fish. *I hate myself. I hate myself. I hate myself.*

"See you on Monday," says Finn, turning to wave as he jogs off, probably back to some glorious mansion.

"Smooth," Lauren says sarcastically.

I can't speak. The horror of Finn catching me drawing him is too much.

Greg passes the ball to another attacker, who pelts it between a defender's legs and back to Greg, who's run into the circle, near the goal. The angle seems too tight but Greg whacks it to the back of the net. Unstoppable. The goalie doesn't have a chance.

I wish I was like that, invincible, right on target, heading for a new life. Instead, I'm a *mentalist stalker* who secretly draws people she's just met.

I'm never going to get over this, *ever.*

HE CAUGHT ME DRAWING HIM. OHMYGOD, I'M SUCH A *LOSER.*

By Monday morning, after beating myself up all weekend over it, I still can't get the sketching incident out of my head. Walking to school, watching my feet, I'm desperate to disappear, or for school to disappear so I don't have to face Finn. Cyclists zoom past. As one clips my arm, I realize I've strayed into the road and jerk back onto the pavement, cursing the bike as it speeds off.

And then I see them, Finn and his brother, standing among waist-high bushes between two buildings. Are they trying to hide, or get caught, or signal danger to the next tribe? UNDER-AGE SMOKERS HERE. Neon lights.

Finn leans against the brick wall of the doctors' surgery, eyes closed as he sucks a rollie like milkshake through a straw. He looks so good. His blue T-shirt, pushed back by the wind, accentuates his skinny but toned torso. I see a new set of scratches on his forearms. Maybe the Masterson household is a cat household. An evil, scratchy cat household.

Then I get why they're standing like that. They're there

for us normal people to admire as we shuffle past, trying not to miss the bell.

I hope to whatever deity is up there that he doesn't see me.

"Hey! Hey, Carla!" Finn calls. Busted. Why would he possibly want to talk to me after Friday?

1. I'm about as interesting as a pot plant.
2. Lest we forget, I fucking *drew* him.
3. He caught me doing it.

Then I think about it. Maybe it's time to become self-assured, like him. Is this my chance? Start anew as Carla Mark II? Tomorrow's another day and all that? I take a deep breath.

"Hey, tiger!" Finn yells.

I stop, turn, and head straight for him. Nearing the bushes, I take in his baby-face features, long eyelashes and hairless chin. Impossibly handsome. My stomach feels like it's been teleported out of my body onto the roof. Somehow, I walk steadily over, keeping eye contact, like I'm being pulled on a thread. Not tripping up like I'm Ugly fucking Betty. Without my jeans spontaneously falling down. Without, like, accidentally serenading him. It's a freaking miracle.

"Hey," I squeak. *This is it, Carla. Get a grip.* "You like Chemistry." I manage to exhale a lame statement. *Great.*

Finn doesn't seem to notice. Am I red? I feel like I'm totally tomatoed.

"You wanna twos me?" he asks.

"I don't smoke," I say. But confidence rises from nowhere and I take the rollie, hold it for a second, then take a drag.

Boldness jolts me upright. Something awakens inside me. Like I've taken a teeny step from uncool kid to something better. I like it. I feel a bit sick, but I like it. I don't cough.

My rebel gene is kicking in.

"Are you sure about that?" he asks. "Looks like you do."

I shrug, not knowing what to say, and hand the rollie back.

Finn takes a pack of tobacco from his back pocket, flicks it open and pulls out a clump, along with a paper and a filter, which his fingers magically transform into a rollie. I go to take it, but he pulls his hand away. Cocking an eyebrow, he slips the rollie behind my ear, pushing back my hair.

"Since you don't smoke and all, maybe you could not smoke this one later," he says.

"Oh, this is Isaac," Finn says, playfully punching him in the ribs.

"Hey," Isaac says.

"Hey," I say. "Seen you around school."

"Upper sixth," he mumbles. Wow, he really is the strong, silent type. Finn scowls at him. "Young Finlay's my baby brother," Isaac adds.

"Shut up!" Finn thumps him hard in the stomach. "Yeah, we're brothers. Fortunately, I'm the looker of the pair. Who wouldn't fall for this cheeky grin?" He flashes a smile. His deep brown eyes hold a kind of wisdom. Though younger and leaner than his rougher-looking brother, Finn seems to call the shots.

He nudges Isaac and whispers something.

"You'll have to excuse me. Later, tiger," Finn says. "See you in Art. Maybe you can get me from another angle."

They disappear before I can get a word out. As they saunter toward the PE block, I can't help watching Finn. All stride and glide and no problems. I step forwards to where he was standing and lean against the wall. I breathe in deeply, trying to capture some of his easy nature simply by being in the space he occupied.

CHAPTER 7

Miss Tillsman, our Biology teacher, wears colourful, dangly enamelled earrings. She has short, fluffy hair: weightless, anti-gravity wisps just right for sweeping cobwebs. Her chin and long neck are almost seamless, and she smells like a patisserie.

There's something comforting about her scent. Everyone trusts and respects her. I think it's part of a cunning plan to win students over, like when supermarkets pump out bakery smells to entice customers.

Biology teaches that smells are important. Butterflies secrete pheromones to send messages to the opposite sex, but it's more than a scientific *nudge nudge wink wink*. Besides attracting a mate, pheromones warn of danger and mark out territory so that butterflies survive and often thrive in great numbers. Without pheromones, how could they dodge a predator or find a mate? Males would probably fight each other to the death over territory, and where would the butterfly population be then? At big fat zero. That's where. Pheromones are an evolutionary trick; a secret, secreting ingredient that keeps the world going round and the sky full of flashes of dancing jewels in summer. Basic biology. Miss Tillsman's in on the smelly secret. She uses Belgian buns to break us. How can you answer back to a sweet feather-haired teacher who smells like pastry?

She's also a good teacher. She makes things interesting. Lauren says they did an experiment investigating the rate of osmosis in potatoes, and with the spare ones, she made them all chips for lunch. No one forgot that lesson.

I sit between Lauren and Sienna. We spend the lesson modelling the human respiratory system, making lungs from balloons and plastic bottles and discussing what happens to the bronchi during an asthma attack. Greg is blowing up balloons and letting them fly about the room.

A red one soars, squeals and lands on Sienna's shoulder.

"Juvenile." She rolls her eyes and flicks the deflated fake lung to the ground. "Don't know what Georgia sees in him."

Lauren starts drawing a diagram of an airway blocked by mucus and constricting muscles.

"Oh no, wait, I do," Sienna continues. "He lets her style his hair and pick his outfits. They spend their lives preening each other like monkeys, and presenting themselves as the hot couple."

"Style over substance?" I venture.

"Exactly." Sienna blows hard into a spirometer, then checks the reading on the plastic cylinder. "Well, what do you know? I'm not asthmatic."

"That's unfair, Sienna," Lauren jumps in. "Aside from the fact that he has the attention span of a gnat, he's excellent at hockey, skateboarding, can play the guitar..."

"Sounds like you fancy him."

"Not even a little bit. I'm just saying he's not a total loser delinquent."

Sienna shrugs.

"What about Finn?" I ask, careful not to look either of them in the eye and let on about my little crush.

"You like him, don't you?" Lauren asks, pausing mid-bronchi-annotation. Clearly, I'm rubbish at hiding things. First rule, don't mention your crush by name. Rookie mistake. *How can I save this?*

"Just curious about the social workings of Thorncroft. Still getting my bearings."

"Lauren used to fancy him." Sienna smirks.

Lauren throws Sienna an evil glance. She taps her biro on her book. Her eyebrows do the trick my dad's do. Together they could put on the Incredible Anti-Grav Eyebrow Show and make millions! Fleas could ride tiny bikes and do wheelies between the hairy caterpillars.

"You did?" I ask, intrigued by the first juicy bit of gossip since I arrived … but also, and I know this sounds stupid, a little jealous.

Lauren shifts on her chair. "It was a moment of weakness in Year 10. I broke my finger in basketball and he took me to the school nurse. I was crying. He calmed me down. I was probably concussed. He can be quite charming." She scrunches her hair behind her head.

"You can't get concussion from a sore finger," I say, raising an eyebrow really high too. Perhaps I'll join the face circus and be a millionaire as well.

"Anyway, so what if I *did* like him? He has more to

recommend him than Greg, in my opinion. He's intelligent, funny, sporty … helps damsels in distress. Just never expect him to be on time for anything. He wouldn't know a watch if it bit him on the ass."

I'd bite him on the ass.

"And, she said it herself, even Greg's not *that* bad, so Finn must be practically Gabriel Grayson," Sienna says.

"I love Gabriel Grayson in that movie *Last Night in Manhattan*," Lauren adds.

"We all love Gabriel Grayson," I say. I'm struck by how easy it is to talk to these girls. I'm not at all nervous around them. I feel like I could fit into this puzzle, no problem. "Hey, do you want to do something after school? Go into town?"

"Can do," Sienna says.

"What about the market?" Lauren suggests. "Loads of food, second-hand books, records. Not exactly Portobello but it's something to do."

We agree to meet up later and walk over together. I'm actually looking forward to it. This is where I belong. This is where I fit.

At the end of the lesson, I nervously await the results of yesterday's impromptu test on the cell cycle. Lauren and Sienna get a *B+* and an *A*, respectively.

Tillsman puts the paper face-down in front of me. I get a lump in my throat, but needlessly. Turning over the test, I see an *A* in red pen with the words, "Well done, Carla."

Hello, Smugville.

At lunch, in the common room, Finn beckons me over to where he and Greg, Georgia and Violet are sitting.

Sienna raises her eyebrows. "What do they want with us?" she asks.

"Carla, need your opinion on something," Finn calls from the middle table.

"Ah, let me rephrase, what do they want with *you*?" Sienna says.

"No idea," I say.

I wander over, trying to saunter the way Violet does, effortlessly, weightlessly. Isaac looks me up and down with curiosity, maybe a little contempt. I probably look like a prize twat. A hint of a scowl creeps on to my face, my brow furrowing of its own accord. I'm never good at hiding emotion. Silent-type Isaac seems good at masking every emotion except disapproval when he sees me. But I can't let it get to me.

Finn gets up, rising to my eye level, then sits on the table with his feet on the bench and a hand on Georgia's shoulder.

"Georgia here is turning seventeen in mere months," he says, "and she's throwing a huge party to celebrate." I'm being asked to a party. By Finn Masterson. "Only thing is, she's struggling with the theme, layout and all the interior decoration and I thought, being completely void of artistic talent myself—"

"Except with hairstyles," Isaac says, deadpan. Finn ignores him.

"And excuses," Slinky says. " 'Sorry, I'm late Mr Wilkinson' " – he mimics Finn's tone perfectly – " 'the queue in Starbucks was ma-*hoo*-ssive.' "

"And yesterday, with Martinez," Violet adds, batting her lashes. " 'You mean we have to come to school *every* day?' "

The band of beautifuls all cracks up.

"I can't believe you said that," Georgia says. I don't know whether to laugh or not. Joining in might be some sort of cool-crowd encroachment. So, I just stand on the periphery like a lemon. Do I risk a giggle? *Stop over-thinking. Just do it.* I let out a burst of laughter… To my utter, dire and crippling embarrassment, it's *after* they've all *stopped laughing*; a lone, stark sound that seems to echo off the walls and slap me in the face. It draws all their beautiful, popular eyes onto me. Self-loathing ensues.

"Awkward," Violet says, throwing Finn a look that asks, *Why are you talking to this socially inept freak?*

My hands start to shake. My face is hot as the sun's core and probably redder than the surface of Mars. Acne craters add texture. *Fucking hell. What's wrong with me? Ugh.*

Note to self. The following behaviours are socially unacceptable:

1. mentalist stalker drawings
2. laughing when everyone has moved on with their lives
3. drowning kittens
4. wearing double denim.

"So anyway," Finn continues, picking up where he left off. I can hardly look him in the eye. "I thought perhaps you could turn your exceptionally talented drawing arm to the cause and doodle a few possibilities for a theme in that sketchbook of yours."

Not an invitation. A commission. I guess it's better than nothing.

"Yeah, maybe… OK, um, sure," I say, and turn to

Georgia. "Do you want to" – I think about asking Georgia to come over to mine to talk about it, but what if she takes one look at my non-Lotto-funded house and decides I'm sort of, I don't know, poor and scummy? Not good enough? No, it must be neutral ground – "come to my form room after school and we can look at some options? A2."

"Great, thanks. You're a lifesaver," Georgia says.

Back at the table with Sienna and Lauren, I face the firing squad.

"What about going to the market?" Sienna asks.

"I couldn't say no, could I?" I say apologetically. "Look, it'll only take half an hour, probably less. I'll meet you there."

"You could have suggested another day," Sienna says, with a hint of moodiness.

"Sorry, I wasn't thinking. Brain-melt. Those guys are pretty intimidating."

"It's OK, we'll wait," Lauren says. "I've got Geography to do for Wong anyway, and that abstract for Paluk. We can go to the library."

Who knew making friends could be so complicated? *Choose a side, and stay there, Carla.*

CHAPTER 8

Before meeting Georgia, I run to the toilets. The white tiles shout with graffiti and the mirror is milky where it's not been cleaned properly. I wipe it with tissue and take a good look at myself.

I've never bothered much with my hair. I brush it and scrape it back, but seeing Violet with her wonder-locks cascading like a diamond waterfall over her shoulders, and Georgia with her amazing waves bouncing around her heart-shaped face, I feel suddenly inadequate.

I pull out my hairband and shake my mane free. It's a sort of nothing brown, except I guess it can look golden in the right light. I have a tousled just-out-of-bed thing going on… It'll have to do. I hope she won't notice my split ends. I rummage for some eyeliner and attempt a black flick. Apparently it makes your eyes look bigger. I get one lid just perfect but muck up the other and look lopsided. I try to even them out but the flicks just get larger and larger until I look like a bad Cleopatra impersonator.

I rub it off and try again. Better this time.

I don't have any blusher so I pinch my cheeks to make them a bit rosier. I suck on my lips to inject a bit of colour.

In the mirror, I see *someone*.

Maybe, like this, I'm not so invisible.

I wait nervously in A2 for Georgia. It's like a job interview, a Friendiview. Here's the ad:

POSITION: Friend

LEVEL: Popular

Outgoing group seeks new blood. Experience required, preferably in similar social circles. Would make exception for charismatic newcomer.

Sense of style mandatory.

Must have own GHDs.

Candidate should demonstrate value to group. Are you great at telling jokes? Can you help with party planning? Do you know someone who works on the door of a club and can get us in under-age? Are you rich?

Would suit class clown, rule-breaker, fittie or sports fanatic.

Oral Hygiene Deficients need not apply.

I chew the skin around my thumbnail, then stop. Nail-biters need not apply.

I need to keep my fingers busy, so I get out my sketch-book and flip it open.

I don't know much about Georgia, except what I've

seen and what I've learned from Lauren and Sienna. She likes vintage glamour, sometimes alternative, bold colours and patterns. She's a risk-taker with clothes – confident, but graceful... I use a soft pencil to rough out the shape of a Cairns Birdwing butterfly: its vibrant colouration, vivid emeralds, shocking yellow and a splash of scarlet, all held in a lace of black. The Cairns Birdwing makes a statement, edgy but elegant in its flittering dance.

I use metallic pastels, blue, a little green, and a pearly white to capture the iridescence of its wings, smudging them with my fingertip.

Georgia arrives after about ten minutes. I instinctively wipe my pastel-covered fingers on my jeans and close the book.

"Hey," she says, tossing her bag on the floor. She pulls out a chair and sits down.

"Hey," I say.

Georgia's wearing red tights, cut-off denim shorts and a NASA T-shirt. Her hair looks pretty wild and effortless, but now she's up close I can see a million little grips pushing it this way and that.

There's a faint whiff of hairspray, and oranges and vanilla.

I don't have time to feel awkward: she launches right into it.

"So, thanks for doing this. I can't draw for shit and I've totally hit a wall with it. I want the party to be this magic space with, like, different areas, for people to think they're in another world, you know?" But she doesn't stop for an answer. "Here are the room dimensions." She hands me a photocopy of a building plan.

"It's huge."

"Yeah. Pretty big. So I know I want loads of fairy lights everywhere."

"It'd cost a fortune to fill this place with lights."

"I'm worth quite a lot. I guess you heard. Do you want paying or something –?"

"Course not. I just meant … this isn't dressing up someone's front room, this looks like a massive warehouse."

"– because I can go right now if that's what you're interested in." Georgia reaches for her bag.

"No, look, I don't care about that. Sorry. I mean, it's cool that you—"

"Jesus, Carla, I'm just messing," she says, taking out a notepad and pen.

"Oh," I say, but inside I'm wondering why someone with bucketloads of cash *doesn't* just get an event planner. Georgia smiles, but I don't risk a laugh after my epic fail in the common room earlier.

"But I hate talking about it. Like, my world changed overnight, whoop-di-doo. It's cool but I was fine before… I'm the same person, but now people see me and think, *Look, the girl with the money.*"

"Don't take this the wrong way, but—"

"Doesn't a massive party scream money?" Georgia sighs. "I didn't actually *want* a big party, but it's what people expect … and it'll be fun. I want to give something back. I could have left this hole and gone to private school, but why leave and have to make friends all over again? That would be *horrible.* My friends are what's important. And they, like, deserve a good time."

I think about expectations: Georgia, throwing a party because it's what she thinks people want from her; and me, changing my hair, such a little thing, just to be liked. I think about my assumptions about what makes us worth something – personality, hair, clothes, self-belief – things I wish were different about me, but who am I reinventing myself for? My head's spinning. I just want to be *better* than I am.

I look at Georgia, surprised by her honesty. "What? Have I got something on my face? I knew this was a shade too far," she says, rubbing at her lips.

"No, nothing like that. I guess, I just wasn't expecting you to be so" – *nice? normal? unbitchy?* – "open about stuff."

"Yeah, well, it's just the way I am. I probably talk too much. Can't help but let it all out." And true to form, she moves from topic to topic: "Your hair's different."

"Yeah. Hairband snapped. Going freeform."

"Oh," she says. *Is that a good "oh" or a bad "oh"?* "So it's not a warehouse but under the railway arches. There's this huge space, usually used for performance art, installations or whatever."

I nod along.

"We could have fairy lights along here." Georgia runs a manicured finger down one edge of the building plan. "And the bar here."

"Maybe a seating area in this bit outside," I add.

"Yeah, a chill-out area."

"What about laying down some fake grass and making it like a magical garden type thing."

"I love that idea."

"And theme-wise, I don't know what you think of this,

but – I mean, not, like, in a five-year-old-princess kind of way, but sort of neons and more stylized shapes, even just taking the pattern as a starting point – maybe it could work," I venture, and open my sketchbook to the bright Cairns Birdwing.

"Yes! Butterflies. You're a genius! Loads of shimmering fabrics draped around, and dancing butterflies projected on the walls. Like this one, really strong colours. Nothing pink. I hate pink."

I'm flooded, overflowing, with good feelings.

"Noted. No pink. What about an acrobatic show? You know, like, circus performers on hoops and ribbons, dancing, flying? Made up to look like butterflies? Cool, macho, non-pink butterflies."

Georgia moves her chair closer, nodding.

"Yes, yes, yes. This is all good stuff. Get drawing."

I sketch out some costumes, stylized butterfly shapes and patterns. We mark where the DJ might go, and then it hits me.

"What if the DJ was in a cage, a birdcage, like this, suspended above the dance floor? Can you do that?"

"I don't know but I'll find out!"

The ideas come fast and furious; before long I've filled several pages with notes and sketches.

"Can you copy this stuff so I can give it to the planner? He's got no clue what he's doing." She widens her eyes. "This will *really* help."

So, there *is* a planner. I'm just the ideas monkey. I check the time on my phone. Almost four. I don't want to keep Lauren and Sienna waiting much longer... "Yeah, of course. But—"

"Want a lift home? Mum's got the Merc outside," Georgia asks.

"Er, may—"

The door swings open.

Sienna walks in. "Hey. You ready? I've done the evil Paluk assignment, and for that, I deserve a bag of chips from the market before they close up. Maybe some fudge, too."

"Yeah," I say.

Georgia shrugs. She replaces her notepad in her bag. "'Bye. Thanks for the help."

"I'll give you the copies tomorrow," I say to her back as she exits the room.

Lauren's waiting in the corridor, bags over her shoulder, a sympathetic look on her face.

"What's up?" I ask. She eyes Georgia making her way down the corridor and out the door.

"Nothing. It's just … I probably shouldn't say this – I mean, we only just met – but … you seem like a nice girl and … those guys sort of live in a dream world, their own little untouchable bubble… They're in trouble sometimes… Do you really want to get involved?"

Whoa. That's a lot of information. Does she think I won't fit in with that crowd? Besides, Georgia was friendly.

"It was only a few sketches. She didn't invite me car-jacking or anything. She was nice."

"I guess Georgia is OK … but…" Lauren shrugs.

But what? Sienna rolls her eyes. "They're just a bit full of it. Come on, I'm literally concave with hunger so let's amscray."

I can't work out whether Lauren is jealous or if she's really trying to warn me. I want to give Georgia, Violet and all that lot the benefit of the doubt. If they talk to me, why not talk back? I want to find out myself what they're really like.

The market is held on a pretty side street off the high street, lined with what my dad would call "chocolate-box" houses. Garden walls are caressed by climbing plants dotted with dusky pink flowers.

Chalkboards and handwritten labels shout:

DELICIOUS HANDMADE SOMERSET FUDGE

SPICED CRAB-APPLE JELLY

LEMON, POLENTA AND ALMOND CAKE

BBQ PULLED PORK ROLLS

Stalls sell all kinds of crafts, books, antiques and clothing, some of it pure junk, but there are a few gems to be found.

The stalls follow the gentle incline of the road, so we can see them all rising ahead of us. Lots of people are milling about; the yummy mummies are out in force, with buggies and babies in slings. A bearded guy hands out leaflets for yoga classes. I notice some brave haircuts.

The sweet scent of the flower barrow permeates everything.

Sienna makes a beeline for the food stalls, choosing thrice-cooked polenta chips with spiced pimento dip. *Fancy.* I don't even know what pimento is. Sounds like a car model to me. *The Fiat Pimento.*

I carry on up the hill with Lauren. Sienna trails behind, eating her chips. We pass a record stall and one with loads of clocks and watches, some ticking out of sync, others stopped altogether.

I pick up a pocket watch, golden with a white face. The tiny hands are still, the intricate movement quiet.

I come over all philosophical. Something about Lauren puts me at ease, like you could talk to her about any problem and she would try her best to solve it for you.

"Do you ever feel like life's going on around you, but you're not part of it?" I ask.

Lauren turns to face me. "How do you mean?"

"Oh, it's nothing." I put down the watch.

"It's obviously *not* nothing."

I sigh. "It's just, like, you go through the motions, day after day, but it's not real? Like you're sleep-walking, waiting for this grand change to happen where you come alive, into your own."

"I think I know what you mean. That there's more out there than this. But I don't reckon it gets handed to you. I think people work hard to get it."

"Yeah, maybe. Do you think, though, I mean, sometimes do you think that there's this ideal life out there, tantalizing you, but however hard you try, you can never quite grasp it? You're stuck where you are. On the edge. Trundling along, parallel to that awesome life that you can't have."

Lauren weighs her answer.

"Not really," she says. "I think life is kind of what you make it. It's good to have dreams, of course it is, but actually, I think the ideal life is just a myth. Say you get all the stuff you want, at that point you'll just make a new list of wants. It's never-ending. You just have to choose to be happy and get on with things."

Lauren talks a lot of sense, but … the thing is, I'm *not* happy. That's the problem. I'm not *at all* happy, and I'm not even sure why. But one thing I do know: I can't sit around waiting to feel happy, for my ideal life to appear before me on a silver platter. Lauren's right: you have to work for things. Waiting is not an option.

Sienna comes up behind us.

"Why can't they just do good old potato ones?" she asks, shoving a polenta chip in her mouth.

"I guess they're trying to show off," Lauren says, taking a steaming chip.

"Get your own!" Sienna bats Lauren away.

"Maybe they're just trying something different," I say.

"Don't mess with the classics. That's what I say."

We continue up the street, dipping in and out of the stalls, picking things up, putting them down. Gasping at prices.

I rifle through some racks of old clothing and find a pair of cut-off, barely there, bum-revealing mini shorts. I put them back. *Not ready for those. But maybe with tights…*

I sift through another rack, find a vest and pair it with the shorts.

"That looks like something Violet would wear," Lauren says, and I don't say it out loud, but I think to myself, *Is that such a bad thing?*

I put the shorts and top back. Pick up a flower-print dress.

"I don't know, it's kind of granny-ish," says Sienna.

"I think it's sort of retro-cool," I say.

Lauren takes the dress and holds it up to me. She pushes a loose lock of hair behind her ear. "I think it'd look good on you."

"Thanks." I smile. I really like the dress, but approval from Lauren cements it for me. The stall owner bags it up and I fish a twenty from my wallet.

"What about these?" I turn around to see Sienna sporting an old-man flat cap and a pair of gold-rimmed half-moon spectacles, her bright red fringe covering her eyes. She's clutching an orange bandeau top and some shiny purple leggings. Lauren and Sienna break into laughter, and I go along with it, but I'm thinking, *OK, not the cap or glasses, but maybe the top or leggings … as part of another outfit… They could be cool.*

Next day I'm in school early to copy the sketches for Georgia. Part of me wanted to hang back, to catch Finn by the doctors' surgery again, but I stuck to my new social rule about minimizing the mentalist stalking.

I can't see Georgia in the common room, and it's almost time for the bell. So I shove the photocopies in my bag and, instead of searching for her, decide to check how my new vintage dress from the market looks, and maybe rearrange my hair before class starts.

In the toilets, I sigh. Yes, I look better, but I'm not used to the reflection staring back at me. I run a comb through my hair, then abandon the sleek look. Tipping my head upside down, I mess it up, make it big, put a few clips in it. I circle my lips with a new red lipstick. It certainly pings, makes a statement.

Out-of-bed look complete.

The door opens and a vision enters. Violet Brody.

I feel like a child caught playing with Mummy's make-up. Trying on too-big heels and tottering about before falling flat on her face. She makes me nervous.

But waltzing in behind her is Georgia, who smiles warmly.

"Hey, Carla," Georgia says.

"Hey," I answer.

"Nice dress," Violet says. "I love that style on you." Wow. Did I hear that right?

"Thanks." I try to hold her attention, looking for a way to be interesting and return the compliment, which, let's face it, shouldn't be hard when Aphro-fucking-dite is before you. "You've got great boobs – I mean, boots, I like your boots." OK, maybe it *is* difficult for a socially inept creature like me.

When I said I was looking for a way to be "interesting", I didn't mean imbecilic... God almighty. I'm sabotaging my own freaking, miserable life.

How can talking to one set of people be so easy and another so tough? They're just people. But tell that to my mind-of-its-own-voicebox.

"I think this one is girl-crushing on me, George," Violet laughs, but with less contempt than last time I embarrassed myself. Maybe Georgia has said something. Could I have actually *passed* the Friendiview? Can I wedge my foot in the door and peer into the Violet Brody and Georgia Presco friendzone? Got to talk, got to laugh at myself, got to *speak up and be heard*.

"No, I, Jesus, I have, like, a dyslexic tongue or something. I hate myself. I'm like the Fount of All Awkwardness, Cringedom."

"You're funny, you know that?" Violet says.

I didn't know that. Funny ha ha or funny weird? At this point, I'll take either.

"I got the boots from some pop-up sale in Shoreditch. They're vintage."

"Well, your *boots* are nice," I tell her and I smile my best lipstick-laden smile. "Oh, here," I say, pulling the papers from my bag and passing them to Georgia. "For the planner."

She takes them with a heavily braceletted arm and flicks through.

"Thanks." Georgia turns to Violet, who's checking her hair in the mirror. "Vi, you've got to see these, for the party. Ohmygod, it's going to be immense. Carla's, like, an artistic genius."

Georgia spreads the pages over the surface around the basin. I try to fend off a wince as the corner of my Cairns Birdwing drawing gets wet.

"Shit, sorry," Georgia says, peeling the soggy paper from the patch of wet.

"It'll dry," I say. "No worries."

Violet surveys the drawings. She nods. "Impressive. But…" She turns to me. "I'm not trying to piss on your parade, but butterflies, aren't they a bit … I don't know, cutesy?"

Ouch.

"Not the way we've planned. It'll be amazing." Georgia

reacts immediately. At least she's on board. And it's *her* party after all.

It's going to be harder work with Violet.

One step forwards, twenty-three steps back.

The bell rings and I stiffen. *Going to be late*. But the girls don't bat an eyelid. Georgia bags the sketches. Violet applies some mascara, checks her profile.

They head out.

I don't move. I'm still processing the last five minutes: the compliment, the criticism, Violet's bipolar responses. It's a start.

I press my red lips together, pouting in the mirror.

Georgia turns. "You coming?" She props the door open with her foot.

"Yeah, coming," I say, gathering my make-up into my bag. I follow them out, into possibly, maybe, what could be the friendzone.

CHAPTER 9

First thing I do when I get home is make some toast. I coat it with an obscene quantity of butter, aching for that first after-school mouthful of soggy, glistening, golden awesomeness. Sat-is-faction.

As I savour the moment, Mum decides to call and rant about me not taking out the bins and *have you done your homework?* and *I hope you haven't just left your washing in a pile on the floor because we have a laundry basket for that, Carla.* I make appropriate noises and affirmative grunts until she seems tenderized. (It's kind of like bashing a steak with a mallet until it softens.)

I retreat upstairs, get my laptop from under a pile of cartridge paper and pencil shavings, and log in to Facebook. Hurrah, a new message!

Hey Kid,

How's life in Londinium? Hope your ma's not going batshit crazy with all the stress. Then again, I know she will be. Stay strong, little one!

Tino and I just saw a wallaby being born. No word of a lie. OMG, it was amazing and only the size of my finger. You'd think they'd be massive. Anyway, it was all pink and hairless and the cutest thing ever. It's great to see new ones popping out because this breed of wallaby is almost extinct. Damn humans and their desire to wear animal carcass! Anyhow... We set traps each day for the furry rascals to monitor them – they're all microchipped, so we can identify each one, take their measurements and a DNA sample. I'm collecting loads of data for my course!

I hope we'll help make a difference. It's hands-on research and fun and rewarding and... I'm going on about it, aren't I? Ha ha. Forget me, tell me what's going on in Lundun!

Off to go get some tucker (they actually say that here. I know, right?!) and bore some other poor soul with outback wallaby conservation tales.

Big love,

Sal

XX

Sal's my cousin, twenty-three, sharp as hell but daft as a brush. Her boyfriend, Tino, is this super-cool surfer dude who rarely speaks, but that's good, because Sal likes to talk. Likes to talk *a lot*. She's the only constant friend I've had. The lucky bugger is on a year out in Australia, leaving me all alone here.

While I'm musing on what to reply, I get a notification. A new friend request. Not just any run-of-the-mill I-met-you-once-when-we-were-nine friend request, oh no, no, no; this is from Finn Masterson himself. Yikes. I'd better do a quick de-tag session of all the bad-angle photographs of me before I accept...

I do a bit of FB stalking on Finn's page. Hit photos. Swoon at perfect lips and smooth jaw, gasp at red raw knees and elbows. WTF? Then it clicks. His status update reads:

Finn Masterson had a mother of a fall today. Wiped out three riders behind me! Ha!

So he *doesn't* have an evil, scratchy cat.

I investigate further down his wall of updates.

Finn Masterson going for gold at the freestyle mountainboard battle in July. Better get training!

Finn Masterson nailed the alley-oop.

Finn Masterson On the track with Greggers.

I click PLAY on the video below and watch a dirt cloud plume into the air as Finn kicks a three-hundred-sixty–degree jump past a shaky lens. The board is long and tapered with heavy-duty wheels. I bet there's some weird name for the trick, but what would I know?

Finn Masterson Switch 180 to late McTwist.

Finn Masterson I take my Burger Flip with fries. Mmm, chips... hard day boarding, time for some well-deserved grease.

I Google "McTwist". It's a real trick. Legs flip-flipping all over the place.

I tear my gaze from Finn's page and pace the room, trying to construct a witty message to send him. My brain fires blanks.

Time to seek advice.

Dear Sheila – ahem – Sal,

Missing you like a leg. Mum is her usual one-woman cyclone system, raining devastation and tormenting the little people (me) with umbrella-breaking shitstorms at every opportunity. I try to take it on the chin but one only has so many umbrellas.

Your work sounds amazing. Post pictures stat. How many wallabies do you catch a day? Is the programme working? Have you seen any other cool wildlife? I saw a rat outside the local coffee shop. Gross. I almost hurled up my croissant.

Now, to business. School is OK, etc., etc., boring crap. Except ... there's this guy. He just friended me on Facebook. Aaaaaarrrggghhh!!! What do I do? I'm out of my depth.

Ah, forget it. I'll admire him from afar. I feel like a dweeb. Yes, I used the word dweeb. So what are you going to do? Sue me for breaching the Use of Uncool Words Act? Go on, I dare ya.

Over and out,

CC

Thing is, I won't hear back from Sal for hours yet…

I'm not exactly worried by Finn's friend request, but I guess I'm thinking, *Am I cool enough, interesting enough? Does Finn think I'm something I'm not? What version of me do I want to be?*

CHAPTER 10

Later I decide to go to the park to clear my head. I like to de-stress by doing gymnastics. I can float into a world where nothing exists but me and the move. Like escaping to a parallel universe where everything makes sense.

I'm just getting existential, thinking, *Who am I, anyway?* when my phone buzzes. New message from Sal. I Google the current time in Melbourne. One a.m. Well, she's always been a night owl.

> All right CC,
>
> Great news, one of the wallabies released last year is preggers! That means the colony is settled and starting to breed independently! Yay!
>
> As for your new guy, he's made the first move by friending you on Facebook. Probably wanted to oggle your photos, ha ha. Wait and see what happens and just be yourself.
>
> Tell me more, tell me more, like does he have a

healthy bank balance and an excellent school record?!

Love 'n' hugs,

Sal

Just be yourself. Good advice. But easier said than done. And do I really believe it? It's never got me anywhere fast before.

The sun is burning through a thin lace of cloud, the air suspended in autumn warmth. Reddish dust clouds around my feet as I pace the path. There are three tired-looking swings, their paint chipped and faded. A lonely roundabout creaks gently as I push it into a spin.

The evening feels like clay, sticky and orange.

I've done gym since I was a toddler. I remember my first somersault when I was four, the world turning as I spun in the air, only it seemed like I was still and things revolved around me. Seeing everything in a different way to other people made me feel special.

I unbutton my shirt and tie it around my waist. Underneath I'm wearing a vest. I draw my hair back into a barely contained blob and fasten it with an elastic band. I try to empty my mind.

I'm brimming with energy.

I pound the grass with my hands, twisting with force and determination, spotting my landings accurately. I do a one-handed cartwheel. I point my toes to an imaginary judge. I bound a few steps and lunge into a round off. Point toe. Grass. Left hand. Grass. Right hand. Grass. World.

Upside down. Legs. Twist. Hands. Push. Spring. Both feet. Grass. World. Right way up. I sense a presence. My vest has ridden up exposing my oh-so-white midriff. I smooth it down with green-stained fingers.

I take a breath.

Then I miss one.

"You're er …" he pauses, "dextrous." Finn is sitting on the middle swing, grinning, eating fish and chips, the harsh, vinegary aroma clawing at my nostrils.

I shuffle on my feet like a loon, and skirt my tongue around my bottom lip. *Just be yourself.* I feel him take me in, look at me from top to toe, taking stock: nervous girl, unruly hair, vest strap off her shoulder, trouser leg tucked into her shoe… I shrink with embarrassment, then think, *He's here, isn't he? Talking to me. Bloody well make the most of it!*

"It takes some skill. Not much…" I trail off.

"No, really, that's some bendy stuff. You double-jointed or some freaky shit like that? You got jelly bones? You made of rubber, tiger?" *He called me tiger! All is not lost!*

"Er, I, um… I used to do gym. Not any more." *COME ON! God Almighty, say something entertaining!*

"You should, you're good." He pulls the chains to his chest, then lets them spring back.

"Nah, I had to pick, gym or puberty. I was pro-puberty." Did I really just say that? Did I say the word *puberty*? Am I going to spontaneously burst into song and start serenading him with Britney's "I'm Not a Girl, Not Yet a Woman"? OH NO.

I feel blood rushing to my cheeks. I cartwheel behind

the swings. I see the school buildings in the distance, dainty like an architect's model.

I run and do another spring. *Must outrun the gaping hole of embarrassment opening up beneath me.* Dive forward roll. Spring. My leg pulls and I feel a sharp twinge in my thigh. It'll ache tomorrow. That'll teach me to do gym without stretching first.

I gently lower myself to the grass and bring my knees to my chest, hugging them tight and feeling that hit of pain as I tense my leg muscles. The silence seems to linger like the warmth in the air.

"Uh … well, yeah, I'm all for that choice. Good decision. Want some?" he asks, offering me his greasy food.

"Ew, no thanks. I hate fish."

He looks slightly embarrassed and I quite enjoy seeing his cheeks flush. He's a bit vulnerable. Like a flash it's gone, cheeky-chappy persona reinstated.

"You into sports?" I enquire, feigning innocence after my Facebook stalking.

"Mountainboarding's my passion."

"That explains the injuries." I point to his lacerated elbows.

"I fractured my hand last year. It absolutely *caned* for weeks. Could stand the pain but not being able to ride really got to me. Set my training back and I messed up the comps. This is my year though. I'm ready."

"When's the comp?" *July. Read it on Facebook.*

"The UK Board Battle's in July, but got a warm-up comp at the weekend. Come watch me win, tiger!"

"I might," I say casually. *I'm so there.*

I get up and do another spring. And another.

"Slow down, you'll tumble right out of the park!"

I muster an upside-down frown. "I like to tumble."

"You're quite the *woman*. Bendy. I like that."

"I just do it now and then. Helps me relax."

"You stressed then?"

"A little. New school. Coursework. Future depending on results. Pushy mother who wants me to be a scientist or a doctor or lawyer or practically anything other than what I might want to be."

"You shouldn't get hung up over that stuff. Havelock and school. It's just another stick in the spokes. You gotta ride that bike of life, tiger. Grab the handlebars and pedal. Forget about them."

"You come out with some bollocks. Really. You do." I sit on one of the swings, out of breath. But maybe Finn's right. I should do what I want.

"You love it, tiger." I steal a glance at him, his eyes wide with excitement. "Hey, can you teach me how to do that flippy thing?"

I take a run and cartwheel. "This?"

"Yeah."

"If you want."

Finn gets up and bins his chips. He starts stretching, pulling one arm, then the other, across his chest. He touches his toes.

"Stand with your legs about a shoulder-width apart and raise your arms."

"Like this?"

"A little wider." Finn moves his legs further apart. "You

might want to hoist your jeans up, so you can move more easily."

"So I don't get my knackers caught, you mean." He pulls his trousers up and tightens his belt a notch. "This is not a good look for me." He grins.

"Arms up."

He lifts them but they're still bent at the elbow. I walk towards him and pull his arms straight. His doe eyes sparkle in the evening light. I catch myself dwelling on them a little too long, caught in the power of those hypnotic pools. For a second it seems like he might lean in and kiss me. And oh, the thought is too much. I move to his side. Probably my imagination.

"Step out with your right leg. Rock from one foot to the other for a moment to get a feel for it. Imagine you're a giant *X*."

"OK." Finn rocks backwards and forwards on the spot, like someone keeps pressing Play, Pause, Rewind, Play, on him.

"When you're ready, build up some momentum. Then put your right hand down, followed by your left hand and kick up to the sky. Think of the *X* shape you're making. Rotate your whole body."

"Oh, just rotate your whole body. It's that simple."

"You should be good at this; you must do flippy things on your board all the time."

I demonstrate the cartwheel again.

"I've got it, I think." Finn hesitates. "OK, here I go."

He throws his legs up, but it's more of a hop than a rotation. I have to laugh.

"Good try. But you" – instinctively I pat him on the back – "might need some practice."

"Diplomatic of you to say, but perhaps I'm not the tumbling type. Unless it's off my board. Thanks for the lesson. Could we have another one, tomorrow at four?"

"Yeah, all right. Maybe I can help you, Mr Masterson, to *master* the humble forward roll."

CHAPTER 11

Next day, I'm marooned on Swoon Island. In Tutorial, I stare at Finn's back like he might grow wings and fly off like an angel. At break, I'm as chatty as a tree stump. At lunch, I can't eat any of the red brick that is Dad's spicy chorizo pasta.

In Biology, Sienna invites me to go to the cinema this evening with her and Lauren.

"It's not the most refined movie but Gabriel Grayson's in it, and explosions," she says, blowing eraser mulch on the floor. "Actually, it's the antithesis of cultural highbrow. But you're welcome to come."

Every instinct wills me to go, and I almost let the "Yeah, sure" slip from my lips but, then… *How could I forget?* Carla's Gym Class is in session at four.

Normally, I'd jump at the chance to get to know them better. But the pull of Finn totally trumps any doubts I have about turning them down. There'll be other movies. But maybe not another chance to be alone with him.

"I can't…" I pause. What can I say? I have a date to show Finn Masterson how to do a forward roll? "I have to do my Biology coursework. I'm really behind," I lie, and feel instantly terrible.

"It's not due for weeks, Carla. What's the deal?"

I've never been good at lying. Once, Dad caught me siphoning vodka into an Evian bottle so it would look like water. I told him I needed it to clean hairspray off my mirror, which I thought was pretty ingenious, until he pointed out that I hadn't worn hairspray since "The Great Fringe Singeing of 2010" when I had frazzled my locks with a sparkler on Bonfire Night.

"Fine, fine." I give in. "I'm meeting Finn. I ran into him last night and he asked me to meet up again tonight."

"I *knew* it," Lauren says.

I bite the end of my biro.

"So is it a date?" Sienna asks.

"No idea. See what happens, I guess."

I look to Lauren, who's staring at me like I've grown a second head and turned purple: weird. "What?"

"But *why* do you like him?" she asks.

"Um, have you *seen* him?"

"Er, yes, but he's not exactly Albert Einstein, is he?"

"You fancy Einstein?" Now it's my turn to do the double-headed purple look.

"No, but let's face it, you won't see Finn's head in a copy of *The God Particle* or *On the Origin of Species* or … *Wuthering Heights*."

"Show me a gorgeous boy with a bookshelf like that and I'll abandon this quest immediately."

Lauren opens her mouth to speak but nothing comes out.

"Didn't think so," I say. In my head I'm jumping to defend Finn, to say he's not dumb, but I keep the words inside. Instead I ask, "Don't you just want to try running in those circles with Georgia and Violet, to see what it's like?"

"Not really. I mean, there's more to life than glossy hair and a big ego. Like getting into uni and finding a career beyond plucking your eyebrows to perfection."

"Can't you be intelligent *and* popular?"

"I'm not saying you can't, but that lot have yet to prove there's more than hairspray and nail glue holding them together. I guess the difference between Violet and me is that I only want my friends to like me. I don't care what everyone else thinks."

Who am I? Why can't I be satisfied with being a Brainy Plain Girl? I get what Lauren's saying but… Is it just something you tell yourself to make yourself feel better? Or is it the truth? I guess I've never felt happy as I am: mid-range, mid-beige, mediocre. Maybe if I try to be friends with those girls, not just to get closer to Finn, but as a way to, I don't know … unlock my potential, I won't feel so down about myself. Maybe if I'm admired by the rest of the school, accepted by Violet, Georgia and Finn, then I'll finally be popular with me.

Tillsman gives out this week's test results. *A+*. Getting better. Intelligent *and* popular. It can be done, I'm sure of it.

In the corridor after class, I notice Finn standing with Georgia and Greg. He's everywhere, a constant thought in my head, and all around the school, on the periphery of my vision. Like a sixth sense, I feel him near me all the time.

He's talking animatedly, but stops when he sees me. Smiles. Georgia catches the look, then kisses Greg and bounds up to Lauren, Sienna and me. She latches on to my arm and pulls me forwards, ignoring the others.

"Walk with me to Psych?" Georgia asks. I don't think I have a choice.

"See you tomorrow," I call to the girls as she drags me away. I feel bad for leaving them, but they have different classes now.

"Sit with me and Finn, OK?"

I feel a rush at this special treatment. Like finally I'm starting to be somebody.

CHAPTER 12

In Psychology, sitting next to Georgia, opposite Finn, I'm distracted. I catch him looking at me more than once. I feel his foot against mine and agonize over whether it's deliberate. In short, I go do-la-la crazy and can't concentrate. Mr Green's been talking for half an hour, but it's only noise. I try to tune back in.

"Why is Bandura's Social Learning Theory too deterministic?" he says.

WTF does deterministic *mean?*

The sun hangs like a canary diamond, glinting. The park is warm and dry. When I get to the swings he's already there. My watch blinks 15.58. He grins at me.

"You look confused." He kicks at the bark chippings with his Converse. "You do remember making this date?" So it's a date!

"Course. I'm just surprised to see you."

"It's four o'clock."

"I know." I sit on the swing next to his. "You're on time."

"You're worth showing up for." *Guh.* The whole world washes with colour twice as bright as a moment ago.

Dear Lovegods,

Thank you for smiling upon me. Amen.

"Ready to learn some moves?" I ask.

"Sure."

Finn proves better at forward rolls than cartwheels.

"Want to try a double?"

"Like, two in a row?"

"No, like where you hold each other's ankles and roll together."

"Sounds a bit advanced, don't you think?"

"It's not *that* difficult."

"Maybe we don't know each other well enough for ankle gropage. Let's start with an elbow or maybe a toe."

"Are you scared you won't be able to do it, Mr I-Can't-Cartwheel?"

"I rarely get scared, Carla. I would, of course, do a double forward roll with you in a heartbeat, but I fear you wouldn't be able to take the weight of my manly physique with your delicate lady arms."

"What a load of bollocks."

"OK, but I could – and judging by my apparently non-existent cartwheel skills probably will – land on you and break your neck, or worse, break *my* neck." He grins.

"Oi! OK, well, I've helped you, now you can help me ... with my homework."

"Homework. That's *exactly* what I want to be doing right now," Finn says. "Are you serious?"

I pull my knees up to my chest and rummage through

my bag. I tug my sketchbook out and send a search party for my pastels.

I go to flip the book open to a clean fresh page, but Finn flicks the cover back down and snatches the book. I'm not that precious, so I skip the standard girlie scream *Giveitback! Giveitback! Giveitback!* But it's more than a sketchbook, more than Art coursework, it's my diary in pictures and words; doodles, poems, lists.

"I could draw you."

"And my manly physique."

"With my delicate lady hands."

The cover is black, corrugated, simple. I'm not that girl who Tippexes guys' names everywhere, draws hearts or calculates our compatibility according to the number of consonants in our names, or whatever. Finn's not going to open the book to find *Mrs Carla Masterson* scrawled everywhere, and *Finn + Carla 4eva* in giant pink bubble writing. No, no, no. Give me some credit, please.

"I want to start at the beginning!" he says. "A woman's doodles say a lot about her."

"Oh yeah?"

"Yeah. A man's doodles say a lot about him, too."

"Is that right?"

"Uh-huh. I'd just like to say, you're welcome to check out my doodles and make your own assessment at any time." We're not talking about drawings now.

"I'll bear that in mind."

"You do that."

"You're an idiot," I say, laughing. He opens to page one: butterflies. Page two: butterflies. Page three: Pre-Raphaelite notes and drawings. Loose papers: shopping list, revision notes I haven't typed up yet and probably never will. Page four: view from my bedroom window, sky like marble, fluid. Pages five to eleven: sculpture designs for my Art coursework, colour tests, notes on the type of butterfly.

"You like butterflies," he comments.

"Your powers of deduction astound me."

"Why butterflies?"

"They're gorgeous. Free. They start as a tiny egg stuck to a leaf somewhere, insignificant, and go on a journey to become this almost magical creature."

I don't say it aloud, but I think, that's what I love most about butterflies: their ability to completely transform, and with such exquisite style. Imagine waking up one morning and being able to fly. Yesterday you were the short, fat kid under threat from the bird bullies. Today you're Angelina freaking Jolie with wings. Complete metamorphosis.

"They're pretty, I guess. Like you."

"Oh, please." I roll my eyes, but can't help feeling flattered.

"I mean it."

"Well, thanks, Casanova."

"You're welcome, Francesca."

"Francesca?"

"In the story. Casanova's in love with Francesca. Not that I'm saying I'm… Well, you know what I mean."

I narrow my eyes at him. It's kind of nice to see him squirm, with his guard down.

"So anyway, could you draw me? Just my face or something," says Finn.

It's one thing drawing him from across the hockey pitch but up close… "I'm no good at faces."

"Why don't you just draw my hands, then?"

"I could handle that." I look at his long, tapered fingers, calloused and manly. Big. I trace my finger across a barely there red line on his palm. "Boarding scar?" Finn nods. I rough out the edges of his fingers, and use different colours to add tone and depth. They look older in pastel. The hands of a trawlerman; powerful, rugged.

"Did you know there's a butterfly called a Chequered Skipper?" I don't look up. His hand, the hand I'm drawing, rests on my left knee. The book sits in my lap. I have a glance-rally between the page and his hand, making sure to capture each contour, each shadow, exactly.

"No."

"And a Scrub-Hairstreak?"

"Ah yes, from the lesser-known family of Bad Dyejob butterflies."

"You're funny," I say, sarcastically. "They have all sorts of names. Red Flasher is one of my favourites for obvious, childish reasons. Daggerwing. There's one called Question Mark. And a Comma. How weird is that?" I don't stop for an answer. "There's even one called Mourning Cloak."

"I assume that one's black," he says. I stop drawing, flick a few pages back.

"Yup," I say, tapping a sketch of a Mourning Cloak. "But I think you'll appreciate this one." I turn the book so he can see another pencil drawing.

"It's beautiful."

"Yeah. It reminds me of you."

"What's it called?"

"Dogface. Not kidding." We fall about, play-fighting, joking. Free like butterflies.

Thank you, Lovegods, from the bottom of my uber-grateful girlie heart.

CHAPTER 13

School is an escape. None of these people know me. I can be anybody. I want to fit in, but on my terms. I don't want to slot in where I've always been: inconsequential, forgettable, nobody. This is my chance – my final opportunity – to shine.

School is an alternative universe where I can be cool and assertive. OK, I was shy at first, who wouldn't be? But then I discovered you can fake confidence, and soon it starts paying off. Act confident, be confident.

In the common room at break, Lauren and Sienna sit dissecting *Heat* magazine.

I pick at a satsuma's white veins.

Lauren flips through the pages. "Look at the size of her bump. She must be carrying a litter. Of bears. With gigantism."

"I wouldn't have picked that wedding dress," Sienna chips in about another story.

"'The happy couple released a pair of doves as a symbol of their love.'"

"Sickening."

"So showy. I bet it's just a money-making media deal."

"I think it's kind of sweet," I say, then immediately regret it.

"Er, clearly cupid's arrow has lodged in your brain and is pressing against some vital nerve, impeding your judgement. It's not *sweet.* It's OTT attention-seeking crap."

"It's only a pair of doves," Lauren says.

"Not just the birds. All that celebrity, fakery, glitter, *look at me, I'm so amazing and I'm so in love!* stuff. It degrades the whole marriage thing. It's all for money and so they can hang on to their fifteen minutes for a bit longer."

"Maybe it's special for them. If it's what they're into."

"I reckon in no time they'll be cashing in on a reality show, then five minutes later it's the divorce, and after that a six-figure dish-the-dirt book deal."

"You're probably right, but I still think the doves are a nice touch."

Sienna opens her mouth to speak again but Lauren cuts her off.

"Date went well then? So what happened?"

I put a satsuma segment in my mouth and mime that I can't possibly talk, I'm eating.

"Come on, Carla. Spill."

I finish my mouthful and prepare to tell the girls about our gym session (why does that sound dirty?) when Finn strides over. Saved.

"Excuse me, ladies. Can I borrow Carla?"

"We've got Paluk in five," Sienna objects, "and Carla was about to tell us something important."

"Nope, nope I wasn't. Definitely no information to relate at all about anything." I shrug as if to say *What you gonna do?* and the girls scowl at me.

I walk with Finn to the corner of the room. His purple T-shirt clings to his chest. His dark hair flops into his eyes and he reaches up and pushes it back.

"I just wanted to give you this," he says, holding out a folded square of paper. I notice the dirt under his nails. Must be from boarding.

"Oh … thanks," I say. "And this is for you." I take out my sketchbook, rip out the drawing, fold it and hand it to him. He smiles widely, touches my arm, then turns to leave.

"Aren't you coming to Chemistry?"

"On time? Never." He walks away.

I stare at the note like it's the freaking Holy Grail, gawking, until I realize I must look like a prize idiot. Lauren taps me on the shoulder and gives me my bag.

"Are you going to open it?" Sienna asks.

"Look at you," Lauren says, then holds her hands to her chest and flutters her eyelashes jokily. "He's so dreamy."

The girls look amused, but at the same time sorry for me. I flash them an icy stare.

"Do you need to go splash your face with cold water? I'll tell Paluk you've got women's problems."

"No, thank you, Sienna." I whack her on the arm. "I'm totally fine and functional. Let's go."

Lauren scoffs. "Be careful, all right?"

"What do you mean?"

"It's Finn Masterson," she says, like his name is

explanation enough. She looks at her watch. "Paluk O'Clock. Come on."

Sienna and Lauren quick-walk to the classroom, weaving through the masses, but I trail behind.

Outside the door, I stop, lean against the wall and unfurl the note.

Tiger,
Meet me at my cat and mouse after school.
66 Buckingham Road.
You've stolen my strawberry tart.
F

The bell screeches, but I'm glued to the spot. The hairs on my body seem to stand on end, and for a second I feel like I'm rebooting, a surge of energy bursting from the core of my chest, through my veins to the tips of my fingers, toes and hair.

"Carla, are you joining us or planning to take notes from outside?" Paluk booms. He's wearing an oversized blood-red shirt; beige trousers flap around his bamboo-thin legs.

"Sorry, sir." Paluk moves aside as I pass. All eyes focus on me, but unlike that horrible first day, this time I'm not bothered. I've never been late for a class in my life. It's kind of exhilarating.

CHAPTER 14

The initial excitement of Finn's invitation dissipates and I get a nagging earworm saying maybe it's a bit soon to be going to his house and also, what does he imagine we're going to do there? Talk about the weather? Catch up on homework? How many other girls has he lured to his room by telling them they've stolen his strawberry tart? I fancy him, sure, but I don't want to look like a desperate, skanky, ho-bag. Still, I get this fluttering in my stomach when I think about being there, lying next to him on the bed…

After school I dash to Finn's house. My earlier apprehension has become nervous excitement and I guess I'm enjoying the kick because my pace and pulse quicken on the way. Finn lives nearer to school than I do, on the other side of the park. And when I say on the other side of the park, I mean ON THE PARK. 66 Buckingham Road is a four-storey end-of-terrace townhouse, its overgrown front garden laid with decorative paving stones; a flight of chunky steps leads up to a glossy red front door with stained-glass panels. Finn's family must be absolutely Lotto-winning-private-jet-fifty-foot-yacht *minted*.

Standing on the top step, I inhale, then breathe out my nerves. I imagine I'm with Finn, sunning myself on our own personal island like Richard Branson, sipping piña coladas…

Reaching for the door knocker, cast like a cat with a mouse dangling from its mouth, I notice a set of buzzers. I press the one labelled MASTERSON.

A super-suave, SAS, 007 type opens the door. He looks like he could have trained police officers, slept with beautiful women every night for the last thirty years, and probably keeps a gun in his sock drawer.

"Um, hi. I'm looking for Finn," I say to the sergeant. "Is this the right house?"

"Hi, you're Carla, right? Come in." He speaks in tones the colour of Merlot, deep and smooth.

"Yeah, thanks." Mr Masterson Senior leads me to another door off the hallway. I head into the house.

I'm beginning to register my surroundings – the ornate Indian lampshade, Hockney prints on the wall, the tiled floor – when Finn comes careering from the living room, dodging his dad like the Stig taking the Hammerhead on *Top Gear*. He grabs my hand and pulls me upstairs.

I follow Finn into his room. His blue-checked duvet is crumpled at one end of the bed and there's still a dent in the pillow where his head has been. I let myself daydream about resting my head there, what it would be like to breathe in his sleepy scent. I imagine lying down next to him, his arm coiled around my waist, his hot breath on my neck.

I force my thoughts onto something else. Otherwise I'll get lost there.

"Nice house."

"Maisonette. Rental. There's a family in the basement and another above us. We've got the garden though, pretty sweet for summer parties."

OK, maybe I won't be on that island any time soon. Not loaded after all. No matter. It's still a gorgeous maisonette.

"Your dad looks like a right hard man."

"He was a marine. Seen a fair bit of action."

"And now?"

"Runs a catering business. He's always liked cooking. He told me this story about when the ship was sailing home – the cook had been killed along with a good chunk of the crew, so he made this meal for the rest of them, the lucky ones. He brought it into the mess and someone had put on the film *Chariots of Fire*, then that song "Jerusalem" came on and everyone was singing and he just burst into tears. So he's not so hard, really. He was only, like, twenty then. I guess being in a war's a lot to deal with. He's been cooking ever since." He looks at his feet, contemplating.

There are piles of *Board Mag* on the floor. His mountainboard leans against the clothes rail, its wheels caked in mud.

I pick up his helmet, and run my finger over the stickers. I hover over a four-leaf clover.

"Isaac gave me that one before my first race, for luck."

"Did you win?"

"Didn't come last." Finn shrugs. "You can sit down."

I sit cross-legged on the bed. "So why am I here?"

"I'm not sure I'm equipped to answer such probing questions about the nature of existentialism. Why are any of us here?"

I roll my eyes.

"You know what I mean. Why did you invite me over?"

"I thought maybe you could help me with my Art. You're pretty good at it." My heart sinks. He only wants to study. "That, and I can't stop thinking about you." *Whoa.*

The walls are covered in mountainboard posters and photos of him and Greg, Georgia, Fat Mike, Slinky and, ugh … so many pictures of him and Violet glossy-coat Brody. Sienna told me her diet is entirely vegan. Seems to me she's been at the Pedigree Chum. No, that's cruel. I don't even know her. I think I'm just a little intimidated by her. I mean, why isn't *she* with Finn? Clearly, there's some history – all these photos…

Look at that hair. Who am I kidding?

He points to a ticket stub Blu-tacked to a mirror. "This is from the Freestyle Board Jam Series, where I got injured last year."

Next to the ticket stub is the drawing I gave him. Here, among all his treasures.

"You're really talented, you know, Carla."

"Shut up."

"You are."

"I want to be an artist, but it's not exactly well paid. Unless you're dead or Damien Hirst. And I don't plan on being either."

"You could be the exception."

"Well, even if I was ever good enough, I can't imagine

my folks would be thrilled. Maybe my dad would be OK, but – not that she's said it outright, I mean, she's hardly ever around to say anything – I get the impression my mum would rather I become a geneticist or work at CERN or something wholly boring like that. Nuclear research is so *not* my bag."

"It's not about her though. It's about you, doing what you want."

"Do you always do what you want?"

"Pretty much."

I think about Finn turning up late for classes, sometimes skipping them entirely, and the way he talks back to teachers. Is it doing him any long-term favours? He's obviously intelligent, but will this do-what-I-want philosophy come back to bite him on the ass come the end of school when he's got minimal qualifications and just a dream of professional mountainboarding to pursue?

What am I going to do if I don't make it as an artist?

"Do you ever wonder what'll happen if we fail our exams?" I ask.

"Not really. I've got my board and I make enough money."

"You've got a job?"

He shrugs. "I don't worry about it." He goes over to his sound dock, slots his phone into place and presses PLAY. I guess that's the end of that conversation.

I point to a picture of Violet. "Did you two use to go out?"

"You ask a lot of questions."

"Sorry. Mum's a journalist. I guess I inherited her inquisitive nature. So, did you?"

"Violet? No way. We've been friends since for ever. She's just a mate."

I nod. "Who's this with you and Greg?"

"That's Dave Compton – one of my ultimate boarding heroes – met him at XBP Mountainboard Centre in Surrey. Soon I'll have another photo for the collection. Tom Kirkman's going to be at the UK Board Battle. Can't wait to meet him. He's a legend. I've been practising the sweetest new trick to show him."

"I see. Cool," I say, widening my eyes.

"Are you making fun of me, tiger?"

"I wouldn't dare. It's cool. You have a passion."

"It's more than a passion. It's my life."

I can't help but laugh out loud then.

Finn sits down on the bed behind me, grabs me around the shoulders and pulls me backwards so I'm lying on his chest. I look up at him.

"The warm-up comp I told you about is tomorrow. You should come. Greg's racing too and Georgia will be there."

He tells me where the skate park is and I agree to meet him.

"You smell like pears," he says.

"That'll be my invisible Carmen Miranda headdress. Made entirely from pears. I'm on a budget and strawberries aren't in season till June." The corners of his mouth curl in amusement. "Or it could be my shampoo."

I want to pull him to me, kiss him, feed him some secret potion that makes him mine and makes him want me for ever and ever and ever. We're inches apart and I can smell the sweet manliness of his neck, his arms, his hair. I smile at the feeling. Intoxicating, powerful, it grips me.

I gulp. I think he's going to kiss me. This is it. Me in my washed-too-many-times-was-white-now-grey-vest-top and elastic-band-tied-back-unkempt-blob hair. He. Is. Going. To. Kiss. ME.

I feel my face flush scarlet.

He leans in. I close my eyes…

The door swings open and I sit bolt upright.

"Oh, didn't know you were here. Sorry." Isaac looks me up and down. "Didn't mean to, er" – he searches his feet for the word – "interrupt."

"Heard of knocking, mate?" Finn snaps.

Isaac's wearing a long-sleeved top under a black shirt. His jeans are loose, baggy, normal. Not like the guys in my year. He has the same coffee-dark eyes as Finn, but behind a curtain of hair. He's attractive, but in a quiet way.

Silence expands between us.

"What do you want, Isaac?" Finn asks, breaking the tension.

"Dinner's ready."

He backs out of the room, and shuts the door.

"Better go," I say. "Culinary disaster awaits at home. Dad's attempting to cook Thai green curry. Knowing him, it'll end up purple and taste of meatballs."

"Mmm, delicious."

"Not all of us are lucky enough to have a dad who's good with a wooden spoon." I pick up my bag and head out, hovering in the doorway.

"See you tomorrow," Finn says, lying back on his bed.

CHAPTER 15

Finn slouches against the wall, one arm around my shoulder, his mountainboard under the other. "Glad you survived your dad's cooking. How were the Thai purple meatballs?" he asks.

"Good actually. Neither purple nor meatballs. Not exactly green curry either, but one step at a time. That Jamie Oliver book I got him for Christmas is starting to pay for itself."

Georgia's rocking an emo-chic look: biker boots, Ramones T-shirt, shocking pink Kate Spade handbag. She and Greg are against the wall, entangled in a pre-comp kiss … and then some.

Are they always like this? I mouth to Finn. He smiles, shrugs, then pushes Greg's shoulder.

"Head in the game, Greggers," he says.

"Come on, baby, let's get a drink," Greg says, pulling Georgia towards a refreshments van.

Finn steps away from the wall and sets his mountainboard on the ground.

His helmet sits like Lego hair, covered in stickers like MASTER OF DISASTER in fluorescent orange, GOT DIRT? in bright blue, and the grass-green four-leaf clover. He taps his head. "This is new," he says, pointing to a black smush.

"Erm..." I wrinkle my forehead. "OK, but ... what is it?"

Finn scratches his head under the helmet. He chews his wrist guard.

"I really do need help with Art. Fuck. I drew it. Last night after you left. It's a butterfly. For you," he says.

"Aw, that's sweet. Thank you."

"You're just giving me the sympathy vote for my terrible drawing skills."

"No, I mean it. I do," I say, but something else has caught Finn's attention. Boarders are taking their places for the first heat.

He looks to a far-off place, shielding his eyes from the sun. "This is it, Carla. First comp of the year. Just got to keep focused, breathe deep and have fun," he reassures himself. He bites his bottom lip. "The top three get automatic places in the UK Board Battle in July. All the best riders from the South-East are here. I've got to beat them. I *will* beat them."

"So how does this work?" I ask.

"It's slopestyle. Kind of like a downhill snowboard run, but without the snow. Riders pull tricks off dirt jumps, rails, wooden kickers, sometimes even half-pipes. It's pretty intense. You can get up to fifty kph! So sweet when you land the big tricks. We get judged on speed, style, technical difficulty and originality. I've got buckets of that. Been working on some wicked new jumps."

We stand, silent except for gasps as other riders land incredible jumps or crash to earth in spectacular, bone-crunching fashion. I gulp at the sight of a shredded shin. I'm afraid Finn might get injured and miss the UK Board Battle, but he's calm.

The loudspeaker crackles. "Finn Masterson. You're up next."

"Go get 'em," I say. "Grab, spin, flip or whatever it is you do!" I grip his arm. "You nervous?"

"No point being nervous. Just got to do it. Believe I can do it." He clenches his fists, like a strongman, bares his teeth and growls, *"Grrrrr!"*

"You'd better go. They're calling you."

The blanket of fog that hovered over the grass this morning has lifted, sucked away by the sun, making way for Finn. He swaggers to the start line with a confidence that to me is such a commodity: confidence without arrogance. Self-belief. The downhill course stretches before him, a winding track dotted with jumps to land, rails to grind, each a goal to achieve. To him those obstacles are opportunities, points to be won.

Straight off the mark he whips up speed like a racing greyhound, swinging to the left and hitting a dirt jump. He twists his body, bending his knees behind him, reaching his arm backwards to grab the middle of the board and spins a 360. His whole body changes shape as he lands, synchronized bones and muscle, his own personal suspension system. He grazes a rail, front wheels in the air, skimming it like a surfer riding a wave. He bounces off it, crouching, pinching the front of the board between his fingers. I'm in awe. I'm in love. Jump after rail, he owns the course, defying gravity with amazing balance. When he somersaults, I imagine what he sees: the world turning, land and sky reversed, like when I do gym. I understand exactly why he loves it. He slides the board horizontal, skidding to a stop at the base of the run. Whistles and applause greet him. He unfastens his helmet. Grins. He disconnects his feet from the board and strolls over.

"You did it!" I congratulate him. "You were the best out there yet."

He takes me by the waist, raising me high, looking up into my eyes. "Ha ha! I did it! It was you. I thought about you, nothing else. My body did the rest."

The boardercross race is next. The finals. "Berms, rollers, doubles, triples, drops, step-ups and step-downs. Four riders race a four-hundred metre track. First to the bottom wins. Simple as that," Finn tells me.

"Simple as that." I smile.

He returns to the line-up, meeting Greg.

The gun goes off, but Finn doesn't forge ahead. He's third in a chain of four, Greg lagging behind him.

Back with me, Georgia lets out an ear-shattering whistle. "Powerful instrument you've got there," I say.

"Sorry."

My jaw and temples tense as Finn swerves a corner, his board gliding around a ridge of mud, but any doubt is unfounded. He is consistently brilliant. Like a breakdancer, snaking and dancing his way down the hill with tight-lipped concentration. Usually his attention flits about. He fidgets through ten minutes of a Chemistry quiz or Psychology coursework, itching for the next thing. I don't think he's ADHD or anything, but active, vocational. Academia frustrates him; it's too immobile, too indoor, too sedentary. People learn differently. If I'm visual, well, he's kinetic.

Under my breath, I will: "Come on, Finn. You can do it. Come on, Finn." I wait with Georgia at the sidelines. Her form of encouragement is more audible, like her personality: unabashedly loud and clear.

"Woooo, yeah! COME ON, GREGGERS. RINSE THEM!"

She lifts her polka-dot top as the riders zoom by, flashing a fluorescent pink bra and GO, GREGGERS! emblazoned across her stomach in red lipstick. One competitor gets distracted and wobbles on his board.

"Er, I think that's cheating," I say.

"I'm not competing. How can it be cheating?" I don't bother with the conversation about morals. Instead I sum up the sentiment in a single look, and she gets the hint. "Fine," she says, rolling down her spotty vest. "I'm still going to cheer at the top of my lungs though. GO ON, BABY! GIVE THEM A FACEFUL OF DIRT!"

I open my sketchbook to a clean page, dove white and daunting. My pencil, a cylindrical UFO, hovers above the barren landscape. I land the point and begin to draw Finn on his board, arms outstretched, full of energy, wheels spinning. Grey lines flow, spreading organically across the page, over the crease of the spine and onto the next. I draw as fast as he boards. With a 4B, I fill in the shadows, strong and definite against those rapid strokes. I pocket the pencil, then study the picture. It moves, still animating on the page.

"Whoa! Ooooh! Owww!" the crowd choruses. The rider out in front stacks a jump, tearing up the grassy slope and face-planting into the ground. The rider next in line can't avoid getting tangled in the crash. Finn thinks fast, powers off the wooden ramp with battering-ram force and sails over them, victorious. One of the fallen riders limps off the course, cupping his nose and mouth, blood trickling through his fingers and over his wrist guards. The other rider gets back on his board, but it's too late. Finn screeches to a halt fifty metres away at the finishing line. He high-fives Greg, who skirts around the crash to claim second place. Finn's got what he came for. Racing with precision, skill and, above all, flair, he's earned himself a place in the UK Board Battle in July.

CHAPTER 16

A hand shakes my shoulder.

"Huh?" I say, pulled back to reality.

Even though the lesson is almost over, my pen has yet to touch my Biology book. Lately my brain seems stuck on a Finn Masterson loop. I glance at the board: The Role of Micro-organisms in Recycling Chemical Elements in Ecosystems. I catch Miss Tillsman's eye, then frantically scribble, anything, so she thinks I'm working.

"I asked if you wanted to come with us to see the Lovettes on Friday night?" Lauren says.

I really should start paying attention. "Oh, yeah, sure. Who are the Lovettes?"

"They're a Motown revival band. Like the Supremes," Sienna chips in, "but don't let that put you off. It'll be good. The organizers do up the hall like a sixties dance and there's even a tin-can diner outside. Everyone dresses up. I've got a black and white polka-dot dress and three red petticoats to go under it. It's going to be like, skinny, skinny, skinny," Sienna runs her hands down her torso, "and then BAM, out at the waist in a skirt explosion."

"Isn't that more fifties?" Lauren asks.

"It's more awesome, is what it is. Carla, you have to come."

"Hmm," I nod.

"And Gabriel Grayson is going to be there. Naked."

"Sounds cool," I say, drawing butterflies in my Biology book.

"Carla! Are you even listening?"

"Sorry. I, um, yeah, the Lovettes. Sixties dance. Friday."

"Yeah. Seven o'clock. Do you want to come by my house first to get ready? Say, five?"

"You need two hours to get ready?" Lauren raises an eyebrow.

"I'll have you know I don't just wake up looking like this. Like some people. You look like you only need two minutes to get ready."

"Ten minutes, actually. Four minutes of teeth-cleaning, two minutes of face-washing, one minute doing my hair, three minutes to eat breakfast."

"How very regimented. I bet you have a timer. Carla, I can do your hair in a beehive."

"Not a chance. But I will come."

Miss Tillsman returns this week's test. I shove it in my bag without even looking at the mark. The bell rings for the end of the day.

CHAPTER 17

I'm just turning into the park after school on Tuesday when POW, here he is, breathless from running. That's sweet. He was trying to catch up with *me.*

"Carla, there's a big party on Friday at Fat Mike's house. You know the hefty guy that looks like he'll burst out of his shirt like the Hulk?" I know who he means. "Um, yeah, so you should come." Finn swings around so he's in front of me, walking backwards.

"Yeah, I guess, maybe..."

Friday night. Damn it. FRIDAY night. The dance.

"Come!"

I need to stall.

"I'll have to ask my p—" And then I stop. Am I actually going to say: *I'll have to ask my parents*?!

Can't say no, though, can I? I'll find a way to be there. I'll find a way if it means picking up the house, transferring it next door to Mike's and climbing undetected through the attic space. "I'll be there," I say, in my best nonchalant voice.

"I knew you wouldn't take much convincing, tiger. Got to go, majorly late."

"Late for what? Off somewhere interesting?"

Finn shrugs, winks, spins around again and bounces off down the road.

What am I going to tell Lauren and Sienna?

CHAPTER 18

Sugar. Flour. Eggs. Milk. Butter. I'm weighing out ingredients for a "please let me go out on Friday night" cake, but I'm undecided which event I'll be attending.

No-brainer: I agreed to the dance before I got the invitation from Finn. So the dance it is.

No-brainer: I've been personally invited to Fat Mike's party. I have my foot in the door; it could open to reveal a whole new me.

I scan the recipe, our family iPad propped against a jar of coffee granules. Equal quantities of butter, flour and sugar, it says.

Our retro scales are more for decoration than cooking. They have a cream-coloured base and a white dial with a red hand that swings across its black digits. I fill its silver bowl with flour, stirring up a white cloud. Let's think about the pros:

SIXTIES DANCE	FIAT MIKE'S PARTY
Chance to get to know Lauren and Sienna better.	Chance to get to know Finn's crowd.
Get to dress up.	Finn asked me.
Errrrm... I guess it could be fun.	I could turn up, and people could say, "Hey, who's she? She looks great," and Finn and I could dance together and I could make a witty statement that makes Georgia and Violet crack up and by the end of the night we could be ... I don't know ... somewhere approaching friends. And I might be a different me.

I guess it all boils down to this:

I *said* I'd go vs I *want* to go.

I pour the flour into the mixing bowl, replace the silver bowl on the scales and set about weighing the sugar.

Intelligent *and* popular. In equal measure.

I think about what it would be like to dance with Finn, to have him swing me around, graze my hips with his hands. To lean in and … and…

The sugar cascades over the rim of the bowl. Am I a terrible person for wanting this?

"You're not going." Mum sinks a ship in my gut.

"Come on, I'm old enough to stay out. On a Friday."

"Carla, be sensible. You hardly know these people. They could be up to anything."

"I know, if only I could get to know them better

through some kind of social gathering, like a party, on a Friday night…"

"What's got into you?" She glares at me with these bulgy, fiery eyes. "You have coursework. And exams." Her face goes all birdlike and scary for a second, then relaxes.

"I got an *A* in my Biology test." Three in a row. Opened it when I got home.

"Fine. Ask your dad."

That's practically a yes. Carla 1. Mum 0.

I've got an Art assignment due in on Monday, but Dad doesn't have to know that. Besides there's the whole of Saturday and Sunday to work.

I find Dad in the lounge, reading the paper.

"I have to go, I *have* to go." I push down the newspaper and practically shove a slice of Victoria sponge in his face. I'm being cheeky, but he doesn't mind. "Eat the cake. It's special, 'please let me go out on Friday night' cake." He melts like butter. Not like I'm manipulating or taking advantage; he just understands. "How else am I supposed to fit in and make friends?"

"What did Mum say?"

"She did her crazy fire eyes and played the schoolwork card. Then she said to ask you."

"She's stressed, love, with the new job and everything. And she wants you to do well. So do I. But…" He does his zero-gravity eyebrow trick. The little brown tufts reach the summit of Mount Dad. He puts down the paper and takes the cake. Sighs. He takes a bite of yellow sponge. "You *will* be sensible, won't you?"

"Course. Aside from the alcohol abuse, drug-taking and

casual sex, I'll be a regular little Virgin Mary." I love joking with Dad. He's like the anti-Mum. He knows I'm messing around. He *knows* I'm being sarky.

"Be good, Carla."

"I will." He does the eyebrows thing again, questioning me. "I *will*, Dad," I say.

I'M GOING TO THE PARTY!

This is possibly the best day of my life so far. I'm not only going to the party, but Finn's picking me up and we're going together. I mean, I don't know if it's a date or anything. We have to go with his brother, Isaac, who's driving, and I think we're taking Slinky, too. But Finn asked me to go with them and he seemed pretty fired up, and oh, I can't wait! Butterflies, butterflies, butterflies, flying around in my stomach…

On our way to Fat Mike's place, Finn passes me a beer. I down it. I guess I'm nervous about going with him, meeting new people, fitting in, et cetera, but mostly I'm excited.

"Got any more?" I ask Finn.

"Plenty more where that came from." He chucks me another.

In the rear-view mirror, I catch Isaac's eyes on me. They flick away instantly. *He's a cautious driver, looking out the back window, right?*

The bass from Mike's place is pounding, his house a huge sound dock, a giant, thumping street-speaker.

I knock on the door. Mike answers.

"Hey, guys." He nods at Finn, Isaac and Slinky.

"Mastersons. Mr Slink. Get in here. Miss Carla. Welcome, one and all."

We're hit by a wall of sound. Wonderful noise. Liquid music. A flowing stream of happiness. Outside was heavy with vibrations, but inside, inside it's melodic bliss. You know what? I've never felt this way about music before. Actually I've never really been into music. Sure, I listen to the radio, when I'm revising or whatever, but if anyone asks me what type of music I'm into, "Uh, all sorts, I guess," is my standard response. Not any more.

The bass is making the whole place hum and I'm humming with it. Like all of us here are connected by an electric charge that keeps sparking, beat after beat, pulse after pulse. I feel the music running through me like a current. The beat repeats, building to a crescendo until I think it can't get any more intense, then, BOOM, a new mix of other-worldly sounds drops, pulsating my ears with pleasure.

I've heard this type of music before but never really "got" it. It was just a load of electronic white noise, but now it seems so much more. Maybe it's the beer or the masses of people or the fact that I'm at a party at all, but some cosmic alignment has come into play and the music finally makes sense. I feel joy in my core. I'm pumped. It's like I've been trying to pick a lock with a matchstick. The pins weren't aligned. I didn't understand the mechanism. I didn't have the tools. But now Finn has given me the key to a whole new world.

In the front room, Finn grabs me around the waist and tries to rape my ear with his tongue.

"Get off!" I shout, fake pissed off. But it's actually kind of funny.

Isaac throws me another look.

Nothing's really happened between me and Finn yet. Maybe Isaac's scoping me out to make sure I'm good enough for his baby brother. What does he make of me?

For that matter, what does Finn make of me? Does *he* think it's a date?

The answer is beer. Ninety per cent of what people joke about when intoxicated is an expression of their true feelings. Beer will produce clarity. Questions to answer during an alcohol-induced confidence boost:

1. Is this a date?
2. Why is Isaac glaring at me?
3. *Is this a date?*

"I'll get us some drinks," Finn says, his hands on my hips, his face close to mine. He lets go and starts to duck and weave through the crowd. I wish he'd take my hand and lead me, protect me, but he doesn't. He forges ahead into the mass of people, but the feel of his hands on me still lingers. *Mmmm*, warm, weird and *aaahhh* … the combination of the beat, beer and hands makes me tingle. I feel a little high. I want more.

I want Finn.

It's a big house with big rooms and a big crowd. I swing around in the mix of moving bodies, and feel like I'm being sucked into a hot vortex. The music jumps. A body knocks my bag off my shoulder and I sink to the ground to find it. Sweat forms on my neck. Legs tower around like I'm in the undergrowth of a living, dancing rainforest.

From the canopy, a hand reaches to rescue me. I breathe a sigh of relief. As I'm pulled upright I see the hand belongs to Isaac. He gives me a look of concern, but like I'm a burden. I bet he's thinking, *Oh, no, I'm going to have to take care of this one.* I wanted it to be Finn's hand; I think it shows on my face.

"You all ri—?" Isaac begins.

But then Finn appears.

"There you are. You OK?" It hits me again – fresh excitement coursing through me like electricity. Here he is, in all his glory, hair so thick and soft you could weave it and wear it as a winter coat; skin that positively glows. Forget Superman's laser-beam eyes, Finn could bat his eyelashes and melt metal.

He pulls me through the swirl of sweaty people. He's strong. If Isaac's arms are twigs, Finn's are fully grown branches. Redwoods.

"Come on, tiger." His lips curl into a cute grin. Menacing. Exciting. But still so cute.

"Dance with me."

Finn bounces and jumps and it's like the whole room is one entity pulsing together. What would it feel like to have Finn's hands on my waist, on the small of my back, to have those arms pull me close? What would it be like to bury my head in his neck and smell his scent? What would it taste like to kiss him? Would his kiss be gentle and soft or full of urgency and passion? Finn's eyes sparkle with excitement as he dips and sways his head. Coming closer to me, his breath is hot on my ear and my stomach dives.

"Let's get some fresh air," he says.

We weave our way to the back door and find Slinky rolling a joint in the garden. Although I've heard he smokes a lot, I'm surprised he's being so obvious. Finn settles on a white plastic garden chair next to Slinky and pulls me to sit on his lap.

It's dark and the clouds threaten rain. The garden is a long, narrow corridor, black as tar, except where the half-moon illuminates and, further down, candles blink like distant stars.

Slinky passes the joint to Finn. "Ladies first," he says, handing it to me. I have a long toke. I don't cough, though it grates in my throat. I haven't smoked weed before. Can you do it wrong?

I feel a bit light-headed, but I'm in such a good mood that it passes quickly. I'm feeling better than ever, actually. I have a big pull, drawing it in like Finn did when I saw him smoking outside the doctors' surgery.

He nods to me. "Good, huh?" I nod back and give the joint to him. I exhale, watching the smoke dance fleetingly to the music before disappearing.

Leaning back into Finn, I feel so relaxed. The cold air prickles against my cheeks but the rest of me is warm. Finn pulls his hoodie sleeves over his fingers, forming fists to keep them in place. Impromptu gloves. I'm super-snug against him. I really like the way he feels against me.

Just as I'm getting cosy, he leaps to his feet, taking me with him. "Let's check out the deal in the ring of fire over there." He gestures to the flickering flames, the faraway stars. I jog after him.

At the circle, candles scatter intermittent light onto the group. Fragmented by the flickering light, their faces are broken jigsaws I put together in my head.

My blood is on fire. Not in an angry red-hot way, but happy, up. I settle on a patch of lawn. It feels damp, but that's OK. Everything is OK. I'm here with Finn, at a party, smoking and enjoying a few tinnies. Everything is *definitely* OK. I turn to the girl next to me, Georgia with the mess of curls. She's smiling and cool, wearing a leopard-print top, black leggings and a thick slick of red lipstick. "Hey, what's up?" she asks.

I say, "Hey. Nothing's up, it's all good. What's up with you?" Georgia says it's all good with her. She comes at me then, right in my face, invading my personal space.

"How *you* doing tonight?" I feel like I'm missing a trick, like I'm the last to get the obvious joke. Or maybe I'm just paranoid, like Slinky... I've had a few big tokes. Seems like she means doing something other than sitting in this circle of light. Something other than weed and booze.

"Um... Just..." I'm doing ... nothing... What does she want me to say? "I'm OK, thanks," I say. Georgia looks taken aback, like I'm weird. Like I'm a total dullard.

I feel so good just being here, but ... I'm missing something, something these guys are looking for. Maybe I can do something else ... but what else is there...? I'm a cute bunny rabbit who's wandered into the lion's den. More alcohol. *I need more alcohol.*

The beer says anything's a good idea right now. My head says I have an assignment due in on Monday, and this isn't the time for that. Or is it? My name is Carla Indecisive Carroll and I'm a non-commitalist. Whatever.

Georgia is already pretty pissed. She's got my arm in a lock like a woodwork vice and starts to chisel away at me.

Where you from? Do you know this song? What's your middle name? What you studying? What, what, what, what, what, what, what you doing here then? Did you come with Finn?

Jesus, she's the fucking Riddler. It's like being in a hit-and-run with a question truck. A tanker has crashed, spilling questions all over me, so many weighing me down I don't know which to answer first, but… As her eyes dart about, and her mind jumps from subject to subject, I realize she doesn't really want answers at all.

"Have you met my boyfriend, Greg?" She points to Greg, who nods and raises a hand in acknowledgement.

"Yeah. At the boarding comp, and he's in my Biology class." I shoehorn in an answer. She tosses her hair.

"Do you like this bracelet?" She jangles a silver chain with red and blue gemstones in my face. "Where's your T-shirt from? Is it Topshop? I saw a really cute top there yesterday."

Before I've even half thought what to say she's rammed another question into my ear. Strange. I don't think she means to offend. She's just chatty, in the mood. Happy to talk, but not to hear. I'm envious. I'm too polite not to listen. I wish I was too confident to care.

"Ohmygod, I *love* this song!" Georgia blurts to no one in particular. She jumps up, nodding and swinging her arms, and starts dancing. On her own. Right there in the middle of the ring of fire. But what happens next takes me by surprise. She just smiles at everyone, her candle-lit grin stretching in a dark half-moon across her face. And that does it. We all get up and dance with her. Like, crazy movements. Dad would call it throwing some shapes. It's magic, awesome. And I think, hell yeah! HELL YEAH!

I get a good look at the others. Greg, tall with blond hair, dancing close to Georgia: he has really white trainers. He whispers something to Isaac, who's come down the garden and joined in. I didn't think Isaac would be the crazy dance type, but I guess when the moment takes you… I smile at him and he smiles back. Violet sways to the music, like a goddess.

There are others, too, but then my attention is seized by Finn, who's spinning in circles and air-drumming and kicking and going and going and going. Hitting the air, over and over like he's the one making the music. He has this look in his eyes. *He owns the music.*

He catches me staring, and pulls me to him. We dance, and I own the music too.

The song ends and another phases in. Finn, Isaac, Violet, Georgia, Greg and I veer off to a secluded corner, under one of those trees with long thin branches that hang to the ground like a giant open umbrella. There are no candles here. It's kind of mysterious. A lighter rips, *shhhrip.* We have light.

Finn spreads his jacket on the ground. "Don't want you getting a wet bum, tiger." He gestures for me to sit with him. I collapse into his arms. Normally I'd be too shy to just fall into him. He might think I'm a clingy sort, but I'm full of beer and it seems like the most natural thing in the world.

I'm cool with just watching and listening. Like I've been allowed into some secret world. I feel like I'm popular. I sit, they talk, I listen.

"It's time!" Greg announces.

"Oh, yes, oh, yes. What have we this week?" asks Finn.

"Doves, mate. Same sort we had at Citrus a couple of weeks ago."

It's a cloak-and-dagger operation. *What are they doing?* I mean, is *everybody* doing this? Am I just a late bloomer? The last to hear the big news? Drugs are in again? Er, hello? The eighties called and they want their narcotics back...

I could never imagine doing it.

"Nice one, thanks." Finn knocks the little white pill back with a swift slurp of beer.

"A dove for my love." Greg hands one to Georgia and she swigs it down.

"Ahhhh..." she says with a drunk giggle.

Violet swallows hers.

Then Isaac has one. They all seem so unconcerned. No biggie, I bet they think. The clock has ticked its way around to me and now the alarm is sounding. It's my turn. What should I do? What should I do? I don't know what to do!

"You want one, Carla?" Greg holds a pill out on the palm of his hand. I feel all their eyes on me. The first day of school, again.

"I ... um ... I've never done one before." Suddenly I don't feel drunk at all. I feel stone-cold sober and scared. I'm scared all right. Scared of what it might do to me. Scared of what I'll do if I take it, or what I'll feel like. What if I'm sick or something, or die like that girl who drank too much water 'cause she felt like she was totally dehydrated and oh God, I should really say something...

"You don't have to," Isaac says. I'm about to say I think

I'll pass, but then they'll probably never speak to me again. Maybe I should drop. Maybe I would feel … fit in. I've never done anything remotely wild, and time is ticking down, sixth form won't last for ever, after this is uni and then adulthood and the Big Bad World and jobs and mortgages and car insurance and council tax. Before that humdrum vanilla life arrives, here's a chance to prove I'm more than a strait-laced, head-down study whore. I can surprise. I can be somebody.

"Come on, tiger, it'll be fun. Trust me." Finn squeezes my arms in support.

"I … er…" I pause again. They must think I've gone a bit loco. Breathe. *Speak*. "All righ—"

"No, mate." Isaac takes the pill from Greg's hand, looking intensely at Finn. "Not if she doesn't want to."

Finn snatches the pill from Isaac's hand and for a millisecond I think he's going to force me to take it. It's right there, in front of my face, heading for my mouth, and then it's gone, bypassing mine and into Finn's.

"More for me, then. I love to double-drop. Right, let's go dance, kids." He pivots my head around to face his, and smirks. He kisses me on the forehead, bounces up off the ground and runs back to the house. Back to the music, the crowd and *fun*. He doesn't even help me up.

Maybe it was a kiss goodbye. I've failed the test. I'm such a fool! Why didn't I have the guts just to do it, like everybody else?

I feel humiliated. I don't want to walk through the party, so I make for the back gate.

"Carla!" Isaac shouts after me. I keep walking. "Wait, Carla. Where are you going?"

"Home," I say, without turning around.

"No, stay. Don't worry about them. It's nothing. I mean, I like to do them now and then, but—" Anything he says just makes me feel worse.

"Forget it. I'm going home."

"Let me drive you. It's a long walk. And it's dark."

"You can't drive. You've had a pill. I'll call my dad to pick me up."

"I'll walk you then. It'll make the trek from yours back to the party *vvvvvery* interesting."

I check my phone, but it's out of battery. "No juice," I whisper, defeated. "OK."

Moonlight shimmers on the pavement. My arms prickle with cold now the alcohol buzz has worn off. I feel a little sick.

"Are you cold?" Isaac asks.

"Not really," I lie. I don't want any more charity from him. Or to throw up on his jacket.

Then it starts raining, like glitter at first, then full-on golf balls. We duck into a bus shelter, but I'm already soaked through.

I wring out my hair and wipe under my eyes with my sleeves. My eyeliner will be everywhere.

Raindrops stick to Isaac's eyelashes and twinkle in the half-light. He looks a little like Finn, but less groomed.

"Those guys are pretty hard core," he says. I shrug. "Don't feel you have to say yes to all that stuff."

He doesn't want me hanging around his brother; I can feel it.

"They seem OK." I feel vomit rise in my throat.

"I guess. You haven't done them before though, right? You looked pretty scared."

What do I say to that? Yeah, I'm a total loser drugs virgin?

"Where did you come from?" he asks.

"As in, which planet?"

Am I completely out of touch with normal teenage life because I'm not snorting something every weekend?

"Er, no … like Birmingham, Suffolk, the moon?"

"Hold on. I think I'm going to hurl."

Isaac grabs my soaking hair and holds it back. I'm not sick but I do let out an enormous burp. Great.

"That was a belter. Feel better?"

"I am so mortified."

"Must be some kind of crazy moon creature if you can make noises like that. Never heard anything like it on earth before. Kinda gross."

"Sorry."

I tell him about Nottingham and Mum's career trajectory.

"I'm going to uni there, if I get in," he says.

"I wished I could have stayed."

"Maybe you'll go back one day. Rain's stopped. Let's go."

He probably wants me to leave tomorrow and get out of his and Finn's lives for ever. It's like I've upset the balance of their social group.

We cross the park. The wet grass glistens under the bright moon.

Isaac is quiet. I'm still mortified.

He walks me to my door, and though incredibly polite, he doesn't seem to want to be with me for longer than necessary.

“Night,” he says, before jogging off.

“Hey, thanks for walking me, and for … you know,” I call out, but Isaac doesn’t even look back.

CHAPTER 19

I can't sleep. I close my eyes and see Greg's hand, the lines on it like a treasure map made of shadows, and that pill, the *X* on the map. What sort of pirate finds the treasure but doesn't take it? I'm BAD at this rebellion stuff. I'm going to drop. I'm going to drop soon.

On Saturday I have the same dream. And again on Sunday, except this time I take the pill. What happens next is ... *beeebeeeeepppp* ... my alarm. Monday morning.

I'm dreading school today and facing Finn and the others. It's not as if I can erase Friday night like a stray line on a drawing. It happened; it's there in permanent marker.

Please don't let Isaac have told Finn about my almost-puke.

I hardly notice the walk in. I'm thinking, reliving, replaying... *Oh God,* there it goes again, on a loop: *Not if she doesn't want to... More for me, then. I love to double-drop...* Finn downing it, and then just leaving me there. I can't get it out of my tiny, embarrassed head. It's tattooed on my retinas, a constant reminder of shameful-wussy-humiliation.

I thought maybe Finn might like me. I was wrong. Now all chance of that is out the window.

Luckily my locker seems intact and slogan-free. Likewise my chair and general desk area. No gum stuck underneath – well, the usual dried-on crap's still there, but no fresh stuff, chewed, soft and sticky, ready to ambush whoever pulls themselves close to the table.

I scan the room for Finn. I didn't see him smoking by the doctors' on the way here.

Eagle-eyed and jumpy, I swear my heart leaps ten feet out of my body every time someone enters the classroom.

He's not here. He's bunking, or ill, or those pills kept him going and he's been on a massive bender... He got in a fight, he got arrested, he, he, he... He just walked in and oh shit, oh shit, *ohshitohshitohshitohshitohshit*... My heart starts jackhammering at a million miles per hour.

Finn swaggers into the classroom, talking loudly on his phone.

"Yeah. I'll be there. OK. See you later, mate."

It's nine o'clock. We're supposed to be in at eight forty-five for register and general teacherial stuff.

Havelock can be a pushover sometimes. Slight tardiness, a few minutes here or there, and you'll get no grief. He's pretty cool like that. But occasionally, he's not in the mood.

My crippling embarrassment is side-lined momentarily while Havelock launches a verbal attack on Finn.

"Do you think you're special, Mr Masterson? Do you think you can stroll into class whenever your hangover allows you to walk again? Hmmm?" Havelock looks at

Finn, eyes afire. Like stars about to supernova. "Hmm? Do you?" He waits.

Finn has on these really, really lush jeans. They're falling low and I can see that *V* that boys have, you know that pelvic *V*, through his sky-blue skater T-shirt, which has a little cartoon man on it, not like a comic or graphic novel character, more like a Banksy stencil. But that's beside the point; his hips just look so good in those jeans. I find myself wondering about the rest of him…

I'm not a total square; I've kissed and messed about with boys before. I'm not a big *V*, but Finn is different. I've never really felt the urge, the want, the passion for anyone before. Now it strikes me like a lightning bolt. My breath catches when I see him. Like I no longer need oxygen to breathe. I need something else. I need him.

"Ted, buddy, a momentary lapse in temporal judgement. I apologize. But I'm here. I'm not queer. And I'm ready to learn," Finn announces to the class, the school, the world.

"It's not acceptable, Finn. You're fifteen minutes late. You know the rule. More than ten minutes late and you don't come in at all."

"Sorry, I was training for the Board Battle. Lost track of time."

"Time is a concept you don't understand, Mr Masterson. Take a seat," Havelock bellows. Veins appear around his temples like worms wriggling under his skin.

Finn throws me a wink before sitting down a couple of rows in front.

I feel like Havelock's watching me. Maybe because I'm new or whatever, but he saw the wink, and I know he's concerned, because after class he keeps me back. He gives me a look I've seen before: the disapproving, thoughtful pose adopted by my dad when he's about to tell me *Be careful. He's trouble. You don't need that. You're better off focusing on your studies*... And yep. That's the gist of it...

"Carla, I looked at your Art proposal. It's good. Really good. If you can follow it through it'll be an excellent project." *If* I can follow it through?

"You don't think I can pull it off?"

"Course I think you can. From what I've seen, your sketches and the plan, of course you can do it. But..."

"But what?"

"It's crucial that you give it time and avoid too many distractions." *Distractions*...

Havelock's right. I could do something amazing. I had this idea about a butterfly sculpture in metal and coloured glass and did a bunch of pen and ink sketches over the weekend, amid all the shame and recurring visions of the pill on Greg's hand. Actually it was kind of an escape, drifting away in my own world, just me, the inks and the colours.

"I'll do it." I look him right in the eye.

"I know you will, Carla. I know. But keep focused, OK?" Havelock pads down his brown cords with his palms and smiles. Positively Cheshire cat. But his eyes are unconvincing. He's saying it, but not *sure* of it. He doesn't think I can do it. But he's wrong. I *will* do this project. I will Pepsi Max this project.

"OK," I say. And mean it.

Finn's waiting for me outside the classroom, Violet too, her hand on his arm, her smile wide. Just old friends, I tell myself. Violet reaches into her pocket and gives him something.

"What was that?" I ask as Violet disappears.

"Just some money she owed me for the beers on Friday."

"Oh."

"Look, I need to talk to you, but no time now." Finn glances at his watch.

"Late for something?"

"Always," he says. "I'll call you tonight."

I really did mess things up by not taking that pill. Finn and I aren't even going out, officially, so why do I get the impression I'm heading for Dumpsville?

It seems Havelock needn't worry about that particular distraction.

Then I realize Finn doesn't even have my number.

This is turning into one craptacular day.

In Art, Finn's nowhere to be seen. Havelock's in full vein-popping-taking-no-shit mode and has commanded we work in silence. Lauren sits next to me as usual. I nudge her, try to provoke a smile, but she carries on with her work.

At lunch, I try to find Lauren and Sienna, but they're not in the common room. I could do with someone to talk to. I text Lauren: *Where are you guys? x*

I sit down at the central table.

My phone vibrates.

The question is: Where were you? Oh, that's right. You ditched us for Finn and that lot. The Lovettes were awesome btw.

Shit. I text back.

So sorry, slipped my mind. And my phone ran out of juice.

Lame excuse, I know. But true. x

I eat my sandwich alone. No Finn, none of those guys comes in. No Sienna. Not even a text back from Lauren. I feel bad about missing the dance. I'm taking a guilt trip to the bloody moon and back.

Later, I'm peeling potatoes for Dad's famous Monday-night sausage and mash when the phone rings. I put down the knife, wipe my hands and wonder if, by some miracle, Finn knows my number, like it's been transferred there by some sort of mind osmosis. Or if it's Lauren or Sienna, wanting to make up. It's just an insurance salesman.

I text Lauren again.

Pls let me make it up 2 u. x

I resume my task. The rule is, if you help cook, you don't have to wash up.

Thoughts creep into my head.

Finn's into drugs. WTF?

At my old schools, the druggies were total drop-outs. I don't want to end up like that.

How could they do that to themselves?

But what if it's not so bad? What if it's just propaganda and most people cope fine?

It could be media scaremongering. Only extreme cases get on the news.

Do I want to risk it?

Shit. I cut my thumb. A bead of blood grows.

People use knives all the time. It doesn't mean they're going to die.

Oh, I don't know what to do!

* * *

I sit pushing my mash around the plate, watching telly with Dad, a programme about lost tribes. The TV's new, and obscenely large. It practically takes up a whole wall, but Dad loves it. "Look at the picture quality. The colours are so vivid."

The light is off so we can enjoy the programme "cinema style"; the glow from the screen flickers over the room like we're at a disco.

About seven o'clock, my phone jingles. It's a number I don't recognize. Lauren's home number probably. I leave my plate on the coffee table and head to the kitchen for some privacy.

"Be quick. Your food will get cold." Dad's voice echoes down the hall.

"Hello."

"Carla, it's Finn."

"Oh, hi. How did you get this number?"

"Facebook."

"Course."

"You really should change your privacy settings. Anyone can see that picture of you with a beard when you were little."

"What beard?"

"You know, you're wearing a gold leotard and that 'you've been Tango'd' tan. And a beard."

"Hey! I was a lion; that was my mane! I was six years old. My first gym competition. We had to do a floor exercise to music and I picked 'The Circle of Life'. I was really into *The Lion King* back then."

"Here I am, thinking you're a tiger, but you're a lion all along. I'm only joking. You look really cute. Bet you came first with that costume."

"Fourth, I think. A sunflower came first." There's a pause. "Are you ringing to break up – and I mean, not that we're … together… I me—"

"What are you on about, tiger?"

I lower my voice, mindful of Dad in the next room. "Because I wouldn't take the pill. You ran off. Don't you think I'm a total lame-ass?"

"I went to get drinks. When I got back you were gone. It doesn't matter about the pill. I just thought you'd like it. They're fun."

"So you haven't been plotting my exile from the group?"

"Not at all. Just the opposite. Have you been fretting over this?"

"No. Maybe. Just a little. A lot, actually. OK, it's all I've been thinking about." Way to stay cool, Carla. "So why did you want to talk to me?"

"I thought maybe you'd give me the pleasure of your company this weekend at the Dirt Junkies mountain-boarding festival. There's loads of punk and ska music and an outdoor cinema. Plus some epic riders will be there."

"Oh. OK. Great. Is everyone going?"

"No, just you and me. A proper date." My stomach does a bungee jump.

"I could teach you some boarding moves, if you like? Pay you back for my cartwheel training?"

"Because cartwheel training went so well? Tempting," I say, trying to regain some composure. To have Finn so close, helping me balance, holding me steady on a mountainboard is an opportunity too good to miss.

"Carla, dinner!" Dad calls from the living room.

"Well, it'd be rude to turn down a free lesson."

"I'll get my dad to drop us there on Saturday morning."

"Perfect."

"Perfect," he says and hangs up.

The next afternoon, in a free period, I wait for Lauren and Sienna in the school library. Last night, after talking to Finn, I called Lauren to apologize for missing the dance. I couldn't take the silent treatment. Sienna wouldn't answer my calls, but Lauren seemed OK when I explained about Fat Mike's party.

"But you only get one free pass."

"I won't leave you in the lurch again, I promise."

The library is always three degrees too warm and smells of pine and polish. A row of wooden tables runs down the centre of the room; ceiling-high bookshelves tower either side. A bank of ancient computers lines the far wall.

Lauren and I sit at a table halfway down, near the Science section.

"It's understandable. Finn's" – she searches for the right word – "charismatic. But you should've called."

"Sorry. I wasn't thinking straight. I really like him." I twist my bag-strap around my finger, nervously. What if I've ruined things with the only real friends I've made, for the sake of a guy?

Sienna appears with an armful of books on genetics.

"So are we doing this Biology assignment or what?"

"You're still mad."

"You stood us up."

"I'm a total loser. Sorry."

"I just don't see what's so great about him. Aside from his looks. He's so into himself … and … sort of obnoxious."

"I don't see that. I see confidence, sure, but he's not excessive with it. Don't you think it's kind of sexy?"

"I'd find a dirty sock sexier than Finn Masterson."

It gets me thinking… Is it Finn's confidence that I crave for myself, or is it him? I've got all these mixed-up feelings.

1. Lauren/Sienna vs Georgia/Violet
2. Finn vs Finn's Confidence
3. Old Carla vs New Improved Carla

Can't I have it all?

"I brought you something."

After not getting through to Sienna last night, I had to do something to fix things, so I went online and ordered a book I thought she'd like. I paid the extra for next-day delivery and picked it up at lunchtime.

I hand Sienna the parcel and she rips through the packaging.

"It's about this caver searching for the deepest cave on earth. He spent months almost two vertical miles deep," I say.

She flips through the pages.

"All is forgiven."

"Are we good?" I ask Lauren.

"I should've ignored you longer. Maybe I'd have got a present too."

"Funny you should mention that," I say, presenting her with a package.

"Ooh, gift time! I was only joking, you know."

"I'll have it if you don't want it," Sienna chips in.

Lauren unwraps the paper. *Gabriel Grayson: A Walk in the Clouds.*

"It's the revised biography. With extra content. Not exactly *On the Origin of Species* … but…"

"Perfect weekend reading," Lauren says. "Thank you."

I wrack my brain over what else I can do to make it up to them both.

"Come on, we can finish the Biology later. Let's go for some cake. I'm buying."

We walk to Adriano's, a pretty little Portuguese café perched on a corner between a launderette and household clearance place. It's on my side of the park, down a side street from the posh shops. Its bright walls are half-tiled in white, yolk-yellow and cobalt-blue, and dotted with rustic paintings. Fresh flowers and wine-bottle candlesticks sit on scrubbed oak tables.

I get a soya latte for Lauren, a caramel macchiato for Sienna and a flat white for me, plus a plate of mini pastries: chocolate, lemon, coconut and custard.

"Who cares what people say? Clearly you *can* buy friendship." Sienna launches at a custard tart with her fork. "So what *did* happen at the party?"

I pick at some dripped candle wax.

"Um…"

I wonder whether to tell them about the drugs, but I know they would just warn me off.

Lauren slurps her coffee, then scoops a mouthful of coconut cake.

"Was it amazing? Did you and lover boy dance in the moonlight?" she asks.

"Actually, I went home early. Isaac walked me. Though I don't think he likes me much."

I shovel some chocolate cream pastry.

"Why do you say that?" Lauren asks.

"He gives me the evil eye every time I'm with Finn and he barely talks to me. He only walked me home out of pity. You could see on his face that he resented it. He just wanted to be back at the party. Maybe he doesn't think I'm good enough for his brother."

Sienna points towards the window.

"Hey, look, there's Violet and Georgia. I bet they're all here, your new posse."

My face burns. I want to go over and join them, but I can't. I promised and I meant it.

"Don't you want to go over? Talk about 'banging tunes', and who's fittest on *Loaded in London*?"

"I told you, I'm not ditching you again."

"Wait a sec. Rewind." Lauren spins her finger anti-clockwise. "Why did you go home?"

I can't tell them about the drugs. Can I? They look at me, expectantly.

"Let's just say I peaked a little too early."

"You mean you puked too early!"

"Something like that," I say, that explanation definitely preferable. It *is* partly true.

CHAPTER 20

I spend most of Friday night swearing at my wardrobe, cursing each garment for being too small, too big, too retro, too frumpy… This morning I settle on black jeans and a blue top to match my eyes. Not very inventive, but practical for a festival. A skirt wouldn't be great for mountainboarding. I fear I'd flash one of Finn's boarding idols as I inevitably crash from board to ground.

I loop a curl around my finger. I decide to wear my hair down, and put some shine spray in it. My first venture into hair products since "The Great Fringe Singeing". Not exactly Violet-Brody-blinding but it looks OK.

A car horn sounds outside around eleven.

I go to tell Dad I'm leaving. He's installing a new amp for the massive beast that is our telly. His head appears from behind the shelving unit.

"Ooh. What's this in aid of?" He gestures at my hair.

"Got bored of having it back."

"Right." Eyebrows up.

"I'll be gone all day, but I've got my phone."

"Have fun. Hope he likes it." Cringe.

"See you later."

The doorbell rings as I open the door. Finn smells like lemons and sweat, not gross, but intoxicating. He definitely has a chemical power over me.

"You look great. Hope you don't mind but Dad had a catering emergency... Isaac's driving."

"Course not." Lie. "What's the emergency? Did they run out of Waldorf salad at a wedding?"

"One of the chefs broke his ankle. Dad had to step in."

"Step in. Ha ha."

"That was bad, sorry."

Finn opens the car door and I slide into the passenger seat.

Isaac mumbles, "Hello."

It's forty-five minutes to the festival site. Isaac grips the wheel, eyes on the road. It's only a Micra, but kitted out well, with speakers in the boot, heavy-duty stuff. I say something about the music system and with a glint in his eyes, Finn becomes animated, trying to explain the technicalities – subwoofers and bass frequencies – but it's all over my head. The little Micra has a lot of loud love to give, that's all I know. Finn finds a song on his phone, presses PLAY, and the headrest begins to vibrate.

Finn starts dancing in the front seat, then unbuckles his seatbelt and clambers into the back with me.

Isaac isn't impressed. "Can you turn that down? Trying to drive."

"Moody today, aren't we?" Finn lowers the volume, clicks the belt over his lap and drapes an arm around my shoulder. "Drive on, Master Masterson."

Although the volume is right down, Isaac seems more agitated than ever. It's a relief when we arrive at the festival gates.

Isaac parks and gets out with us.

"Are you coming too?" I ask, confused.

"Someone's got to drive you home."

"Oh." I can't believe Isaac Moody-son is crashing another date.

Finn takes his mountainboard and helmet out of the boot and stuffs the knee-pads, elbow-pads and wrist guards into his rucksack.

After getting our wristbands, we wander around. There are BMX bikers on a half-pipe and mountainboarders on rails and ramps. A massive crescent-shaped stage dominates one corner of the site, while in another, live coverage of stunt skaters plays on an enormous screen overlooking a hollowed-out amphitheatre.

Food vans line the field. The smell of cut grass and chips fills the air.

Isaac heads off to watch the bikes.

Finn puts on his gear, does some jumps, then tackles the rails. I sit on a patch of grass nearby, watching the riders careering down, kicking and flipping, giddy and proud at the sight of Finn's every turn.

A guy in an orange hoodie stops Finn and chats with him briefly. Finn grins at me and walks over.

"I'll get us some donuts. You want anything else?"

"A Coke?"

"Sure. Back in a sec. Can you watch my board?"

"Yeah, course."

"Maybe you should try it out when I get back. Put this on." He hands me his helmet. I trace my fingers over the butterfly he said was for me, for luck.

"I'm not sure my hair will survive under this."

Finn takes the safety-guards from his rucksack. "Get strapped up. We'll have you on those rails by the end of the day."

"Ha! You'll be lucky."

"Be right back."

I encase myself in safety gear and strap my feet to the board. So glad I wore trainers.

I haul myself upright and shift the board forwards a little. It's much harder than it looks. I almost topple, but all that gym work pays off and I regain my balance. I lurch forwards, arms outstretched like a surfer. The board rolls faster and I wobble, struggling to keep vertical. Eventually I slow down enough to bend and unhook my feet, but…

"Shit!"

I fall backwards, hitting the ground with an almighty thud.

"Need help with that?"

Isaac kneels down to undo the catches. I take off the helmet and shake out my hair.

"Thanks. Now I see the point of the suit of armour."

"Where's Finn?" Isaac asks, folding two blades of grass into a tiny concertina.

"Getting some food. He'll be back in a minute." I glance over to the donut stall, but I can't see him. Maybe he went to another one.

"I'll stay until he gets back."

"I'm all right on my own, you know."

"I know."

But Finn doesn't return for ages. Twenty minutes of agonizing small talk tick by. I sense Isaac's only here because he feels he has to be. Like he's babysitting.

Maybe I can at least find out what he really thinks about me and Finn.

"So, I never thanked you for walking me home from the party. Well, I did, but I don't think you heard. You were off back to Fat Mike's like lightning."

"I was starting to come up on the pill. I didn't— It doesn't matter. You're welcome."

"I think maybe I overreacted that night."

"They shouldn't have offered you the pills." My brain splutters into action as I try to process what he means. That I don't deserve to do drugs? That I'm not cool enough? That they shouldn't be wasted on me? "Finn sometimes conveniently forgets that actions have consequences."

Finn reappears, his hand to his face, wincing. There's a graze below his eye and his cheek is red and sore-looking.

"What happened to you?" Isaac asks.

"Fell off a rail."

"But your board is here."

"I was testing one, from the shop. Bearings were loose."

Isaac exchanges a glance with Finn, then turns to leave.

"Did I miss anything?" Finn asks.

"Just me falling on my ass."

"Sorry, that took ages. Massive queue for the loos, then I just had to try this board. Worked out well, obviously.

But look what I *did* get." He pulls a crumpled bag from his rucksack.

"Mmm, donuts."

"They're a bit squished."

"Still taste the same, that's all that matters. You should get some ice on that cheek. Where's the Coke?"

Finn hands me a can and lays his head on my shoulder. I hold the can to his cheek. He sucks air through his teeth, flinching.

"Very resourceful. Hope you can manage a bit longer without your caffeine fix."

"Sorry if it hurts."

"It's OK. Sorry I left you with Captain Gloomy."

"No worries. I think I have some paracetamol in my bag."

"Isaac give you a headache?"

"No. For you."

I root around for the painkillers.

"I've been thinking about what you said about pills."

"Yeah. They're fun. You'd enjoy it."

"Don't you think about side effects?"

"It's just like a hangover. Completely worth it."

"I'm not sure."

"There's really nothing to worry about."

"I guess … it's just… In PSHE lessons, and on TV, we're always told drugs are, like, evil, home-wrecking, health-wrecking, future-ruining devil potions or whatever. Taking one leads to another and before you know it you're jacking up under a bridge somewhere and all your teeth are missing."

"Graphic."

"Some of that PSHE life-skills stuff must have stuck."

"This isn't heroin or crack, you know? It's just a little MDMA and coke." Suddenly I feel way out of my depth. Maybe this conversation isn't such a good idea. Perhaps I'm just not the druggie type. All the same, I want to be a new me, and take some risks...

"Georgia's birthday party's in a couple of weeks. You could try it then. I'll look after you."

Everyone will be there. I could show them I'm not a lame-ass after all. Still, I'm nervous. Bomb-disposal-team-nervous. Home-pregnancy-test nervous.

"I don't know."

"No pressure." He gets up and paces back and forth. "Think about it."

I bite my lip. I can't control it when I'm thinking, rolling through the worst-case scenarios in my head.

Puking.

Overdosing.

Making a fool of myself.

What if I end up forever believing I'm a giant purple octopus called Beryl?

What if I die?

Finn seems to sense my concern.

"You'll love it. I promise. It's kind of like – hang on."

He lifts me to my feet.

We hold each other's hands and spin around so fast that nothing exists but Finn and the Impressionist landscape in the background. The whole world blurs into thin horizontal lines, blue and brown sandwiching greens and oranges.

My legs almost buckle so many times, but he keeps pulling me into the spin, until he catches me in his arms and we fall to the ground, exhilarated. He grabs me around the waist and starts tickling me. I laugh like a hyena but I don't care. Squirming on the ground, my hairstyle inflates to an Afro.

"You look like a bushman!" he says, grinning. I raise my eyebrows. "A sexy bushman. Really. A hot, sexy bushman."

"I don't want to be a bushman, sexy or otherwise."

"Ah, but tiger, it's a strong look. Might want to think about trimming that beard though," he says, tugging at my chin. Which, I may add, is perfectly smooth. I punch him gently on the arm.

"Anyway, it's like that, but way better. Oh, and there's something else I wanted to ask you about."

"Go on."

"Maybe we should change our Facebook statuses," he says. *Really? Did I imagine that?* I look at him, roughed-up hair, dark-pool eyes and low-slung skinny jeans. He's so perfectly defined. So absolutely defiant. No one compares.

"How utterly romantic," I reply, oozing sarcasm.

He looks up at me with those gorgeous eyes and teases me, hesitating before...

A million butterflies duck and dive inside me. Without warning I'm high above the festival. The trees, the stalls, the noise and all the people are gone. We're all that exists. Finn's hand is on my waist. I hold his neck, stroking his thick, soft hair. The moment swells; a minute, a lifetime, or just a kiss ... all of the above. Long enough to get my tummy tingling. Short enough to leave me wanting more. Gentle, lingering, perfect. His lip ring making it that little bit more exciting. He draws back and I smile, no longer afraid. Not embarrassed. Happy. He pushes a stray hair behind my ear, and grins back.

Maybe I will drop at Georgia's party after all.

CHAPTER 21

EMERGENCY ASSISTANCE REQUIRED

You'll never guess what! The gorgeous boy – the one with the make-me-melt eyes, impossibly handsome grin and (what I imagine to be) perfectly toned body – kissed me. I fell into it like a dream ... ahhhh ... excuse me while I make a safe landing back to earth...

So, Sal, I need help. Knowing me, I will balls it up at the first opportunity. You're old (ha ha) and wise (ha ha). As "female relative nearest my age", you must advise.

Peace out.

Hopelessly lost in love,

London

Dear Loser,

Excuse me, Lindsay Lohan, you've had boyfriends

before. Man up and stop going so teen-flick on me.

Older and wiser,

Oz

Hey, Sal,

Sorry, sorry, sorry! I've caught "Girlie Unappeasable Lovesick Puppy Syndrome" – GULPS for short. Cover your orifices – it's airborne!!! I will endeavour to restrain myself in any future correspondence ;-)

Off to bed now. Those loved-up dreams aren't going to dream themselves.

Patient 32143

PS Before you ask, of course I don't talk like this when he's around. I'd seem a world-class freak. These sickly speeches are reserved for you. Bet you're happy about that. Ha.

CC

xx

I drift into a silky sleep, reliving a thousand times over that butterfly moment when our lips touched.

CHAPTER 22

I wake at noon after an epic sleep. Best sleep of my life. Perfect dreams of summer days and flying and being absolutely content enveloped me from start to finish. I nuke some leftover chilli in the microwave and then doze in front of a *Come Dine with Me* marathon. Livin' the dream.

I bring Finn's cheeky grin to my phone screen and hit CALL.

"You want to come over?" I ask.

"Well, that depends," he says, his irreverent voice like honey. "Have you got any donuts? Cold cans of Coke to tend my wounds?"

"I might be able to rustle something up. Where are you hurting?" I'm asking for trouble, but can't help myself. It's kind of exciting. Finn laughs.

Here's the thing: I can't stop thinking about sex. I've never felt like this before, like I want to be totally and utterly consumed by this intense … fire. And in *that* way. I wonder what it would be like to have his hands roam over me, to hear his breath catching…

Mum and Dad are out shopping for Alessi kitchen accessories (kitchens need accessorizing too, dontcha know) and faux Moore garden sculptures. I bet they come home with a water feature. *Shudder.* So, the house is parent-free…

"I can think of a hundred cringey answers. You want to hear them?" he replies.

"I do, genuinely. Be creative. I like that," I say. "So, Finn, where are you hurting?"

"I've got a pain in my heart when we're apart."

"Oh, please." I shake my head. "Keep going. This is amusing. Actually, I think I know exactly what the problem is. Have you got a sore little finger? It must be turning blue where I'm wound around it."

"I'm aching all over for you, baby,"

"Ohmygod, that's the worst, by far. Come on. Come over."

"You've twisted my arm. I'll be there in twenty minutes. Get the Coke on ice."

I hang up, quickly run a brush through my hair and change my T-shirt, a spilled-chilli casualty of lunchtime.

Nineteen minutes later Finn knocks. Early. He's *never* early. Except to meet me.

I open the door and he immediately knots his fingers with mine and pulls me to him. His clean, man-musk scent revives me from lazy Sunday afternoon slumber like Victorian smelling salts. "Hey," he smoulders, "how are you?"

"Positively sprightly."

There's electricity between us. The kind of frenetic energy sugar-fuelled kids have on Christmas morning.

Strange how people regress when they're in love … or in lust.

Up in my room, we talk, our words criss-crossing like a plait. Mad, incoherent, but completely right and natural. I tell him my stupid secrets: how I hate dunking my head in the bath in case I inhale bubbles; that I have a horse-shoe-shaped scar on my elbow from when I fell down the stairs aged three; that waxworks freak me out big time, the same as people painted gold all over, pretending to be statues.

"We won't be going on a date to Madame Tussauds any time soon then, will we?"

He says he hates courgettes, cucumber, avocado, aubergine, and all those slimy vegetables. That everyone thinks his favourite movie is *The Shawshank Redemption*, but it's actually *Elf*. How he wishes his dad would get a girlfriend and start to live again.

I tell him I wish Mum was around more.

I curl my legs underneath me like a human pretzel. Mid-sentence, he's kissing me, wanting me, but … just because Facebook declares to the world we're "in a relationship" doesn't mean we have to get straight in bed together, right?

We lie there. And kiss. We cuddle and well… His hands trace my curves, move under my top and I laugh, maybe it's nerves, maybe it's his fingertips gently tickling. He reaches his other hand to silence me, and suddenly, this is serious. My pulse gallops. I grip his shirt, twisting it in my fist, and then all I want is to pull it off, feel his skin on my skin and pull him closer than even that. But…

"Wait," I say. It sounds like someone else; the old me, the invisible girl talking, out to sabotage.

"You OK?"

"I ... um ... just need a minute." I head to the bathroom. Splash some water on my face, careful not to smudge my new make-up. Look myself in the eye. *It's no big deal,* I think. *You wanted this.* My gaze drifts and I catch myself looking through the window to the garden below, calculating the distance to the ground. You're just scared. Looking back at the mirror, I straighten my top, take a deep breath, plaster a smile on my face, then go back to my room.

Finn's sitting up, hair wild, eyes sparkling, reading my sketchbook. He smiles openly in that way of his. "You really are very good at the art stuff. One talented girl." He cocks his head to the side. "Everything all right?" he says. "We don't have t—"

It's my turn to put a finger to his lips to quieten him. Because we do have to do this. To keep him, for me to make that leap from invisible girl to someone, we do...

I kiss his neck, then his mouth. He pulls at my lips with his teeth, just gently.

This is happening. Mountains move, icebergs melt, volcanoes erupt... And vaguely, I'm thinking: *Nothing could be better than this, could it?*

He touches my neck, kisses my eyelids... His lush, full hair sticks to his forehead, and I brush it aside. He smiles. Even though he's right there, he's not near enough; the feel of him, the smell of him, everything about him so achingly moreish.

"Tell me everything about you that you wouldn't tell your mother," he says.

I reach behind me for a pillow and hit him with it. And I'm happy, really I am. Except for, I don't know, this kind of … lost feeling that washes over me.

CHAPTER 23

"I *hate* suits," Dad mumbles under his breath. I scan the room through the slightly open door. He's sitting on the edge of the bed, half a glass of red wine and a dog-eared copy of *Shantaram* on his bedside table. An empty wine glass sits on Mum's table, next to a well-thumbed copy of *How to Get What You Want and Get It Now;* her Prada reading glasses lie among the pages of this week's *Nature.* Dad fiddles with his silver cufflinks, light bouncing off them and dancing on the ceiling.

The alarm clock flashes 20:17 in red retro digits. I hear Mum in the bathroom, fixing her face, flossing her teeth, washing the purple wine tint from her lips.

"You need help?" I ask Dad, going in to fasten his cuffs. "Where you off to?"

"Oh, some prize-giving thing for Mum's paper. They're up for Newspaper of the Year." He doesn't seem too happy about spending the evening with Mum's schmoozy colleagues. Networking, they call it in the business. Being tossers, we say in the real world.

"Yeah? Cool. Free fizz and nibbles. What's not to like?"

"Hmm." Dad sighs. I finish the cufflinks. "Thanks," he says.

"It's Georgia's birthday thing tonight."

"OK, love. Are you staying over?"

"Probably."

"Well, take your key in case you change your mind. We won't be back until late."

"OK."

"You've been in a better mood this week. Have you attracted a following of impossibly handsome suitors? Made it onto the gym team?"

I shrug, trying to act casual, but can't hold back a smile. I'm chirpy as a bird on a blue-sky morning. My head is filled with Finn, Finn, Finn...

"You know you have, Carla, dancing about the place like a loon. I saw you knee-slide on the kitchen floor to some 'song', and I say 'song' in its loosest sense. It was more of a *dook-chooka, boom boom*." Dad attempts to beatbox in a cripplingly embarrassing manner, for what is quite possibly the most excruciating eight seconds of my life thus far. *"Bleepety-bleep, umcha, umcha, doof doof doooo—"*

"Please stop that."

"I'm not complaining. Just wondering what's brought about this miraculous transformation."

"Oh, nothing really. I'm my usual melancholy self inside. I promise."

"If you say so." Dad gives me a nudge, and a look that says, *I know this is about a bloke.* He won't push it though. Plus, telling him would mean telling Mum and sparking the whole focusing-on-my-studies talk. *Ugh*… I'm not up for that. I have a night to prep for. A date with fate – hot boy, pills, music – I'll take that over fizz, nibbles and networking any day.

CHAPTER 24

Georgia's parents are flash with cash, and Citrus, the huge venue under the railway arches, has been transformed for Georgia's party. It's beautifully decorated with my designs. Silver sculptures, like giant glinting teardrops, hang from the vaulted ceiling, where a million fairy lights wink. The butterfly acrobats twist and turn on ribbons and hoops, my drawings brought to life. The DJ box is high overhead, a giant birdcage on a monster Meccano scaffold of steel girders, just like I pictured it. It's a wonderland. Clearly nothing's too much for Glen and Lucy Presco's birthday girl.

My stomach is churning, nerves and excitement mingling like guests at a dinner party; Beer Confidence and Speak Before You Think will undoubtedly join the party later.

The epic space is heaving, bodies dancing, bouncing everywhere.

I clock Georgia in the corner with Greg, chatting animatedly. As usual she stands out from the crowd, wearing zebra-print leggings, oversized geek glasses and her trademark red lipstick. Greg's long arms caress her tiny waist and I think how odd they look, him so gangly … everything about him narrow, stretched to 110 per cent in some unfortunate twist of genetic fate … and her so pert. Like a grasshopper going out with a ladybird. Weird.

Finn heads to the bar with Slinky so I go over to Georgia. "Happy birthday. The place looks amazing," I say.

"Thanks to you," she says, smiling.

A glass smashes behind her and I look over to the commotion. Finn and Isaac are arguing. Finn slams his fist on the bar, slopping his beer onto the black granite surface. Isaac rolls his eyes and chucks him a bar towel. Finn takes the throw to the chest, and lets the cloth fall to the floor. Isaac glares at him, exasperated, raises his hand, then bends to pick it up. He catches my eye, and seems about to speak, but doesn't. He whispers something to Finn, then walks off.

Finn winks at me, and I wander over.

"What was that about?" I melt as he swings an arm around my shoulder.

"What was what about?" He acts unaware.

"You and Isaac. The bar abuse."

"He's just being a dick. Nothing, tiger. Ignore the moody bastard."

"Didn't look like nothing." I snuggle into the nook of his shoulder, burrowing for information buried inside him. Reconnaissance closeness.

"Who knows what's up with him? He's acting weird. I mean, he *is* weird, but weirder than usual. He must be bipolar or something. Best mate one minute, angry bastard the next. Throws his toys out of the pram at every little thing."

He cups my face and I plummet into his eyes. "I just said we should do a couple of lines, then double-drop tonight. No point messing about … and he flew off the handle."

My heart starts to race, thinking about drugs. I put the Isaac thing to one side. Whatever the deal is with him, it's that: *his* deal. *His* problem. It's not going to ruin Finn's and my night.

"Forget him," Finn says, half-heartedly, eyeing the streams of spilled beer snaking across the granite and merging into one pool.

"Hey," I say, shaking his shoulder. "He's in a mood. He'll be fine. We'll find him later and he'll be right as rain. He's probably just stressed about exams."

"Maybe." Finn sighs. I've never seen him so distracted before, but at least it shows his sensitive side. I like that. Still, this isn't the time or place for bust-ups. This is the time and place for booze, drugs and over-emotional chats with people you've only just met. This is a party after all, not *The Jeremy Kyle Show*. Feuding brothers can wait for a suitable daytime slot.

A maze of breeze-block corridors leads to another room, white-walled and dusty, with high arched ceilings, like a warehouse. Lights tumble around like a giant kaleidoscope, flashing, fading, glinting, fracturing, shapes shifting, colours intensifying. It's awash with colour, music and dancing. The room hums with energy. Finn pushes through to the bar and orders two beers. I take a swig, feel it run down cold inside me. Condensation from the icy bottle trickles onto my wrist.

I push the hair from Finn's forehead and can't help smiling.

"Dance?" he asks.

"Yeah!" I say, and he pulls me into the hot, airless kaleidoscope. Lasers paint on a canvas of fake smoke. People dance so closely packed that you're touching someone on every side, but nobody pushes or shoves.

Finn draws me close and I hold his waist.

He mouths something but I can't make it out. "What?" I shout, gesturing to my ear. He yells back but it's muffled in the bass of the music. He takes my hand and we snake through the tangle of bodies to the edge of the room. Finn pulls back a drape, revealing a door.

"VIP secret passage," he says. "Bypass the masses."

Fluorescent lights buzz overhead as we make our way down a corridor. We emerge through a fire door into the cool, fresh air of a courtyard – the magical chill-out area I'd sketched. Flowers and tiny lights wind through trellises. Handcrafted, rustic wooden seats dot a carpet of fake grass. It's a paradise.

"Like the place?" he asks, taking his baccie packet from his jeans pocket.

"Love it. Inside's a maze though!"

"You'll get used to it. Come back here if we lose each other," he says, holding a filter-tip in his lips. He pinches some brown-mulch-baccie, evens it out in a paper, adds the filter and expertly rolls the tobacco into a thin tube. He hands it to me, lights it and rolls one for himself. I light his and pocket the Clipper. "But I won't lose you," he promises, "and you're never going to lose me."

I scan the courtyard. People are talking, laughing, joking. It's dark but I've seen at least ten people wearing sunglasses. Some girls are really made up and others just wear jeans and trainers. I smoke my rollie, not intimidated by the pretty girls. Breakthrough!

"All right, kiddo, shall we smoke these, then drop or do you want to do a line first?"

"Uh..." I hesitate.

"God, your face! Ha! Don't worry, tiger. I'll protect you. You'll like it. It'll help. Then just forget about it and enjoy."

"All right, Super Finn, Protector of Nerdy Girls."

"You making fun of me, are ya?" Finn ducks and weaves his head, squaring up to me, playfully.

"Course. Fun's good."

"Yeah, well, you've never had this much fun." He cocks an eyebrow, discards his rollie and off we go again, back through the labyrinth towards the toilets.

Duh-doom-duh-doom-duh-doom. We run up some white stairs to a white room with white toilets. The music still thumps loud, but muffled here. The loos are unisex; or, if they aren't, no one's paying attention to the rules.

Violet comes out of a cubicle, looking worse for wear.

"Is she all right?" I ask.

"Yeah. She's all right. Aren't you, Vi?"

"I am now I've found you," Violet says. My blood boils.

"See you later. Go get some water," Finn instructs.

Violet staggers downstairs.

"She was totally flirting with you."

Finn shrugs. "She's more pickled than an onion. Three sheets to the wind." Finn holds open the door to a cubicle. "Madam," he says and I step inside, excited, nervous, both.

Finn reaches into his pocket and brings out a small plastic bag filled with white powder.

Oh, *shit*.

The reality of the drugs, physically right there – not part of a seedy TV drama scene or fly-on-the-wall documentary – and my total lack of experience, not to mention the whole illegality of the situation, hit me like a ton of bricks. My moral compass starts twirling and my head starts spinning. Information from years of PSHE lessons I'd hardly been listening to suddenly asserts itself. The file marked DRUG FACTS lays bare its contents:

– Sharing needles can give you HIV/AIDS and hepatitis.

– Sudden death can occur on the first use of cocaine.

– Ecstasy inhibits the body's ability to regulate its temperature and can cause dangerous overheating.

Granted, these are extremes. I'm fairly sure Finn isn't about to whip out a crack pipe, but still… *Am I really going to do this?*

Finn tips some powder onto the ledge behind the toilet. It's a bit lumpy. Is that normal? He takes a twenty from his wallet, places it flat on the powder, then presses his bank card over the note, crushing the powder into finer particles.

I'm out of my depth. My breath falters. Beer rises in my throat, then falls away again.

"Wait," I say.

Finn stops and turns his attention to me. Blood seems to drain from my face and pool in my shoes. I must be dead white.

"What is it?"

"I … I'm not sure I can… I mean, do we have to?"

"You don't *have* to. But you *want* to. Believe me."

I want to. Yep. I do. I want to do it, I remind myself.

"I just want us to have a good time," Finn says.

Leaving the note over the powder, he sits on the closed toilet, wraps his arms around my legs and tugs me forwards to sit on his lap. "We can do it together."

My hands are trembling, but I try to ignore them.

"OK," I say.

"Good call," Finn says, releasing his arms. Their warmth lingers on my waist as I stand up. My whole body tingles with anticipation, but I can't help wondering where my not-so-moral compass is leading me. Good call? Could be the best choice of my life. I'll probably have the Best Time Ever and that'll be the end of it.

Maybe I won't seem like such a vanilla hanger-on to Violet, Georgia and that lot. *OK, Carla, just fucking get on with it and reap the rewards, not just tonight, but at school on Monday.*

Putting the note aside, Finn meticulously divides the powder into two long, narrow lines, using the card. It's impossible not to watch: I might get tested later or something... Also, it just seems such a bizarre act. Are people doing this all the time in pubs, clubs, at home? All this fuss over a little white stuff? But what do I know? I guess we're about to find out.

Finn tucks his hair behind his ears and I think he looks cuter than ever. A little glaze of sweat makes him glow. His head bobs with the beat as he takes the twenty and rolls it into a cylinder, a little pipeline...

"I'll show you how," he says.

I make a mental note of his technique. He holds the note between his thumb and forefinger, the end of the note-tube just inside his nostril. In one swift sniff the powder disappears. Just like that. Gone.

"Your turn." He holds out the note. "Ready?"

Um, NO. I shake my head, but take the note.

Sudden death can occur on the first use of cocaine.

I bite my lip, breathing in, hoping to activate something within, the alcohol perhaps, anything for confidence. But it's time, it's going to happen and then it *is* happening...

I risk a glance at Finn, hoping for further advice. He's wiping his nostrils.

"Breathe out first, then breathe in sharply through your nose," he instructs.

OK. I can do this. I step away from the stall wall and it's right in front of me, so silly, so small, so...

I lean over the line while he holds my hair back. His fingertips send a shiver down my spine.

Sudden death can occur on the first use of cocaine.

I exhale, put the note to my nose and breathe in, trying to suck up the powder. It's at this moment that I realize I haven't even asked if it actually *is* coke. *It could be any freaking thing. MDMA? Mephedrone? Ketamine?* I did some research online... It's surprising what people will put up their noses. Anyway, too late now. I've agreed to do it. The little white line vanishes, like dirt up a Hoover. Zoom, suck, gone.

I don't know what to expect. Fireworks? I don't think it's affecting me much. A cool, hard, but not harsh, sensation as I snort it. Then numbness at the back of my throat: the "Chemical Drip", Finn says. Otherwise ... nothing.

I blink a few times. What was I worried about? And what's all the fuss? It doesn't seem that great to me. I do want another beer though...

Yeah another beer would be good you know it would feel good to drink another beer loosen me up and then maybe we could have a dance or a smoke or whatever it doesn't matter but we should really get out of this cubicle we've been in here ages and the music sounds pretty good we should probably dance I think we should dance let's get another beer and then dance...

Blink. Blink. "Yo, bad influence. Let's get a drink. It's thirsty weather," I say. Finn scans the ledge, making sure he's pocketed all his things.

"Yep. Let's amscray."

I unlatch the cubicle door and kick it open. Suddenly I feel determined. On a mission. I grab Finn's hand. It seems so natural. I remember where the nearest bar is, and lead him there. I smile at the barman and order two beers. I pay.

Although it's late I feel really awake. The place has filled up even more since we went to the toilets and everyone's dancing. The music sounds good and I feel so in control of it. Like this is my music. And my turn to dance. So we do. The music pulses and I pulse with it. But now that we're dancing, I feel like talking. *We can do both. Yeah. That'll work.*

"Hey, so how did you get into this has it been long where did you find out about this place I really like it there's such a mix of people and the music's good I mean I'm not used to this kind of music but I like it it's good."

"Yeah, I used to come here with Isaac all the time. He's laid off it a bit recently though, but he can be a proper wreckhead at times. He's a dark horse! So yeah, you call me a bad influence, well, Isaac was mine. Big bro, you know, he was cool."

"Ah, so the bad boy has an even bigger badder brother."

"Something like that. But he's a bit of a lame-ass these days. He actually turns up for revision sessions."

"Call the police he dared try to pass his exams CRIME CRIME!"

"Ha ha! Yeah! How very dare him!"

"You get on well with Isaac then look out for each other it must be nice to have a brother." I'm speaking so fast…

"Yeah, he's a mate and a kinsman." Finn straightens his back and takes a deep breath before leaning into me, saying, "But he don't half annoy me sometimes. I think he might like you, Miss Tiger. And I don't like the thought of my bigger badder brother liking you."

"Mr Masterson I can assure you I…" My head starts to feel a little woolly, and not bad, but, but, but, um, I think I just feel a little drunk and I guess I'm still awake but it's not quite the same. "I can I assure you Mr Masterson that … um … that…" I breathe in, deeply.

Isaac. Isaac staring at me in the car and fighting with Finn and HOLDING BACK MY HAIR WHILE I ALMOST VOMIT. He couldn't. He hates me. Doesn't he? I'm just a girl taking away his brother's attention… No, I don't believe it.

OHMYGOD. That's it. Isaac *likes* me.

Regaining my composure, I say, "I only have eyes for the one brother," but my mind is whirring with thoughts, with chemicals, with a whole mess of crap that's fighting for my attention. Got to focus on Finn.

"And which brother would that be?" He smirks.

"Isn't it obvious?" I mirror his silly smile, and although I don't feel as confident or clear-headed now the initial buzz is gone, I still have the conviction I need at this moment. I don't wait for him to answer. I just kiss him. Certain and easy, a natural kiss I'm in control of from start to finish.

"Mmm, some more sweet, for my sweet? A little pick-me-up?" Finn says.

"Yeah. I think so. I think it's wearing off. I didn't really feel like it was anything but now it's worn off..."

"It's a funny one, coke. Like not knowing what you've got till it's gone," Finn says, referring to that old Joni Mitchell song. "But I've got another treat for you, tiger."

"Yeah?" I look at his perfectly formed neck and high cheekbones, smooth and rough all at once. Stubble dots his clear skin. Whenever I look at him I feel like I'm falling into this great black hole, like I could fall continuously, just thinking about him. I can't explain it. I could drink him in for ever and still be thirsty.

I blink. I open my eyes wide. "We can do that. I'd like to. Feeding time for the tiger."

"Raaa!" He bites my ear and my breath catches. Rushes shoot through my body and I wonder how I will feel after more if I feel like this now. It will be amazing. It has to be.

The artificial light bounces off my skin. In the mirror I look dull, like I'm seeing myself through blue-tinted sunglasses. Wiping a black tear of kohl liner from the corner of my eye, I start to feel ugly, but shake it off. Got to be hot. Got to be in control, ready for anything, that's how Finn wants me. And I want that too. I want what he wants. A cubicle door smashes against its wooden frame and Finn glides through it, nonchalant and King of Everything. He kisses my hand and pulls the door back.

"Madam." He bows and waves me into the cubicle. There's something ironic about it. I feel like royalty. We're doing this special secret thing, but in a two-by-four-foot box with sticky floors and a strange acidic smell, urine probably. Our royal box.

We do another line of coke. Finn says it will help me "get in the spirit". I don't say no because it didn't seem to do much the first time anyway. Can't have too much of nothing, right? Finn reaches into his pocket for a greyish package, which turns out to be about ten pills wrapped in clingfilm. I notice the pills have indented heart shapes. That's got to be a good sign. My heart pounds. I can't believe I'm doing this.

Am I really going through with it?

Finn has waved a wand over me and I'm under his spell. I'll do anything.

"Drop now?"

"Yeah." I nod approvingly. "Is it like being drunk?" I ask, and immediately feel like a dunce. Finn doesn't notice.

"No, not really. Sort of. It's wanting to talk and dance and appreciating everything that's around you…"

"Sounds like some hippy dippy shit to me."

"Just wait, Carla. You wanna be happy? I can make you happy. This will make you H. A. P. P. Y!" He places the pill on my tongue and offers me his beer. I take a gulp and swallow it. Just like that.

Finn necks his pill, too. His hair falls away from his face, then flutters back over his eyes. They glint under the harsh light. He shakes his fringe to one side, leans in and kisses me. I taste the saltiness of sweat.

"I'm going to make you love me, tiger. You'll love me in half an hour!"

I'm not scared. I want to love him. I think... Maybe I already do. I can feel it growing inside me. A force of nature gaining speed and strength. A hurricane about to rip through me, and him. I don't need a heart pill to tell me that.

He gives me a long hug before we head back to the party, happy, joking, awake, together, on fire...

Half an hour later, the pill floats inside me like a lifeboat adrift, firing distress signals. Beacons of nausea, flares of discomfort in my stomach, alarm bells in my head. But Finn says it's OK.

"It's only natural, tiger. Give it ten minutes. You'll be right as rain, I'm telling you." His words fade in and out, like I'm underwater and he's shouting from the edge of the pool.

I feel strange and hot and sick. The lights seem to flash more slowly, their colours bleeding together in an intense haze. I have a sip of beer. *Oh God, oh God, oh God, ohmygod what the fuck is happeningwhatthefuckishappeninginging...*

"All right, tiger, you look a bit peaky, let's go for a smoke and a sit down. You'll be fine in a minute." Finn grabs my wrist and we weave through the crowd like a motorbike in traffic. I feel like everyone is watching me. Can they see something is wrong? Can they? *Is* anything wrong? I flick through emotions like I'm sampling food at a buffet. I'm scared. What's happening? But I'm safe, Finn will look after me. Rationalize, Carla. People are looking, but then again, are they? I'm awake, and starting to feel … something … something else … something better … but holy fuck am I scared…

"Sit down," Finn instructs, moving an empty bottle from a wooden seat. I lower myself clumsily and lean against the trellis-covered wall separating us from the street. The barrier between me and running home. Oh God, I want to go home.

"Can you take me home, Finn? I don't like this."

"Trust me. Just wait."

"I feel weird."

"Good weird?"

"I dunno. Just weird."

"Just your adrenalin pumping. You'll adjust." He strokes my cheek sympathetically. "My first time I felt scared, too. But then you feel great. Let's find you a distraction."

He passes me the cigarette he's been rolling. I hold it between my teeth while I feel for the lighter that's still in my pocket. Before I can pull it out of my jeans, Finn's hand clamps down on my thigh.

I spot Greg and point him out to Finn.

"Hey, mate, you got fire?" Finn turns to Greg, who removes his thick-rimmed sunglasses and hooks them onto the neck of his navy and white striped T-shirt.

"Sure," he says, smiling, and pulls a lighter from his black skinny jeans. He smiles and crouches beside me to light my rollie. I immediately feel more at ease. Greg has a friendly face: strangely round cheeks for someone so slim, thin cherry lips and wide, dark eyes. His blond hair tumbles forwards like the crest of a glittering sun-soaked wave.

"You having a good night?"

"Yeah, yeah, yeah, real good. You?"

Greg nods. "Been out here most of the time though!"

"I know," Finn says. "You get caught in the net. Always the way. Too many good-looking, fun specimens of person out here! Where's the birthday girl?"

"Dancing. That girl loves to dance."

Greg brushes the gold wave back from his face, then lets it crash forwards.

Everywhere I look people are laughing, joking, having the Best Time of Their Lives, and you know what? I'm starting to feel pretty damn good, too. I interlock my fingers and click them back. I feel...

Suddenly I begin to talk. With a deft flick of the tongue, I'm verbal. Verbal and animated.

"You, er, mean to come out dressed as a sailor or was it an accident?" I verbanimate. Greg and Finn have twin expressions of mock-shock. Their mouths hang open. But Greg doesn't seem at all bothered by the not-so-veiled insult. It's just banter.

"I like this T-shirt!" Greg pinches the fabric and pulls it out from his chest; he ducks his chin, eyeing the stripes. "It's an ace shirt!"

"It is. It's, er, shipshape."

"You're on fire, tiger!" Finn says, and then leaning close, in a low voice, "I can see you're feeling better. I told you so." I can do nothing but smile.

"All right, let's leave Sinbad alone. He lent us his lighter after all," I say, winking. "I guess you've got to get back to the ship and mop some decks, reel some nets in—"

"Batten down some hatches," Greg interjects with a cheeky smirk.

"I reckon we've dropped anchor out here long enough. You coming in for a dance?"

"Nah, mate. Catch you later. I'm liking it with the good-looking, fun specimens. I feel at home!" Greg says, slipping his sunglasses back over those wide, dark eyes.

A film of sweat glistens on Finn's brow. I ask him if he wants some water. We get a bottle between us. Leaning against the wall of the dance room, I drink in the people filing past. They seem straight from the pages of *Vice*. I recognize some from school but most are new to me. Maybe they're from Georgia's model agency. Wannabe Lesley Arfins mixing with lager lads. You can be anything here. You are free. Free.

"What's free?" Finn says. *Shit, I said that out loud!*

"I was just thinking how there's such a diverse group of people here. How you're free to be who you want to be." I scan the room. A tall beardy guy slyly smokes behind a ten-foot stack of speakers. A girl with too much hair and bug-eye glasses chats with a dude in Nike hi-tops and Teddy-boy tie. Another guy wears a T-shirt reading, I FACEBOOKED YOUR MUM, his hair backcombed to retro perfection. A few randoms work the Day-Glo look.

"I mean, look at her," I say, pointing discreetly to a girl

in floral print with knitting needles around her neck. "She gets the thumbs-up for her twist on granny chic. But the bloke she's talking to, he's wearing Adidas trackies circa 1996. You wouldn't exactly put them together."

"Beauty of the dark, Carla."

"I guess. All sorts of crazy things happen in the dark, right?" Words fall out of me and it feels good. Free. This place feels free. I hope the night lasts for ever.

Finn kisses my neck softly. I feel alive. Weightless. But I make him stop.

"Not a pretentious crowd at all…" I don't even know if that's sarcasm or not. I get it though: these seeming misfits would never speak ouside the walls of this club. Their paths wouldn't cross. But here, they are the same, all out for a good time, all collaborating to make it happen. United by a common goal: to get wasted. Am I making sense? I'm thinking too much. I shake my head again. Thoughts fall out.

"Some are, but we're all friends here!" Finn says, a giant grin spreading across his face. And I know why; I can see it all around, in the faces of the mixed-bag crowd.

A tune builds tempo stealthily, gathering speed, energizing … and then kicks in with a thud, and my guts twist with delight. My heart skips a beat. My head feels suddenly clear. At this moment there is nothing but this room and this feeling. Finn joins the chorus of "ohhhs" praising the DJ, who's nodding, flicking switches, turning dials, whatever it is they do, working his magic. He looks across his people, and grins. Commander of an army. King. God. He's sly. He knows what he's doing. I catch the eye of granny-chic girl, who's dancing, faux-knitting to the beat. She mouths "Yeah!" to me and I do the same. YEAH! YEAH! YEAH! We're all the same. This is fucking madness and I love it!

I've never danced so much in my life. Not caring how I look, not being able to disguise my joy. I'm in abso-fucking-lute awe of the DJ and think to myself: *Why haven't I done this before?* What have I been doing all this time? I was a shy animal cowering in the corner of my cage. Now the door is open. Beyond that door is a world. And I'm dancing in it. Like a prize twat. But a happy, free twat who doesn't give a shit what you think…

While we're dancing Finn reaches into his pocket and pulls out the cling-filmed packet.

"Open wide," he says, putting another pill on my tongue. I swill it down with some water. Anything to keep this feeling alive. Finn swallows one, too. A song I recognize but don't know the name of comes on. It doesn't matter; I still know the tune, the words. Lost in Finn, I watch him like no one else exists in the room. He smiles and sweats and moves. He's done this a hundred times, drugs, clubs, the party thing, but still I feel special to be with him. Maybe for him it feels fresh and new with me? I want to grab him and say, "Hey, you! I want to be with you always!" That's silly, we hardly know each other. But something about him and this moment makes me think we'll last for ever.

CHAPTER 25

Whoever said all good things come to an end is an idiot. Sure, things ebb and flow like the tide, but they don't disappear completely, right? I hope I'm right. Finn makes the hand signal for "Let's go for a rollie" and we head to the smoking area, now flooded with morning light. It flicks a switch in me. I'm turning off. Shutting down. Game over. Knockout. Exhausted.

"Carla?"

"Hmm?"

"You want the rollie or not?"

"Oh, yeah, yeah, yeah." I take the rollie from Finn and have a long, hard drag. I cough, but I'm not embarrassed. I'm tired, but still pretty high. "I can't believe it's fucking daylight. What have we been doing all night?"

"Having a blinder, tiger!"

"I think we did all right." My lips curl upward.

"All right? You fucking loved it."

"I did."

A strange look pans across Finn's face, serious and

calculating. Do I look rough? Is my mascara gothed? Do I look like I should be in a body bag after staying up all night? I search his face for clues, then duck my head into my knees, hiding, but he touches my cheek, turns me to face him, kisses me.

We walk home, full of our own majesty. King and Queen of London, England, United Kingdom, World, Universe. As we amble across the bridge, the river stretching out for ever either side of us, I feel like I'm flying. Not crazy LSD "I can fly!" nonsense but, I don't know, just happy and soaring in some other place. Some secret place where it all makes sense. A parallel universe, but better. So much better... I feel confident, pretty, and I have the guy. Un-fucking-believable. This is amazing!

I don't want it to stop. I don't want to stop being this girl. The beautiful girl in the foreground, not a smudge of paint in the background. Health damages be damned! New friends, new experiences, this new life: it's going to be a masterpiece.

I wonder if the London Eye is moving. It can't be. Must be the drugs playing tricks. We're hand in hand, me silent and him singing "Water" by Traction:

Like a breaker I could carry you, thrill you, together we'd ride. Or I could draw you under, let you drown in my depths. Fill your lungs with me, drink me in and never leave.

I do have to go home though, don't I? I have to sneak in, at least be there. It won't matter if I'm not very vocal later, as long as I make an appearance. Anyway, Mum will probably be shopping/working overtime/on a business trip/networking/researching/generally not around. Delete as appropriate.

Finn lends me his old iPod so I can listen to some tunes if I can't get to sleep. I hope to be comatose in the near future but, although my body is tired and empty-feeling, my mind is still click-click-clicking...

Finn.

Finn.

I did coke.

I did pills.

Have I damaged myself? Don't think about that...

Think about Finn...

CHAPTER 26

I don't feel well. Understatement of the year, the decade, the century. After exactly zero hour's sleep, Sunday is just an extension of Saturday. I lie in bed for ages, waiting for my stomach to stop churning and for my thoughts to switch off. I can't relax. I repeat, *Lights off, nobody home*, vainly trying to convince myself I'm done thinking for today. But … although the ecstatic feeling is long gone, the crazy thought process and wide-awakeness persist. Stop this ride! I want to get off!

I'm in conflict. Body wants to shut down; brain wants to talk. Right now, it's chattering pretty damn loudly.

What if Isaac never accepts me as Finn's girlfriend? Or he makes Finn choose between us? Finn won't stop talking to his brother… And does Isaac *really* fancy me, like Finn said?

Isaacgate is coming. I can feel it.

And besides all *that* churning around in my head, *this*:

HOLY CRAP, I TOOK DRUGS.

THEY WERE AMAZING.

THANK FUCK, I'M STILL ALIVE.

OHMYGOD, I FEEL AWFUL.

Was it worth it? Now it's over, feeling the pain of the comedown, the epic hangover, I'm not so sure.

I confide in Dad that I had a bit to drink on Saturday night. I can't really hide that I'm a wreck, so I have to say something. He laughs. "That'll learn ya."

I fall asleep mid-afternoon, but wake at one thirty a.m., six hours ahead of schedule. Not good. I try to get back to sleep but my body refuses. I shift under the sheets, fluff my pillow, take some painkillers. Still awake. Then BEEP-BEEPBEEPBEEPBEEP... Siren of doom, most hated sound in the known universe. Why is it that now, at seven thirty a.m., when I actually have to get up and resemble a human being, I feel compelled to hibernate for ever? OH GOD. I have to go to school, and if they ask me what I did this weekend I'll just crumble and cry because I am a sleep-deprived-shell-of-my-former-self wreck of a person today.

7.37 a.m.: Dad calls, "Carla, are you up?"

7.42 a.m.: He shouts again. No answer.

What do I do?

1. Lie: Pull a sickie, which, in the current circumstances, won't exactly be a stretch of my acting talent.
2. Tell the truth: I have a two-day hangover.

Um, obviously I'm going with Option 1.

Did I hear that someone was off school with a stomach bug? A virus? No, too specific. Nausea and sore throat? Headache?

7.46 a.m.: Dad taps on my door.

I pull the duvet around my neck. It smells like dust and shampoo. I straighten my pyjama top over my stomach and rub my feet together in an attempt to get comfortable. I don't want to lie to Dad, but … it's not *technically* lying because I feel like death, yet it *is* my doing. I am, just a smidgen, in the wrong.

Suck it up. Go to school.

I sit up in bed. The walls spin. I'm not going anywhere.

Lights off, nobody home. Go away, conscience.

I made this happen, but to be honest, the guilt card is totally trumped by the grim death card. I can't go to school like this. I don't want to show my face in the mirror, let alone a classroom.

"Carla, you'll be late if you don't get up now."

I rummage in my portfolio of physical abilities for "constructing sentences and speaking aloud". I swear it's like I have to switch a skill off to allow another one to switch on. Honestly: turn off "balance and spatial awareness", turn on "listen and assimilate information". Multi-tasking is a no-go after no sleep.

"Not feeling well, think I should stay home," I croak.

"What's up? Can I come in?" he asks, brimming with concern.

No, don't come in.

"Yeah, come in," I say. "Feel sick. Bit of a headache."

Dad hesitates, weighing up what's best to do on his invisible parenting scales. A cough, forlorn expression and "Dad, please" tip them in my favour, but he isn't stupid.

"Carla," he says accusingly. Yet he feels my forehead and adds, "You *are* a bit warm." His eyebrows rise like helium balloons. "I'm such a bloody pushover. Don't tell your mother I let you stay home. And no more boozing. Even at the weekend."

Dad disappears downstairs. Five minutes later, he's back. "I rang school. If you're up to it later, you can get your assignments online."

"OK," I say.

He gets my laptop from the desk. "Don't download too many movies."

He kisses me on the forehead, then exits with a gust that whips my door shut.

I screw up that last atom of guilt like a receipt for a top I couldn't afford.

Lights off, nobody home…

CHAPTER 27

Bang, bang, bang…

I wake to the sight of rolling credits.

Bang, bang, bang…

The door.

I cocoon myself in my stripy duvet and stumble downstairs. I feel fuzzy, scatty, a sandwich short of a picnic. Halfway down, I duck to try and make out who's at the door. For a millisecond I'm convinced it's Finn, come to see if I'm all right. He has the same dark hair, the same fair, smooth skin and dark eyes, but Isaac's rougher around the edges. It's got to be Isaac. I mean, Finn's no Ken doll, he has style. He has a metrosexual emo chic thing going on, but it's a controlled, deliberate roughening of his edges, whereas Isaac just doesn't care if he looks good or not.

I open the door to the face of someone trying to do a hard sum: perplexed, awkward, in pain. *There's no way he likes me.*

I cough an opener. "Hi." *Not my best line…*

Isaac surveys me like he's looking at a building for the

last time before pulling the demolition lever.

"I, er, came to check on you. Finn said you were sick." He doesn't look me in the eye. I twist the corner of the duvet in my fingers.

"Couldn't sleep last night. Coming down with something. Best keep your distance."

"Bet you'll be feeling better by tomorrow."

"What do you mean?" I ask, watching his dark hair flap in the wind, exposing a few little furrows on his forehead. He's always in his head, thinking, analyzing, calculating…

"Just… Saturday night" – Isaac descends into mumble – "going pretty hard and…"

Dramatic pause. I'm freaked at the length of the silence.

"Anybody home?" I say.

Nothing.

I sigh. "I feel like a giant slice of death, if I'm honest."

"Look, um…" He shuffles his feet, then looks right at me – in a scary making-me-wish-I-wasn't-home-alone kind of way – and starts projectile word-vomiting. He just wants to get it over with and go home. "Carla, I came because, well, Finn couldn't. He asked me to. He's gone with Slink to some way-out board shop for bearings. It was a favour for him. I'll let him know you're OK. You can go back to sleeping or whatever."

"OK, well, yeah, I'm alive. Report back to Finn. Thanks for stopping by," I say, and wait for a nod or a "Later" or a wave goodbye, but…

I scan his face for life-signs. *Nada.* Zero. Flatline. Blank. He's forgotten how to end conversations. I'm too tired to cope with the complex workings of the male brain, and I need to be lying down, or with my head in the toilet right now, so I break the deadlock with "See ya" and shut the door.

I slump into a pile of duvet on the hall floor, listening for the thud of his footsteps to fade away before returning to the man I actually *do* understand and can guarantee will always supply the happy ending, my romcom husband, Gabriel Grayson.

What was *that* about?

CHAPTER 28

"You can do better than this, Carla." Havelock's words pinch me at the back of the neck. A guilt grip. I *can* do better, he's right. It's only mocks though. Just fake exams. What will happen if I fail my fake exams? I won't get a fake job, earn invisible money and afford a fictional car? I'm saving my *real* energy for *real* things, conserving my brain for something that actually counts. Things are going so well with Finn, and he deserves my time, too.

Havelock leans against his desk. Sighs. Looks to me for an explanation.

I wave my white results transcript in surrender, with its list of descending grades: A (Art) to F (Biology). With C, D, D between.

"Sorry," I say. It sounds *pitiful*. "I guess exam nerves really got to me."

He shoots me a bewildered, concerned look, but I think he buys it.

"Are you sleeping and eating OK?"

I don't answer, and look down at my tatty Converse. I

guess my clothes are getting a bit baggy.

"I understand exams can be stressful – some stress can be good, motivational. Try not to let the pressure overwhelm you." Havelock opens a file and removes a sheet of paper and I'm thinking, *Great, more homework.* "Here are some ideas on managing stress," he says, handing me the piece of A4.

Guilt tightens its grip. Should've done more revision.

In Psychology, I open my textbook and try to concentrate on Bowlby's Theory of Attachment. Finn's wearing a V-neck black T-shirt and his emo jeans. I can't get over how perfect this all is. I mean, aside from the odd homework dodge and lesson skive, everything is pretty darn good. Finn straddles the back of his chair, swinging around to face me. I could dive right into him. I want to. A smile steals his entire face, holding it captive. I love that his emotion is right there, raw, taking over his whole body. And mine. He locks me in a staring match, with those beautiful coffee-bean eyes, an ear-to-ear-grinning–stare-down. I'm one hundred per cent guaranteed to lose this contest. Five. Four. Three. Two. One. Heart to jelly; can't look at him any longer. *Have* to get on with some work.

I pick up my pen, write the date on the lined pad and draw a perfectly straight line under it. I check whether the biro has made a dent in the page below. It has. Of course it has, you idiot. *Notes. Got to make notes.* I read the first paragraph, absorbing nothing into my supposedly sponge-like young brain and have to read it again. My phone vibrates in my pocket. Text from Finn, sitting a metre and a half away. Still staring.

Good work, tiger. Havelock totally believed u. Meet up tomo? xxx

I look up, fighting the urge to climb over the table so I can be nearer to him. I quickly construct a reply under the desk, glad of my fast texting fingers.

Maybe do sumthin in the eve? School tomo! xxx

I've barely sent it before the reply buzzes back:

And? xxx

I finally manage two pages of half-arsed paraphrased plagiarism. The mild sense of achievement this brings is dangerous. I deserve a reward. Breaking from the notes, I let my mind wander. Finn and I have seen each other almost every day since Citrus. He's told his mates I'm his girlfriend. It feels fluid and easy, as if it's always been "us". Will bunking one day really matter? In the great scheme is it really *that* important? Probably not.

So what if I'm a little late to class because I'm talking to Finn or if I take a day off here and there. I can still get the grades. That's all that matters as far as I'm concerned. At school, after only a few months, I'm someone else. A new me. A tiger.

After school we go to Finn's to do some revision, supposedly, but instead watch *Avengers Assemble* and eat peanut M&M's.

In the kitchen, I pour some juice and Finn nukes a bag of popcorn. As the microwave dings, alarm bells begin to chime in my head. I look out the window at his neglected lawn. My stomach flips at the thought of all the work I need to catch up on. Xylem. Phloem. Biology. Bowlby.

Baudrillard. Psychology… Exams looming…

"Catch!" Finn chucks the popcorn at me and I empty the packet into a bowl.

I gear up to tell him we have to see each other less and revise more.

"Um, right… So … we should really get the Psych done now," I say, a little tetchy with him for the first time. "The Bowlby presentation is Monday." I give him my best sickly sweet, do-it-for-me smile. I hold his hand as he shuffles his feet, undecided, swinging his gorgeous, strong arm to and fro. "Pretty please. Let's just get through the first bit."

But then he kisses me, sending a shockwave through my nervous system and I sort of forget…

In his room, as the seventeenth peanut M&M ricochets off my forehead, I realize we won't be getting any work done today. Finn is wearing his black Fenchurch T-shirt that says "I should wear a crown because I'm royally f#*ked up." His arms look toned and strong, like a swimmer's or gymnast's. Contrasting with his bear-like forearms, his biceps are smooth and not *too* big. My eyes wander over him until he flicks another chocolate peanut in my direction.

"Oi, kiddo! I'm trying to work here," I exclaim, cutting him an icy glance. "Stop this tomfoolery at once!"

"Tomfoolery, eh?"

"Yup."

"Who is this Tom? I'll have him! Only Finnfoolery allowed here!"

"There's no Tom. It was said purely for your amusement.

An underused word. We should bring it back. Like 'rad'. I want to bring rad back."

"Let's bring in Finnfoolery, too. It'll be rad," he suggests.

"OK," I agree.

"Rad."

"Cool."

"Rad."

"OK."

"Rad."

"Stop this Finnfoolery!"

"But it's totally rad!"

"Stop it."

"OK, rad."

"Stop it!"

"Rad."

"I've changed my mind. Let's leave the word rad in the past, where it belongs. Send it to Room 101, with blancmange and hair scrunchies and—"

"I think I'm a little bit in love with you," he says.

Ohmygod.

Tingles. Check. Skipped heartbeat. Check. Heart stopping altogether. Check.

"I'm a little bit in love with you, too." Flatline. Get the defibrillator.

His kiss resuscitates me.

"I mean it." Finn speaks to my eyes, my cheeks, hair and mouth, scanning all of me. "OK, then," he says, plonking himself on the bed and leaning forwards, assaulting my body and senses with his eyes and gorgeous musky man scent. "Let's do the revision, but to compensate for this wholly uncharacteristic burst of nerd-dom, I expect you to wear a fabulously low-cut dress on Friday."

I push him on the shoulder, provoking a yelp. "Oi, mister, that ain't rad!"

"All right, all right," he concedes. "It doesn't have to be low-cut. Wear a short skirt. I'm easy. Whatever you want, tiger!" He recoils, anticipating another assault. I draw back my hand, for effect. "Not the face!" He laughs. "I'm teasing you! You'd look hot in a brown paper bag."

"You're unbelievable!" I say, eyes wide, heart pumping fast. He leans back onto the pillow, nodding in agreement. "What's Friday, anyway?" I ask.

"Violet's having a select few over. Nothing big, just a cheese board and a bottle of red," he says, grinning. Definitely won't be cheese, that's for sure.

"Ha. Sounds delightful," I mock.

My heart races. I try to concentrate.

"OK," I begin. *"Attachment is an emotional bond to another person,"* I read from my crib sheet. *"Psychologist John Bowlby was the first attachment theorist..."* Finn sits up. Edges closer. I try to focus. *"His psychological model..."* He kisses my neck. The words blur. *Connectedness. Support. Trust.* I put the paper down to give Finn my attention.

All I can think is, *He loves me. He loves me. He loves me.*

CHAPTER 29

My brain has decided to no longer accept information about Biology. An invisible anti-Biology force field bounces it off my head. Not even in-one-ear-and-out-the-other. This is a dangerous condition considering I have:

1. a test next Monday
2. coursework due in a month
3. total lack of interest.

Give me Rothko, Vermeer, the beautiful mess of a Jackson Pollock or the cut-and-paste prints of Jamie Reid. Not Energy Flow Through Ecosystems… What has that got to do with Thermodynamics? I don't get it! *Ugh*.

"I don't understand this," I tell Miss Tillsman after Monday's lesson. "I'm really worried about the exams."

"Carla, you just have to give it some solid attention. I know you're bright. Self-discipline. Put some effort in if you want results."

"I'm trying."

"Not hard enough, it seems. I know what you *can* do. Your early coursework was superb. What's happened?

Are you having problems at home?" *Cringe.*

"No … I'm just tired, I guess. I'll try to keep on top of it."

"Come to Biology Club on Fridays. It might help." *Biology Club?* Is she nuts? I might as well tattoo NERD on my forehead and give myself a wedgie.

Friday. Violet's get-together…

"I have plans this week."

"If you're serious about passing, Carla, you need to come – if only to catch up."

Well, I'll skip it this week. Already made plans. It'd be rude to cancel. It's only a test. I'll be totally clued up for the exams, no problem.

The rest of the week is a whole bunch of nothing. Boring crap. It's all about the weekend. Friday's finally here and I'm *so* excited. I survey the contents of my wardrobe, and toss a few new things onto the bed, ready to road-test them. Finn's iPod is in the sound dock. I click onto Traction, select "Water".

The song starts slow, quiet, then builds, and the beat kicks in.

Like a breaker I could carry you, thrill you, together we'd ride. Or I could draw you under, let you drown in my depths. Fill your lungs with me, drink me in and never leave.

After Traction, I listen to a set by a DJ I've never heard of, but the bass reminds me of that first wonderful night, and the feelings come rushing back, flooding my senses … the incredible highs… In a few hours, I could feel that way again. It's exhilarating just thinking about it.

I turn up the music. It thumps.

I find some ripped black tights, a lace of ladders down one leg. OK. I pull on a new skirt and T-shirt, and start on my make-up. I want big eyes – big smoky eyes – and a flash of red on my lips.

There's a knock on my door.

"Come in," I say, still looking in the mirror. I see Dad in the doorway, reflected.

His eyebrows do their thing. I get the message, and reduce the pounding bass.

"Thanks. Where you off to?"

I consider my answer.

"Cinema."

"Who with?"

"Finn."

"Oh."

"Problem?"

"No. No problem. Just asking."

"OK, then."

"I hear the door."

"That'll be him. See ya."

I take a last look in the mirror. *Here I am, world.*

Outside, Finn wraps me in a hug. Isaac is loitering with Slinky and Fat Mike, leaning against the front wall. Slinky's already smoking a joint. I only hope Dad doesn't smell it. Isaac looks as sullen as ever, kicking at the moss between the bricks of the wall.

As we walk away Mike hands me a beer. It hisses as I open it. Finn offers his hand and I go to take it, but in his palm I feel something. He says nothing, just kisses me on the cheek.

I wait until we're out of my road before putting the pill in my mouth, as subtly as I can, then knock it back with the beer.

I bet Violet lives in a palace. I bet she has her own pet white tiger and a staircase of gold and fifty servants catering to her every whim.

As we turn off the high street, I realize I'm mistaken. She lives in one of the chocolate-box houses. Pale blue, Violet's house sits between a pink one and a yellow one. Window boxes burst with floral colour. The epitome of picturesque – well, as picturesque as they come in South London, twenty minutes from the city. It's not a big house by any stretch, but small, perfectly formed, bijou. To one side, down an alley, I make out a distinctly normal-looking back garden; patio, slightly overgrown grass, sagging clothesline, even a few gnomes dotted about. I *did not* have Violet pegged as a gnome person, but it's her parents' house after all. They probably do the accessorizing. And she thought my butterfly sketches were cutesy?

I finish my beer, crunch the can in my hand, and place it in the bin outside her house.

Mike raps the door. Violet appears.

"Hey," she says, "you're all here." She smiles and comes in for a hug. Not like her, but I go with it.

"Carla, let's find Georgia. She's around here somewhere." Violet pulls me from Finn, towards the kitchen. I follow her, feeling torn. Torn from Finn, torn between him and the chance to connect with these new mates.

"I didn't know you were coming," she says, "but I'm glad you're here."

In the kitchen, Georgia throws her arms wide. "Heeeeey!" She pulls me into a hug. "Want a drink?"

"Yeah. What is there?"

"Vodka."

"Sounds good. You'll have to let me go to get it."

"Nooooo! Hugs are soooo good." She twists to whisper in my ear. "Double-dropped, he he!" she titters, full of warmth and childlike wonder.

"I'll get it," Violet says.

She returns with a full glass, complete with lime wedge and mini-umbrella.

Georgia releases me. I wince as I sip, but drink it anyway.

Definitely more than vodka. OK. It'll help me get in the mood.

"So tell me all about you and Finn."

I lose track of time talking with Georgia and Violet. It's like … I don't know … a blind spot. One minute we're talking and then… No, it's gone.

I sit at the kitchen table, empty glass in hand. Georgia and Violet have moved on.

Then I see it. The music is hurtling towards me. A stream of sound coming right at me. I can see it. Did you ever see *Donnie Darko*? – that's what I'm talking about. I *see* ripples of music.

I stand up, wobbly, and go into the lounge.

The music's thumping, curving, twisting, bending. I can *see* it.

I need to sit down again.

There's a free seat on the sofa, next to Isaac.

"Isaac, Isaac, Isaaaaaaaaaac! Can you see that right there can you see that it's weird ripples floating around the place. I think I can move them sort of like when I look at them they change direction or are they moving in time with the music I don't know it doesn't matter really so how are you?"

Silence.

"Of course I know it's just my imagination. It'll pass I just thought maybe you might have … never mind. Ignore me. How are you?"

A wall of silence fifteen metres thick.

I light a rollie, inhale and get a rush. *Happy, this is what happy feels like.*

"Can't smoke in here, Carla," he says. "Garden."

"Oh yeah, course." I go to stand up, but stumble backwards, circling my arms for balance in classic comic style. Isaac isn't laughing. I steady myself, finessing the move with jazz hands and a muffled *ta-dah!*, the rollie stuck between my lips.

He's still not laughing. Can't get this stone to bleed. I stagger to the back door, strangely OK with the stumbling. It must be beer confidence, drugs confidence.

"Maybe I should take you home," Isaac says.

"Why? I'm fine." *Fine and dandy.* "Have you seen Finn?"

Isaac sighs. "Bedroom."

I move for the stairs.

"Carla."

"Yeeeeeesss?"

"The rollie. You can't smoke in the house."

"Oh," I say. I spot a beer can on the coffee table, put the rollie in and let it fizz out.

The stairs are changing shape, thick, thin, high, low, tilting one way, then the other. I cling to the handrail to pull myself up.

I hear Georgia's voice from behind a door and push it open.

Violet's sitting next to Finn on the floor, carving up lines on the back of a French revision book.

"Hey, you." Finn smiles. I crash onto his lap, planting a kiss on his neck.

"What happened?" I ask.

"You conked out for a minute," Violet says. "Happens to all of us. Like Greggers here."

Greg's half-asleep, hand on stomach, head against the wall, long legs outstretched on the bed. Georgia's bouncing cross-legged on the mattress, like when you play Fried Eggs on a trampoline. Greg is inevitably bouncing with her, looking pale and ready to hurl at any second.

"He's just sleepy," Georgia says, flicking her mane-like hair.

"Rack up one more," Finn instructs. Violet doesn't look up, but does what she's told.

"Well, this is cosy," Finn says, looking into my eyes. I hear the *ssshhhhoosh* of Violet's line disappearing. She passes the book to Finn and he does his. *"Merci beaucoup,"* he says, and passes the book to me.

The lines look *massive.*

I push my nose from side to side and sniff. Got to be in it to win it, eh? I snort it like a trooper, and hand the book to Georgia.

"Brrrrriing, brrriiinggggg! Gregory, this is your wake-up call!" she says, nudging Greg awake. He stirs, and takes the book.

"That's what I call room service," he says.

Immediately, things change. I'm awake. AWAKE. Zip, ping, chemicals. VERY AWAKE. JUMP-STARTED AWAKE.

Greg is miraculously revived. He and Georgia bounce out of the room for a dance.

I stand up.

"Shall we dance?" I ask Finn. My heart's galloping.

"Yeah." He turns to Violet. "Coming, Vi?"

"Let's all go," she says, holding out a hand to be pulled up.

A few hours later my heart starts to sink. The clouds have cleared, leaving a sky of sapphire. The wind wraps around the trees in the garden as if choking them. We huddle together on a fluorescent orange blow-up sofa on the patio. I imagine we're floating, adrift at sea on our inflatable tangerine life-couch, bobbing up and down in epic darkness, freezing water lapping at our ankles. Just another ridiculous thought emanating from my subconscious. Silly ideas flash on and off in my head like a faulty light bulb.

God, shut up, brain. Everything's normal.

Finn's got hold of my hand, tight, reassuring me. I shiver, freezing, no longer wearing my beer coat. He wraps his jacket around my shoulders, and whispers, "I love you, tiger." I look at him, but … I have a *bad* feeling. Might just be paranoia setting in, but something isn't right. The world's askew. I can't see straight. People seem crooked. Like I can see the dark side of people.

Shut up, brain. Everything's normal.

I just rest my head on him, thinking how crazy my body feels, full of all these chemicals… I feel … helpless.

My mouth's desert dry. I sip some water, then take a long slug, draining the glass, but it feels foreign in my stomach and I don't think it'll be there for long… *Vomit cometh.*

"I'll get us a water refill," he says.

I watch him walking away, rubbing his temples.

Georgia comes into the garden, and sways unsteadily above me, a can of Red Bull in one hand and a spliff in the other. Seems contradictory to me, but she dances to the beat of her own drum. Her red lipstick has rearranged itself into a map of Australia, smeared and colonizing the skin above and below her lips, but she still pulls it off. Don't-give-a-fuck-chic.

"Have a toke," Georgia says, offering me the spliff, smoked almost to the roach. "You look like you could use it."

Can't talk. *I feel broken…*

"Thanks," I manage. My voice is someone else's. I am someone else. Is this what I wanted? I wanted to be someone. But *this* someone? I don't like it. *Fuck, fuck, fuck.* I really don't like it. Will I feel this way for ever, so out of control, so God-awful?

Maybe the weed will help relax me. I take a drag. "I'm feeling a bit messy," I say.

"Yeah. Me too, honey. I've been bouncing off the walls tonight. Comedown's starting to hit me now. Got to do this slowly, land it like a plane."

I swing my legs from the sofa, making room for Georgia. She slides next to me, rubbing my shoulder to keep me warm. I finish the spliff and stub it out on the side of a giant terracotta flowerpot, where a gnome sits, fishing.

Finn reappears with water.

"Thanks," I say.

He takes my hand. It feels cold and sweaty. Like melting ice.

My head pounds. I'm sick and spent and sad and empty.

"Let's get you home," Finn says. I think that's a very good idea.

At home, stars bounce around the white-walled cube. I hunch over the bathroom basin, then stand bolt upright, roll my shoulders out, then hunch again. Can't decide. Do I feel sick? Am I just hungry? No food since yesterday lunch. I tried to have dinner last night, but nerves had shorted out the circuit that tells my brain to eat. Anyway, eatin's cheatin' when you're going out.

I nearly fall into the mirror like Narcissus. Eyes glassy and avian, I'm staring at a scary stranger. Not a bewitching beauty, definitely not a bird of paradise, but a strange creature who looks a bit like me and occasionally thinks the same thoughts.

My nostrils are caked in crap. I blow them out.

Head against the white tiles, I close my eyes and tiredness overwhelms me. Like a chainmail suit, it weighs every limb, yet, agonizingly, my brain still finds thoughts to keep me awake and my heart is going crazy fast. *Fuck, fuck, fuck… I knew this would happen. Why did I do it again?*

This is so messed up.

My internal organs have turned themselves inside-out and are making a bid for freedom. I can't stop it. Acid rises, choking me, then projectiles into the bath and all over Mum's fancy soaps. The loofah is coated. I'm surprised it doesn't disintegrate. Whatever's coming out of me is corrosive, fucking battery acid, and my raw throat gets more raw. I retch until nothing more comes, and my ribs ache from heaving and crunching over the hard edge of the bath.

I twist the taps and let the water fall, washing away the sick; then dunk my head under the water. I'm not even afraid of inhaling bubbles. I put the plug in.

I don't wait for the water to rise, but haul myself into the tub, fully-clothed. The water gets too hot, but I can't find the energy to turn up the cold.

A drop of red swirls in the water, and then another. I put my hand to my face and bring it back to see blood. Nosebleed.

I feel tears pressing like hot pokers. Can't stop them. No control. My body's being driven by someone else, someone evil, sadistic and cruel.

Fast-flowing tears mingle with blood.

This is it, the end. I wish… *I wish I was dead. Don't think that. It'll pass. It has to. Don't think that.*

Just make it stop. Let me feel normal again.

Shit. Shit. Shit. I think I'm going to have a seizure or something… My heart's racing. I'm so tired but it's still hammering on without me … too fast … too much…

Sudden death.

Heart attack.

Cocaine.

Paranoia. Got to just be paranoia. I'm fine, right?

Yeah, I'm fine.

I'm telling myself I'm fine.

Oh God. Talking to myself.

It's just paranoia.

I mean, I'm fine, right?

The steam rises, and then and then…

I hear hammering in my head. *Bash, bash, bash.* No, not my head. The bathroom door.

"Carla? You in there?" Dad calls. *Bash, bash, bash.*

"Um." My voice is a rasp. The water's cold – mind-bendingly sub-zero freezing. I pull the plug to let it drain. My soaked clothes cling to my hollow body, an icy suction suit.

"Just a minute," I manage, panicking.

I hear footsteps fade away, peel off my clothes, wrap myself in a towel. My teeth chatter.

I crawl across the landing to my bedroom, embedding carpet grit in my palms. I'm a drunk, cumbersome animal. So far from human.

I lie, fixated on the ceiling, and click PLAY on Finn's iPod.

My heart dances and aches for him all at once, all the time…

Like a breaker I could carry you, thrill you, together we'd ride. Or I could draw you under, let you drown in my depths. Fill your lungs with me, drink me in and never leave.

CHAPTER 30

I read somewhere that the body has no memory for pain. That's why women can go through childbirth over and over again. I think maybe it's true, because something's messing with my head, telling me the comedown wasn't *so* bad and *didn't you have a good time? It was worth it, right? Come on, body,* my brain's saying, *you had fun, didn't you? Let's do it all again!*

I'm having a schiz-out. All I want is for the weekend to come round again.

Next time I gobble down chemicals and my dopamine levels plummet to a dopa-minus, I may change my answer, but now, it all feels in the past. It's fucked-up crazy shit.

What am I doing?

It's totally worth it, isn't it? I believe it. Sort of. *Goddamnit.*

In school on Monday, I can barely talk. The text in my book is a blurry word jumble. My head's a desolate thought graveyard, except for two that kick and scream to be heard:

How long until I can do drugs again?

Are you out of your mind?

Finn drapes an arm around my shoulder. I lean into him and could drift off to sleep, right here, right now … I could fall… Paluk eyes us from the front of the class. *Wake up. Got to wake up.*

"I was thinking, this weekend we could hang out, just the two of us," Finn says.

"I think that's a perfect idea."

"I've got these new pills. I've heard they're amazing."

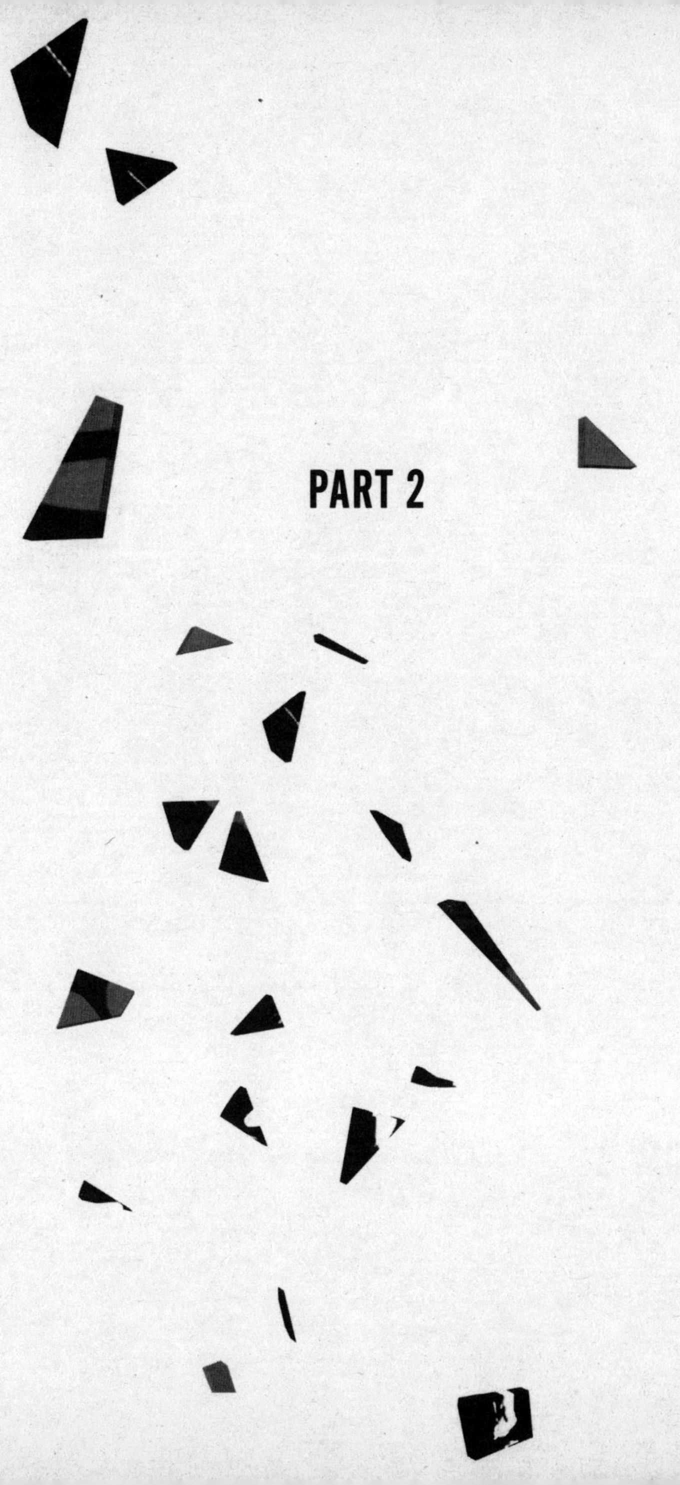

PART 2

CHAPTER 31

This is January:

This is February:

This is March:

Full

of

h o l e s.

It's been a while since I sat with Lauren or Sienna at school.

I haven't been avoiding them, it's just we've been running in different circles. Parallel paths, not crossing. Same place, same age, different lives. Still, I find myself missing them. Missing normality.

I thought I wanted this. I do want it, but can't I have both?

Lauren/Sienna vs Finn's crowd

Can't I have it all?

I find Lauren and Sienna in the common room at lunchtime.

"Hey," I say.

"The ugly duckling returns," Sienna says, looking me up and down, "a beautiful swan. Nice ribs."

I clutch my middle. I guess I have lost weight. Dancing burns a lot of calories.

"I'm not here to fight. I thought ... wondered if you wanted to come over, after school."

"Finn busy?"

"No ... I just... Look, don't make this hard. I'm trying to... Never mind." I turn to leave.

"Yeah, we'd love to come over," Lauren says. "Wouldn't we?"

"Fine. That'd be nice," Sienna says, tight-lipped. "But don't think we're going out car-jacking with you."

"Sienna!" Lauren says. I swing around.

"You don't *have* to come," I say to Sienna.

She shrugs. "We'll come."

After school, we walk across the park towards my house, but I'm too tired to cartwheel, too knackered even to form proper sentences, let alone flip and twist my body in the air. I'm always tired these days.

We go up to my room and stick a film on, but end up chatting and completely ignoring it and it actually feels kind of nice. I've been severely neglecting them recently. Sienna has every right to be mad.

A packet of Jaffa Cakes and a tube of Pringles later, Lauren asks if we can talk about something more serious. I assume she means revision, but no.

"Are you all right?" she asks.

"What do you mean?"

"Since you got with Finn you've been pretty wrapped up in him and that's cool. It's new, it's exciting, I get it. But you're exhausted and you're not turning in your work and … I don't know" – she looks to Sienna for support – "you seem kind of fuzzy."

"Fuzzy?"

"Like you go so mental at the weekend that you're hardly recovered by Friday and then you go out and do it all again," Sienna says.

"Oh."

I feel myself prickle. Is it really that noticeable?

"You think I'm a dirty chemical-head," I say.

"No… Just… Why do you do it to yourself?"

I avoid the question. "You didn't say that about Georgia or Greg or Finn when you introduced them. You said they were popular. You even said you liked them."

"Well, they don't get so" – Sienna searches for the right word – "messed up as you. And we thought it was just a crush. We didn't think you'd *actually* end up going out with him. "

"Oh, great. Not only did you think Finn was so out of my league it would never happen, you also think I'm a total weakling who can't handle the after-effects of a couple of nights out."

We're supposed to be doing these things, aren't we? These are the best years of our lives and all that crap.

"It's just you've got more to lose than they have. We're worried about you. It's not really my thing. I'm not exactly a waster, like yo– like that lot. I spent Friday night watching *The Great British Bake Off* and balling my socks. But *you* don't seem to cope so well with the after-effects. That's all I'm saying."

"I'm fine. Like you said, you don't know anything about it." Anger wraps around my head and chest.

"Finn's corrupting you." Coming from Lauren, this hits me in the gut.

"Before you know it," Sienna says, "you'll be working a life sentence at Asda, still getting wrecked at every opportunity, while Finn Jr steals money from your purse to go out and get trolleyed with Daddy down the pub every night."

"You paint a pretty picture, Sienna."

I want them to stop talking. I want to put my hands to my ears and scream to block them out, but something stops me. Am I fighting with them … or me?

"I didn't see it before but Finn's charm is just an act," Lauren says. "He's always thinking about himself, how things can benefit him. Does he tell you why you're his perfect girl? Or does he just flatter you? Does he show an interest in your life at all? He's good-looking, sure, but what about the rest? I bet he can't even list your AS-levels. How can he love you if he pushes you to do things that jeopardize your future? Think about it."

Stop talking, please stop talking.

I don't want to think about it. Finn and I have made a perfect little world and no one can destroy it. I feel cold, like the room has just dropped five degrees. I tense all over, barriers up. Too late. The ideas are already setting up camp in my mind, lighting a fire that's bound to spread until it consumes me. I bring my hand to my cheek, wiping a tear.

"I think you should go."

"I didn't mean to upset you but you've got to wake up. He's bad news."

I thought they were my friends.

Yet … I don't think I'd be so mad and upset unless I was beginning to think they might be right.

I think about the changes I've made to fit in with Finn's lifestyle. It's what I've wanted, but somehow, I don't feel like myself any more. And what has he sacrificed for this relationship? I can't think of a single thing.

I try to shake off these thoughts. *He loves me. He loves me. He loves me. He said it and that has to mean something.*

CHAPTER 32

Last night Finn and I stayed up doing pills, just the two of us. It seemed like a good idea and I wanted to feel close to him and prove Sienna and Lauren wrong: we were in love, and I could do whatever drugs I wanted and get by just fine, thank you. That was yesterday. Now at school, reality is kicking in with a crash and a wallop and an almighty BANG and I can hardly keep my eyes open.

I sit at a desk with JACK BRACER IS SHITE IN BED etched into its surface, and get out my textbook.

The words blur: *Unit 2 – Biological Psychology, including stress, factors affecting stress, coping with stress, managing stress.*

Relevant, at least.

Where's Finn? He's supposed to be here.

Finn, Lauren, Sienna … they're from different worlds, and I'm in this weird limbo between them. I mean, they're all important to me. I wish we could all be mates. I even dared entertain the idea of Finn and Sienna being friends – until I realized Lauren and Sienna will never again think of Finn as just the charismatic joker, the nice guy with the slight problem with authority. Now they see him as someone else, someone darker.

How can I say to Finn, *My friends think you're driving me into the ground with all the brain-melt drugs and sleepless nights out gallivanting? They think I should show you where to shove it…?* I don't have the words.

Plus, I guess I don't want to end the dream, even if it's turning into a nightmare.

I yawn.

Concentrate, Carla.

I read somewhere that we remember ten per cent of what we read, fifty percent of what we see and hear, and ninety per cent of what we say and experience. Maybe if I read the page ten times I'll retain it all. What if I read it aloud twice? Will that work? Maybe if I just focus instead of procrastinating about how best to learn it, I'll actually remember some of it. I get my head down and fill it with words like *hypothalamus, pituitary, adrenal* and *neurotransmitter.*

My head drops forwards. I could close my eyes, just for a second…

It's April and bright but summer hasn't quite taken the bait yet. We're still fishing for it in the cool waters of late spring. A caterpillar crawls along my wrist. "Hello," I whisper. At my fingertip it forms a chrysalis, then emerges, wings magnificent golds and oranges and purples. It darts and spirals and corkscrews and flits. So beautiful. So graceful… It falls into my palm, grey, lifeless, crumbles to dust…

"Are we boring you, Miss Carroll?" asks Green.

I jerk awake.

"No, sir."

I chew the end of my pencil. Fat Mike taps me on the shoulder. "Finn wants to see you after school. By the fire escape."

"Where is he? Why didn't he text me?"

He shrugs. "Martinez confiscated his phone."

"Oh."

An hour later I'm three-quarters of the way down the page, having copied it out perfectly, diagrams and all. The drawings are impressive, considering how unbelievably tired I am, but the information I've assimilated is minimal.

No sign of Finn in Chemistry. Paluk slaps a detention on me for not turning in an assignment.

At lunch Isaac's stare bores into the back of my head.

I somehow survive Biology. Our seats are allocated for the whole year, so Lauren, Sienna and I sit together in stony silence, still reeling from our argument.

Slinky nudges me awake *three* times in English Lit. I get another detention. This is turning into one craptacular day. All I want to do is *sleep*.

The bell dings and I slam my book shut, grab my bag and coat and leave.

In the corridor, Martinez stops me.

"Off to see that lad of yours? Give him this, please."

He hands me Finn's phone.

On my way to meet Finn, his phone vibrates in my pocket. A text from Isaac.

I'm curious. I know it's wrong but I press OPEN.

Hello, uber-mistake.

Reading your boyfriend's texts will always turn out badly. Dating 101, right?

Mate, wot r u doin? She can't handle it.

What does he mean? It takes a minute but then I wonder, *Does Isaac mean me?* Does he think I'm some loser little girl who can't handle her drugs?

Outside, I chew over whether to mention the text to Finn. I watch the clouds turn charcoal. They've been teasing us mortals with five-minute showers every half-hour for the last week. Leaning against the yellow brick wall, breathing deep, I feel like I'm being fed something wholesome: clean air. I fill my lungs but that brings on the cough I'm getting from all the smoking.

The fire-escape door bursts open. A figure emerges, wrapped in a navy coat and with several days' stubble, rugged and almost wild-looking.

"Isaac?"

"I didn't think you'd come if I asked. I got Mike to say Finn wanted to meet you."

"What's the matter? Is Finn OK?"

"Yeah. He's fine. But, Carla, I can't stand it. I tried, for his sake, but I can't. He'll mess you up. He's just thinking of himself, he can't see that you're fragile. He conveniently forgets that actions have consequences."

Mad fury takes hold, swelling inside me, hot and wild, barely controllable. I swallow hard, attempting to quell it. I'm *fragile*? *Fragile?* I can't *handle it*?

"You don't need to party so much," Isaac says. I can hardly process, let alone respond to, his words. My anger just builds, my whole body buzzing. "I mean, I'm not trying to tell you what to do, it's just … I care about you. You're better than this. Finn, he's only out for himself, instant gratification. Never thinks about what happens next. I don't want to see you hurt, sucked in … but it's happening and … it's agonizing … watching you become the fallout of *his* bad decisions."

His voice becomes soft, but impassioned. "Look at me," he says. I glance up. "I think you're amazing."

I snap my gaze away, downwards; kick a leaf from my shoe, then look up again, searching for truth in his eyes.

Fuck, fuck… He means it. He really means it. The rage inside me shifts to confusion, excitement, a spectrum of emotions. My pulse is a battering ram, punch-punch-punching.

"You're amazing, and you don't even know it."

Isaac hesitates, summoning courage, but he's come this far; there's no stopping him now. I can feel his heat, his breath across my cheek, the tingling there.

"Something inside you is breaking," he says. "I can see you trying to patch it with Finn, the drugs, all of it. But I know, I *know*, it won't work. That stuff, it's just a crutch, a cloak, a hiding place… It's not *real*. You start to believe you need it all to be … you. You don't, Carla. You don't need all that. You're already … I mean, just the way you… Everything about you is … is … already perfect. You're funny, really quick, did you know that? You're hands-down the best draw-er I've ever met, and I think … you're exceptional. I can't stop thinking about you."

Time stands still, life on PAUSE. We contemplate each other, with all the "what ifs" and alternative-universe scenarios where things might have been different between us. I feel like helium, floating.

But no. I'm nothing without… What am I but the invisible girl?

I press PLAY, time resumes and I plummet to earth.

What am I thinking? My mind's playing tricks on me. Twisted as a double helix. All I want is Finn. Not Isaac. I'm amazing? Whatever! Isaac's playing a game. Trying to manipulate me into breaking up with Finn. I take myself off MUTE.

"What are you talking about? I'm fine. I'm OK. I *can handle it*." I stretch the words to their most emphatic. I shove Finn's phone into Isaac's hand. I want him to know I've read his message. How dare he stick his oar in? He gives me the evil eye all year, hardly says a word to me, then spurts off a load of crap about me getting my act together? Out. Of. Order.

"I care about you, Carla. Don't let Finn destroy you."

I feel hot and my chest starts to thump. *Breathe, Carla.* "Look, Is—" I begin, but I'm cut short. Finn appears in the open doorway, gripping the frame, fuming. A pulse of adrenalin zooms around my body.

"I can't believe you're trying it on with my girlfriend!"

"I'm not trying it on. I'm just sick of you not listening. She deserves better. You'll hurt her."

"I'm right here!" I interject. Can't take this verbal slanging match. Kids fighting over a toy. "You're just trying to mess things up for us!" I shout at Isaac.

"No, Carla, I'm not," he replies. But I don't want to hear it.

Finn clenches his fists, steps out of the doorway and squares up to Isaac.

"Oh yeah, you're concerned about Carla's welfare? Whatever, mate. You're jealous. You're just jealous," he insists.

"I'm not listening to this," I say, but neither hears me. The blood's running too hot and thick between their ears.

"Why are you trying to ruin things? We're fine. I love Carla. Leave it. Just go, will you?"

Isaac shakes his head. They lock eyes, stubborn as each other.

Finn's body expands like a balloon, his ever-so-red, perfect lips twitch. "Go!" he shouts again. "Get out of here!"

"I can't, mate. I can't. Wake up and smell the codeine. She's not used to it," Isaac adds, unruffled, like a sea refusing to whip with the wind.

Finn shakes Isaac's shoulders, trying to force a reaction. "*Fuck's sake, Isaac.* It's none of your bloody business," he says, ramming his brother backwards.

Isaac lunges at Finn, sending him crashing into me. I scrape my arm on the sandpaper surface of the brick wall and sink to the ground. Pinpricks of blood appear like a rash.

"You're the one hurting me, Isaac! This *is* too much for me to handle!" I roar. I pull myself up and charge between them, brimming with weird energy. *I just want to be calm again. Got to get out of this. Everything's OK. Don't panic.*

I head towards the school gates.

Isaac calls after me, "He's going out with you to get back at Violet for cheating on him last year!"

What the hell?

I turn to see Finn rush at Isaac, pinning him against the wall.

"Sorry. I had to tell you. And there's something els—"

"Fuck off, Isaac!" Finn presses his arm against Isaac's

neck. "He's lying, Carla, I promise you. I love you, tiger."

Havelock appears, sweat on his brow, his rolled-up sleeves revealing thick, dark hair on his tanned arms. He rounds the corner carrying a bag of footballs. Probably been covering a PE lesson.

"Finn! Isaac! What's going on?" he yells in his taking-no-shit voice.

"Nothing, sir."

"Wait for me in my room." Havelock turns to me. "Carla, come here. Now."

But Havelock's not important.

"You're a liar," I say, hardly knowing which brother I'm speaking to.

I start to run.

"Carla, wait!" Finn calls out. But he doesn't follow me.

Havelock shouts my name. I keep running.

CHAPTER 33

I run to the shop for a Coke and a packet of Doritos, as if they're the magic formula to solve all my problems.

"That's two pounds fifty." A ruddy-faced woman with deep wrinkles like a satellite shot of the Grand Canyon holds out a hand expectantly. I root around for some change and find a two-pound coin but that's all. Out of nowhere tears form and fight to get free. *Not now. Don't bloody cry now.* There's an awkward silence as she watches me frantically search for coins, sobbing all the while.

"Carla, what's up?" I'm startled to hear my name. I wipe my eyes with my sleeve, smudging black on my shirt cuff.

"You OK?" Lauren asks.

"She's short by fifty pence. Just leave the Coke, love."

"It's not about the stupid Coke."

Lauren pays the cashier and leads me out of the shop towards the park.

I open the can with a *tssszzzz* and gulp it down in three. After all that, my appetite's gone and I can't face the Doritos. Typical.

I well up again, feel my body begin to reject the Coke; my stomach turns icy, my throat burns.

A wind circles us like a buzzard, ready to swoop and snap with cold at my bare neck. I turn to the green expanse of trees. And throw up. "Sorry about that."

Lauren pulls out a pack of Kleenex and I take one.

"It's OK. You missed my shoes."

I pick at the peeling paint on the roundabout frame with my fingernails, flicking it to the ground. Lauren sits on one of the seats and I sit next to her, pushing against the ground with my feet until we gently spin.

"So what's going on?"

I stall, thumping my feet on the bark chippings, sending splinters of wood flying. The roundabout stops. Lauren looks at me, concerned.

I let my head fall into my hands, then recover myself.

"Finn's a prick," I say, admitting it to myself as much as Lauren. "He's using me to get back at Violet. Isaac said so. But *Finn* told me they never went out. He's lying, right? And another thing: Isaac likes me."

"He does stare at you a lot. *And* he came to check on you when you were ill."

"To rub in the fact that I felt bad after Georgia's party."

"No, it all makes sense. He was fighting with Finn at the party because he didn't want to see you hurt."

"Then why didn't he tell me at the time?"

"He couldn't, could he? You're his brother's girlfriend. I bet it's pretty harsh on Isaac, seeing you with Finn all the time. Must have taken guts to tell you and risk losing his brother over it."

"*Did* Violet and Finn go out?"

"Yeah, for, like, three years, until she cheated on him with some older guy. One of Georgia's model friends."

"*Three years?* He said they were never a couple. That she was like a sister to him."

"If that's how he'd kiss his sister, he's a serious weirdo."

"Shit." Little hamsters work the ticker tape in my brain. "Why did no one tell me?"

"It's common knowledge. Everybody knows."

"Except me. It's not exactly in the school welcome pack!" I sigh. "Maybe he didn't tell me about Violet because he thought I'd worry about her. Maybe he was trying to protect me."

"Why are you defending him?"

"I just thought..."

"What?"

"He said he loved me. I feel stupid now, but I believed him. I'm still trying to believe him. It could just be a misunderstanding."

Lauren shrugs. "You need to talk to him. But be careful, Carla. I think he's a snake."

It's my turn to shrug. "About the other night. I'm sorry. Should've listened to you. I've been a prize idiot. You tried to help me and I threw it back in your faces. I can't believe you're still talking to me."

"What are mates for?"

Maybe real ones don't try to change you into someone you're not.

Right. *Pull yourself together, Carla!* Go home, listen to loud music for an hour in the dark, then emerge again fresh-faced with renewed perspective. That's what I'll do. But it's not that easy, is it?

When I get in, my Spidey-sense tingles and draws me to the kitchen, where I eat three jam tarts. Yes, *three.* I drink some juice and sit at the table examining the grain of the wood. I'm about to go to my room and begin the loud music anti-angst therapy thing, but first stare at my mobile, willing it to ring, using my best Jedi-mind-trick face and waving magic fingers. *Ring, damn it.* A watched phone never beeps, except on this occasion, when it rumbles into life on the table.

"It's me."

"Hello, you," I answer flatly.

"Please don't listen to Isaac. Violet – she's nothing. History. Why would I want to make her jealous? I have you. You're all I want."

Those words would usually melt me but today they make me squirm.

"You said you were never together. But you were, for *three* years. *Three goddamn years*, Finn. Probably worth mentioning."

Silence.

"I don't know what to say." *That's because I've caught you out.*

"Why didn't you tell me? I stood in your room and asked you outright and you denied it."

"I didn't think it was important."

"You lied about it. What else are you hiding?"

"Nothing. I promise."

"Do you want her back?"

"Course not. She cheated. We broke up. End of."

"Then why are you still friends? Isn't that weird?"

"Look, we're not!"

"Finn, that makes no sense."

I hear him breathe deeply.

"I didn't tell you because she says she made a big mistake and wants me back. I said no, but she keeps hanging around and trying it on. I didn't want you to worry about it. She's all hair-flicking and Tango tan and stick-on eyelashes. All style, no substance. She draws on her eyebrows, for fuck's sake. I told her it was over but she can't accept it."

Could this be true? I so want it to be, so Finn and I can remain perfect, but it doesn't add up.

It crosses my mind that Lauren and Sienna might be right about Finn not knowing a single thing about me. If he doesn't, I can't be all that important to him.

"What AS-levels am I doing?"

"What do you mean?"

"You heard me. It's a simple question."

"Um." He pauses. "What's it got to do with anything?"

"It has everything to do with it. What exams am I taking?"

"Er, Art."

"Yeah, and?"

"Chemistry, Psychology." *Three down, two to go.* "Physics – no, the other one, Biology."

"Lucky guess. One more."

"I don't know! Geography!"

"Nope."

"Carla, this is stupid. Just come round, we'll watch a

film and everything will be cool. Isaac's trying to break us up, can't you see?"

"It's funny, I thought so too. Now I'm not so sure. I think he's looking out for me."

"I can't believe he's got to you. I'll kill him for this. He's jealous. He hasn't got a girlfriend and can't stand to see us happy. I love you. I love that you draw butterflies everywhere and that you taught me to do cartwheels and that you're afraid to put your head under the water. I love you. I love you. I love you, Carla Carroll." I can almost feel his breath tickling my ear. I think about the feeling I had when we spun around together at the boarding festival: giddy, high. But was it real love or just a bunch of chemicals pinging about – even before the drugs? Maybe love is only ever a bunch of crazy chemicals raging around inside you, making you do stupid shit and believe anything. Is that real love?

"I…" I want to say, *I love you too.* But do I? "I need time to think. I'll talk to you later."

"Carla, plea—"

I hang up.

CHAPTER 34

In my head, images blur together. I see Georgia dancing in the garden; she looks at me but her eyes have no irises; they're completely white, except for the outline of a heart, like on the first pill I ever took. She grabs my hands and we spin like Finn and I did at the park, but then it's not Finn or Georgia, it's Isaac and we're laughing and when we fall to the ground he's gone. I open my sketchbook and frantically smudge the pastel pictures of Finn's hands, but they reform and reach out of the pages. Just as they are about to wrap around my throat and choke me, his hands turn into hundreds of butterflies that swirl around and lift me up so high. I see Isaac on the ground below and start to plummet, I call out for him to save me, but he doesn't hear, then *vrrruummph*! I wake up as I hit the ground…

I scratch at the sleep that's gathered at the corners of my eyes. I stretch, groan and swing my legs out of bed and into my furry, purple monster-feet slippers before heading downstairs.

In the kitchen I fill the kettle, listening to its whispery *shhhush* and put some toast on, get the blackcurrant jam from the fridge, and the good butter, not the olive spread. Dad struggles with Mum's espresso machine, tutting and turning knobs and dials. Steam jets out and he jumps back.

"Maybe I'll just have instant."

"Good idea."

The toast pops. *Shhhusssh. Snap!* The kettle clicks off. I make Dad's coffee. Lots of milk, two sugars. Not quite a latte but as good as it gets when I'm making it.

"So your mum and I thought you might like to go to Wales at half-term. Sal will be back and you two can catch up."

"What about you guys?"

"Got work. Thought maybe you could get some revision done. It'll be quiet."

"If by 'quiet' you mean completely dead and void of all entertainment, you're on the button. Isn't it like a rule that you have to be over a hundred to live in their village?"

"They let you in at eighty-nine these days."

"Are you asking if I want to go or telling me I'm going?"

"You could do with a break, don't you think…? Your teacher called."

"My what did what?" *Er, not good. Hello, ding, ding, ding ALARM BELLS.*

"Mr Havelock is very concerned that you haven't attended your revision sessions. I answered the phone and not your mother, thank God."

"I'm OK. I don't need banishing to Nowhereville."

"It's this or, well, I'll have to ground you."

"Dad, you couldn't ground a peanut with a pestle and mortar."

"But I can ask you nicely to visit your cousin who I know you miss, do some work while you're there and not make a fuss. It's for yo—"

"For my own good. I get it."

The next day at school is as awkward as wearing double fillets in your bra. Ladies, don't even try it. In Chemistry, Finn makes his usual jokes and grabs me around the waist.

"Come on, Carla. It's you and me," he says and I think about what that means: *you and me.* It seems to me that together we're just a druggie couple. Where will we be in ten years or five years or even one year if we stay as *you and me*? We'll be another couple of wasters without the buffer of school popularity. I want to be the It Girl, but at what price? Is it worth it?

My grades have taken a nosedive.

I can't have a good time without taking drugs.

I've nearly lost the only real friends I've made.

I haven't seen Isaac all day, and weirdly, I feel a little bit sad about that.

Later, at home, I take to the sofa with a duvet, a monster bag of Maltesers and my new best friend, the remote. I channel-hop until I find an old *Big Bang Theory*, then bury myself in cushions to watch.

Something falls through the letterbox onto the mat in the hall. I groan at the prospect of leaving my cocoon, but get up to investigate. There's a doodle in one corner of the purple envelope, not a great drawing, but I make out a butterfly. I recognize the handwriting.

Tiger,

I've been a right Hampton Wick. Let's not bull and cow about it.

But if you like, you can punch me in the boat race.

You're my cloud seven, my only turtle dove.

Please forgive me.

F xxx

I return to the sofa, trying to re-establish cosiness, but can't get comfortable. I read the note a billion times. It says the same thing, but each time I soften and think, *Maybe I'll give him another chance.*

CHAPTER 35

The sun is an ink spot, bleeding reds and golds onto a cyan canvas. Finn's fingers are laced with mine. We lie gazing at the painted sky, picking out shapes in rouge-tinted clouds.

"I see a turtle."

"I see a VW camper."

"A pizza."

"A face with sharp teeth."

"A bowl of Thai purple meatballs."

"I see a problem," I say. "We need to talk."

I tell Finn there can be no more secrets. That this is his only chance. And that, most importantly, we have to stop the drugs. NO MORE DRUGS. Step 1 on my three-step plan:

1. NO MORE DRUGS
2. NO MORE LIES
3. WAAAAAY MORE REVISION

"Course. Anything you want. I won't even touch drugs again. I'll quit. We'll both stop. Right now. For ever." He rubs my arm, his hands warm on my skin. He brushes my hair out of my eyes and kisses my nose.

We get up from the grass and stroll to the playground.

"I thought I was going to lose you," Finn says.

I twirl in the swing seat, twisting the chains into a tight spiral, then release. The park whirls around and around, blurring into horizontal stripes of colour, like a Rothko.

"Never," I say. But for such a short word, it still manages to wrap around my neck and choke me.

Later, I go to the movies with Lauren and Sienna.

"What's Finn up to tonight?" Lauren asks.

"Does Finn have to be busy for me to want to see you guys?"

Sienna throws me a look.

"OK," I concede. "*Battle Cry 3: Do or Die.* Boys' night, in other words. Exerting their masculinity by slaughtering a virtual mutant army."

"Figures."

The cinema is in a big complex, overlooking an atrium edged with shops and restaurants, with a fountain in the centre. Outside, fingers of dim moonlight poke through thick cloud, the only illumination in the otherwise black night. But inside you couldn't tell. It could be one in the afternoon or one in the morning, the light would still be a million watts and bright as burning magnesium.

We climb the escalator two steps at a time to buy our tickets. The girls are, to say the least, unimpressed that I'm sticking with Finn, but happy I'm curbing the drugs.

"Do you think you can just give it up like that?"

"I've got to. To have any chance of passing my exams."

At the snack counter, I order a jumbo Coke and an even

bigger popcorn, practically a bucket. Half and half, salted and sweet.

Sienna gives me a funny look, like I'm mentally disturbed.

"It's like dinner and dessert," I say.

"Gross. Hurry up if you want decent seats."

"Hey, look. There's Little Miss Hair Flick." Lauren points to the ticket queue. Violet is in a trench coat, cinched at the waist, apparently bare legs and six-inch *killer* heels. I'd *kill her* with those heels…

I grab my food and drink and yank the girls behind the pick 'n' mix stand. We huddle like we're planning an ambush.

"What are we doing?"

"Hiding. Duh."

"Why? She's the little ho-bag scamming on your boyfriend. Not that I'm taking his side. He's not worth—"

"You've already made your feelings quite clear. They're duly noted." I cut Sienna off.

She waggles a finger at me. "I think you should get rid of that handsome but poisonous weasel."

"Weasels aren't poisonous." Lauren flicks a piece of popcorn at Sienna and it lodges in her hair. She picks it out and shoves it in her mouth.

"Oh, well, this one got bitten by a radioactive spider or something."

"So Finn is Spider-weasel?" Lauren laughs.

"What are you on about?"

"Never mind," Sienna rolls her eyes. "Violet's the one who's all 'Oh, Finn, I dropped my pen, could you pick it up for me?' and 'Oh, Finn, you look so hot in your shorts', so why are you the acting stealth?"

"You're right. I *should* be telling her to go shove a pineapple up her arse."

"Maybe we could break into her house, crimp her hair and shave her eyebrows off."

"I'd love to see her try to work the Vi Brody charm while rocking that look."

"She'd probably still be hot *sans* eyebrows. I bet everyone would copy it like it was the new fashion or something. Bloody sheep." Sienna thinks for a moment, as if we are seriously considering committing any of these heinous acts. "We could hold her down while you stuff popcorn up her nose."

"Sweet or salted?"

"Half and half. One in each nostril."

They may not be the coolest girls but they do make me laugh.

Violet studies the board with the movie listings, then buys her tickets and heads down the escalators into the atrium. I walk over to the mezzanine balcony. Below me, she struts towards the fountain.

"Are you going to talk to her?"

"I think I might," I say, courage making me stand taller.

I step onto the escalator, the metal stairs humming beneath me, then retreat, stagger back up the moving steps and tumble onto the mezzanine. I whack my wrist on the marble floor but don't feel the pain.

My heart stops. I recognize his walk, his shape from behind, the lazy swing of his hips.

Finn. Here. To meet *her.* WTF???

I mean, WHAT THE FFFFFFFUUUCCCCCKKKKKIIIINNNGGG FFFUUUCCCKKKK??????

My nails dig into the handrail.

Are you freaking kidding me? She's *nothing* to him? *Not even mates*, he'd said.

My teeth clench. Every muscle tenses, as if my blood has suddenly solidified. I'm rigid. LIVID.

INSANE CRAZY-WOMAN ANGRY.

He talks to Violet for a moment. She gives him his movie ticket, touches his face with her perfectly manicured hands, kisses him on the mouth, just a peck, but it's enough. I've seen all I can take.

EYE-TWITCHING RAVING-LUNATIC FURIOUS.

I rub my wrist, welcoming the pain now flooding there, reddening the skin. It's a distraction. And although all I want to do is summon enough strength to rip up the ticket kiosk, hurl it over the balcony and onto Finn's arrogant, lying, little head, I don't. Instead I bite down on my emotion and say, "Come on. We'll miss the film." I grab Lauren with my good arm and steer her and Sienna towards Screen 10.

FOAMING-AT-THE-MOUTH APE-SHIT FUMING.

VOLATILE.

VIOLENT.

VILE.

VIOLET!!!! *Ugh…*

The film is a blur. My racing thoughts are all I can hear, not Gabriel Grayson, not the motorbike chase, not the exploding helicopter, just:

WHAT THE HELL IS HE DOING WITH HER?

HE LIED TO ME.

I AM SUCH AN IDIOT.

CHAPTER 36

Afterwards, at home, I lie awake weighing up the pros and cons of *Finn and Carla: The Sequel.* It's not looking good. Hollywood Execs would not take a risk on this script.

PROS	CONS
So gorgeous.	Knows he's gorgeous.
Doesn't study much.	Keeps me from studying.
Does a lot of drugs.	Makes me feel like I should do drugs when he does.
Makes me feel things I've never felt.	The comedowns are like repeatedly walking into a cactus while throwing up your own lungs and stomach, with a tiny person sitting on one shoulder scraping their nails down a blackboard and another in your head shouting paranoid thoughts over and over until you crack with depression and fall into a broken, sweaty sleep.

Has cool friends.	Sienna and Lauren don't like him.
Awesome mountainboarder.	Can be a show-off.
SAYS HE LOVES ME.	Lied about his ex. OF THREE YEARS.
	Who, by the way, is a totally freaking bona *fide* hottie. (Bitch.)
	Makes me feel like a prize twat for trusting him.

I'm not sure the last pro really counts.

Has anything about him been real?

After a sleepless night, I get up to a dreary day and an even gloomier state of mind. Am I ready for another day of panic-revision, panic-plagiarism, ohmygod-I'm-so-unprepared-for-my-exams-super-freaking-out panic stations? Um, no. Even though I know how important it is for me to get the schoolwork done, it's still second on my To Do list. I feel like … like … *fucking GGGGggRRRRrrrrRRRrrrr*!

I reread the pros and cons list and know what I have to do. But first, I need to find out the truth about Finn and Violet.

In school, I'm on edge. Wound tight, like a jack-in-the-box. I nibble at my fingernails, pulling at the skin with my teeth.

Turning into a corridor, I see Violet and Finn at the other end, heading out of the fire escape. I've geared myself up to end it for real with Finn, but I'm curious, too. Is he really as bad as Isaac made out and Sienna and Lauren say? I have to see it with my own eyes.

I have to see him kiss her.

I have to follow them.

I peel myself off the wall and walk to the corner of the PE block. The fire-escape door is open and I hear the screech of after-school basketball practice. I smell rubber and sweat. I peek at the ducks and dives of the B-team blue vests, and glimpse a red vest A-teamer sink a hoop. Four dozen rubber soles collide with the gym's polished floor like a chorus of chirping birds. *Shreeep … shreeep…*

There's a garage-cum-storeroom-cum-junkpit beyond the Astroturf courts. Everybody calls it the Asbestos Shed. It's a sheltered area, tucked right at the back of the campus. Finn and Violet step inside and I grimace, thinking about what they might do in there, hidden away.

I stop about six feet from the wall of the shed.

I hear talking.

"Twenty. You know it's twenty, Slink. Always has been." Finn's voice, cocksure and commanding, but still with a playful edge, echoes around the walls.

I summon the courage to move closer to the slightly open door. My breathing sounds loud in my ears. Slinky pipes up.

"I ain't got twenty, but look, I got these. Come on. I know you do swapsies sometimes and I've really got to have some smoke for the weekend. Bro. Please. You know I'm good for it almost always." He says "always" like the longer he says it the more true it will become.

"What you got, Mr Slinky, what you got?" Finn rubs his hands together, grinning like an excited shop assistant at a new delivery of the latest iPhone. "Don't keep me waiting, Slink!"

"Knew you'd be game. Survey the goods." The lanky dude pulls out a plastic press-lock bag, teeny-tiny, a couple of inches across. I can just about see something white in it. "2CBs. They're a bit trippy."

"Nice." Finn takes the baggie and gives the weed to Slinky. "There's an eighth there. Here's yours, Vi."

Violet takes a baggie full of pills from Finn.

"My hero." She hides it in her bra, kisses him on the cheek and gets up to leave. I move behind the shed so she won't see me, then start to cross the field, aiming for a gap in the fence where I can get out and walk the long route around the school grounds and back in through the front gate.

No one suspects the butterfly. They never dream that a creature so enchanting could be so deadly. The Monarch is captivating, intricately beautiful; its striking orange and black patterned wings are one of nature's greatest works of art, but it has a secret. During its time as a caterpillar, it feeds on toxic milkweed, making it poisonous to birds and mammals and dangerous to the human heart. If Finn were a butterfly, I know which he would be.

It's all starting to make sense. That day at the mountain-boarding festival when Finn came back with a black eye. A deal gone wrong. And there was that time I saw Violet give him something. Money for drugs? I've been so caught up thinking they were flirting I haven't had room in my head for the truth.

Finn may not be cheating on me.

But he's dealing.

He lied about cutting out the drugs.

This is so messed up.

I schedule an emergency chat with Sal for this evening. I don't tell her about the drugs, only that he lied about Violet and that I saw them together.

"Ditch him. Now," she says, straight to the point as usual. I sigh and she asks, "Do you love him?"

"Thought I did."

"Look, it boils down to this: *You can't be in love if you're not in love.*"

Her voice sounds tinny over the phone.

"That's deep, Sal."

"Hey, people pay for advice like that. You're getting it for free. Seriously, he's bad news. Cut him loose."

"It's just, he's got a hold on me."

"Well, get unheld."

"OK. I'll see you in a few weeks."

"I'll fire up the awesomobile to get you from the coach station."

"You've still got that wreck?"

"Of course. It's been in Mum's garage, sleeping."

"All right."

"All right, what?"

"I'll end it."

"Good girl."

I'll do it. I'll break up with him. I will.

CHAPTER 37

May brings a mini-heatwave. Sweat trickles down my neck as I stand at the foot of the steps to Finn's front door, rehearsing my break-up speech. Its not quite summer but it's typical British weather. Buzzing once, then again, it occurs to me that it's lunchtime on a hot Saturday and he probably isn't even home. He called me repeatedly last night. Eventually, I switched off my phone. I want to do this face to face.

A blurry figure appears behind the glass. Seeing my reflection in the silver of the ornate door knocker, I straighten out my hair.

"Oh, hey." Isaac's hair has grown shaggier and falls into his eyes. Stubble casts a shadow on his chin. He's wearing shorts and a vest, his earphones draped around his neck. His skin glistens with sweat. I knew this might happen: that Isaac could be here. I'd considered getting Finn to meet me somewhere neutral, but on some stupid level I want to see his room again, to smell its boy smell, to commit it to memory, because even if we're breaking up, the relationship has changed me and I want to remember that. To keep the good bits. Like hanging out in his room, laughing and kissing and feeling good, and his touch, and the slow drum of his heartbeat as I lay on his chest, listening. And to junk the rest of it. The lies, the fall from grace... Maybe it's twisted, but it's how I feel.

"Hey," I say.

Look at me. I think you're amazing. The scene replays in my head and my stomach somersaults.

Isaac wipes sweat from his forehead with the hem of his vest. "I've been running," he says, looking nervous.

"Um, OK."

"Do you want to come in? It's three hundred degrees out there. I'll get you some juice. Or we have lemonade. Or—"

"Actually, I came to see Finn."

"Oh, right. Course. He's upstairs."

Isaac moves aside and I head up to Finn's room.

Finn puts down the Xbox controller when he sees me standing in the doorway. Slinky's leaning out the window, smoking a joint.

"Carla, you've got to see this. Finn's found the sickest video on YouTube. This kid's sitting in the park and this eagle swoops down and picks him up."

"It's fake. Got to be," Finn says.

I say nothing.

Slinky stubs out the joint on the outside wall. Ash rains onto the hedges below. Finn and Slinky exchange not-so-subtle looks.

"OK. So I'll be leaving then. See you later."

"Bye, mate."

Finn watches until Slinky's out of the room, then pulls

me inside and shuts the door behind us. He pins me against the door and moves to kiss me but I turn my head away. *Be strong. Got to be strong.*

"Is your phone broken?" he asks, fiddling with the change in his pocket. And the pills. I bet they're still swimming around among the debris in there. A little bag of lies.

I shake my head.

Light slices through the window and plays with Finn's dark hair, turning it a thousand colours of liquorice, plum, chocolate, jet black. My pulse quickens.

"I thought we were OK."

I shake my head. Better to say nothing than something I don't mean, like, *Come here, I want you, I need you.* Those feelings are just a trick, stupid chemical processes making my heart and body want him. But my brain has to take control now.

"If my brother's been spreading stuff about me again, I'll kill him."

"It's not about Isaac," I say. I take a breath. "I saw you with Violet—"

"Nothing's going on with Violet."

"Nothing?"

"No, course not."

"So it was someone else with her at the cinema? Your twin?"

"Shit." Finn rubs his eyes and then his temples. He sits on the bed.

"And it wasn't you selling stuff in the Asbestos Shed and taking pills from Slinky? You said you wouldn't do it any more."

"I sold Violet some Ritalin. She uses it to stay awake, to revise. She gets depressed without it. Withdrawal or something. I'm not *with her* though. Not at all. I just get it for her."

"You're not seeing her, you're just dealing to her. Right. OK," I say, like saying it aloud will straighten it out in my mind, but it just seems even more messed up. "Wow, that's so much better," I say caustically. "Finn, I don't think this is—"

"No, Carla, don't do this. I'll make it up to you."

"I don't trust you. You said you would quit the drugs but I can smell weed. You were smoking just now with Slinky and he gave you those 2CBs or whatever the hell they were yesterday. You're dealing too!" I sit on the bed next to Finn. My breath catches in my throat along with my words, but I have to keep going. "You say you never went out with Violet, but that's bullshit. You're a liar, Finn."

He takes my hand. "Come on, I opened your eyes. I helped you."

"But the thing is, you thought I needed help. Even without all the other issues, the fact that you thought I needed changing says enough."

"You wanted it."

"I guess I did. More fool me. We're done."

"But I love you, tiger."

"Just another lie though, isn't it?"

He shakes his head and I can't tell if it's in response to the question or just exasperation.

Then I realize I'm guilty too. Not of dealing or lying or whatever, but of wanting him to be someone he's not. I wanted the perfect, popular boyfriend. I loved the *idea* of us, but I've been clinging to a fantasy.

He puts his hand on my back and pulls me closer. His eyes are so dark I can't see where the pupils end and the irises begin. Drugs or not, his eyes always look the same. Endless gorgeous abysses. I press my eyelids closed, not wanting to fall into them again like so many times before.

His hand curves around my neck and he leans in to whisper, "No lie."

Then it's my turn to shake my head. *Got to be strong.* I reach in my pocket for his iPod. Place it on the desk.

"It's over, Finn."

On the kerb in front of the Mastersons' untamed front garden, Isaac's washing his car. I do my best don't-try-to-talk-to-me-I'm-in-a-hurry walk but fail spectacularly.

"You OK?"

"Not really," I snap.

"I came out here. I didn't want to, er, disturb…"

"You've done enough of that." As soon as I say it, I regret it. It's not his fault. "Sorry. Bad day. You were right, Finn's not good for me."

I feel the inevitable, uncontrollable shake as I try to resist the emotion and close the floodgates. But the tears just bulldoze through. Isaac goes to put a hand on my shoulder, then takes it away like he can't quite decide what to do. Funny thing is, I don't feel at all embarrassed about him seeing me like this. I do, however, need to get home quick sharp, out of the vicinity of Finn. Out of the Finncinity.

I take a deep breath. "Thanks for telling me."

“Er, no problem. I’m so—”

“No, don’t apologize. It’s me … I’m just…” I sigh. “Look. Sorry for what I said just now but I just broke up with your brother and this is weird, talking to you, and really all I want to do is go home.”

“Yeah, course. You’re right. I, um, hope you feel better.”

But I don’t go straight home. I go to the park and while salty tears stream down my cheeks, I flip and roll and tumble until all my muscles ache and twinge and the sun gets low and I know that once I’m home I’ll fall straight to sleep.

CHAPTER 38

Post–break-up advice: Take pain, screw up pain into ball, throw ball away.

But it's not that simple.

I miss Finn, but more than that, I guess I'm grieving for what I've lost out on – the dream – the *perfect life*. Because that life doesn't exist, does it? So now I feel hollow, foolish, *alone*.

It's like I've come down with a terrible illness. A serious case of Woe-is-me. Symptoms include:

1. snot-pillow. You know what I'm talking about. Crusty-salty snot-pillow. And I don't even change it because that would be like admitting I'm over it when clearly I will stay heartbroken for ever.
2. max-lyrical. Every song I hear is relevant. I find poignant meaning in jingles for cat litter, theme songs to Saturday-night game shows, and every ballad is CLEARLY about us.
3. sadvertising. Adverts featuring puppies/toasters/old people are now as emotional to watch as *Schindler's List*.

4. pine-language. I now communicate exclusively by grunts and shoulder-shrugs.

There's a week until half-term, then study leave and EXAMS.

One more week of Finn. *Just get through it.*

Let me rephrase: *AAaAaaAAaaarrrrggghhhhhhhh!!!!! Kill me now.*

In the common room, I sit with Lauren and Sienna, right back where I started this year. Across from us, Violet drapes herself over Finn. He's not that into it, but he doesn't seem to hate it either. She *is* beautiful after all. Maybe he's hoping it'll make me jealous. And I guess I am, just a little. OK, I am. A lot.

Finn glances at me. My stomach twists.

He passes by where Lauren, Sienna and I sit. Hesitates. Looks like he's about to say something. I drop my gaze. *Can't do this.* He walks on, out of the room, Violet trailing behind him. She stops. Turns back.

"So, Finn's taking me to the Blitz Board Fest on Saturday. Doesn't he look hot when he's boarding? He's so talented."

I can't help but screw up my face.

"You didn't really think it would work out between you and him, did you? That's cute."

I look up. It takes all my willpower to stop myself ripping her arm off and stabbing her in the eye with her own perfectly painted nails.

I'm *breaking inside.*

Violet *actually* smiles. I'm afire. All my muscles tense. I stand up. Look her in the eye.

I say … nothing.

"Bye-bye," she says and heads out.

Thirty seconds later I've got a list of witty remarks filed under "Things I Should Have Said":

1. You didn't think things would work out between you and that shade of eyeshadow, did you? Oh, you did.
2. Sorry, I don't speak Twat. ME ENGLISH.
3. Piss off, you Ritalin-addled whore.

OK, 3 isn't so witty but I wish I'd said it.

I consider telling Havelock about the Ritalin, but why bother? I'm many things but a snitch isn't one of them.

Instead, I head to Paluk for a not-so-fun-filled Finn-and-Violet-filled Chemistry class. Someone links my arm and pulls me into the toilets.

"Tell me everything that's happened," Georgia says.

"We broke up. End of," I say.

"Not *end of.* Maybe you'll get back together."

"I don't think so," I say, checking my make-up in the mirror. I've welled up more than once today.

"Well, you have to sort it before Brighton."

"Brighton?"

"Yeah, results day. Sun, sea and *seriously* loud music. We've booked a hostel. Not that I expect we'll be sleeping much."

Georgia straightens her top, then reapplies her lipstick.

"Not happening," I say.

"We're all going. You wouldn't have to be with him all the time… It's not for ages yet. Maybe things will have blown over by then."

"I doubt those guys would want me there."

"So what? *I'm* asking you."

"I'll think about it," I say, but I'd sooner chew off my own leg than spend time with Finn and Violet.

"It's your day, too, you know."

I shrug. Even before the exams, I know results day will definitely not be a *good* day.

School is like sucking lemons. A rain shower drums on the window of A2. Biology textbooks on my left, Emily Dickinson poems on my right, I try to revise. But all I've amassed is a page of doodles. I tear it out and screw it up. The next page is full of drawings of ladders swirling higgledy-piggledy across one another. Chequerboards heavily shaded. Crosses. Beams of light. What do they mean?

Under the desk, I take out my phone and search online. *Black is associated with seriousness and a bleak outlook.* No shit, Sherlock. *Anarchic doodles suggest coping issues or mental distress.* On the money. *Emotional people who crave love tend to draw rounded shapes, or symbols of femininity and eternity. Those who like to be in control and crave security tend to draw square shapes.* I want to be in control again. Bingo.

A salmon-pink–shirted Havelock peers down at me. I stare at his brown loafers. He crouches down to my level. I die inside as twenty heads turn my way.

He scans my doodles, then taps my book. "See me after class."

I nod.

I wait for the room to empty before facing Havelock.

I know what he's going to say before he says it.

"You all right, Carla?"

I beg the curtains for an answer. I pray to the whiteboard. Should I be honest?

"I'm way behind, Mr Havelock."

"There's still time, Carla. You can do this." I shrug. Havelock continues. "I realize you've been having some, er … difficulties, recently… If you need to talk to someone…"

I die again inside. Cringe. I like Havelock, but enough with the pally-pally stuff.

"I know that, but no. Really, I'm fine. What I don't know is what the Emily Dickinson poems mean, or about gene theory or all the rest, and it's too late now."

Havelock can't think what to say.

"See you later, sir." I make for the door.

"Don't give up, Carla," Havelock calls.

CHAPTER 39

Next day, in the library, I'm in head-down-last-ditch-eggs-in-one-basket-uber-nerdy-revision-freak mode. But I'm so behind that the words on the page make no sense. I may as well be looking at blueprints for the Large Hadron Collider. In Russian. Upside down.

It hits me like a sledgehammer that I'll probably fail my exams.

I want to hate Finn, blame him for the jam I'm in, but I can't. I've got myself into this mess.

I flip the page. Diagram. Unpronounceable words. My brains, splattered across it…

A shadow falls on the book. I look up.

"How are you?" Isaac asks.

"Bloody wonderful. Can't you tell?"

"Fancy going into Central London? Could go to the park and laugh at tourists getting chased by pigeons."

"Better not. Have to revise."

I admit I'm wary of Isaac's motives. Does he still like me? Or is he just trying to be a friend? I'm not sure, but

I *could* do with a friend right now, one who understands, and Isaac … maybe he does understand, more than Lauren, more than Sienna, perhaps more than I do myself. But I don't want to give him the wrong idea…

Then it comes to me: revision, schoolwork, something *platonic.* "Actually, there is something you could help me with." As soon as I've said it, I regret it. I don't mean to, it's just … *complicated.*

"What?" he asks.

"Um…"

Reasons not to meet Isaac:

1. I don't want to give him hope.
2. More drama is the last thing I want.
3. I need time to, I don't know, figure stuff out…
4. I'm not ready to welcome the affections of any new guy, let alone a Masterson. Harsh, maybe. True, definitely.

I think about this whole year; how all along, without knowing it, I've been trying to patch the cracks in my life. I'm realizing that perhaps I'm the one to fill the gaps, not drugs, not a guy. But do I have to do it alone? Can someone help me? Someone who, maybe, seems to get it? Get *me*?

"There's this exhibition in town," I say. "Thought I might go. I've still got a critical piece to write for my Art portfolio. You could come."

"All right."

"Meet at Adriano's later. Four?"

"OK. See you there."

Isaac leans against the wall of Adriano's, reading J.G. Ballard. I've only ever seen him read *Evo* magazine, which

I judge from the cover is about fast, sexy cars, so to see him with an actual book is odd. He looks like a private detective, pretending to read while actually scanning the crowd.

"Hey. Is that for English Lit?"

"No." *Oh, he's into reading then.*

"You like art?"

"I like that you like art. I mean, I heard you like art."

"I told you I like art."

"Yeah."

Awkward.

I buy us a couple of coffees for the journey. We walk the short distance from Adriano's to Bus Stop E in the high street.

We slurp our drinks.

He doesn't say much, nor do I, but I sense there's something worth digging for under his quiet, sometimes distant, exterior.

What would Finn think if he saw us?

Whatever. I don't care. I really don't… Has Isaac told him he's meeting me?

I begin to think this is a bad idea, but see the bus in the distance, then it's here, I'm getting on it, and we're heading to the top deck. It's twenty minutes to town, twenty freaking silent minutes, staring at houses, office buildings, skyscrapers, and not a peep from either of us. Nothing said, but so much hanging there between us.

Just as it's becoming unbearable, Isaac looks at me with a hint of a smile, saying with his eyes what he said before: *You're amazing, and you don't even know it.*

And I'm thinking, *I don't need this right now*, but at the same time…

I feel hot, the heat of the sun drumming through the window onto my skin.

I ring the bell for the next stop as the bus approaches Trafalgar Square.

We amble across the square, past the fountains and up the stone steps, where a gazillion tourists have stopped to eat their lunch and snap pictures of the current art installation on the fourth plinth. This year, a giant blue cock has been erected there. Cockerel, that is, with its chest puffed to bursting. A shining ultramarine gem in a dull grey crown among all the grey buildings. I read somewhere it's supposed to say something about regeneration, awakening and strength, but to me it's a funny, surreal thing, poking fun at the staid bronze statues of men on pedestals.

I wonder what it would be like to have an installation here, for all the world to see. I think it would be kind of great. I think about my butterfly sculpture. I have so much still to do on it, like, erm, all the painting. But if finished, and made bigger … it could be up there.

"Do you like it?" Isaac asks as we pass the sculpture.

"What?" I ask, grinning.

"I'm not saying it."

"Well, then, I can't think what you mean."

Isaac sighs. "Do you like the … um … bird?"

"Yes, I like the massive bird."

We turn left past the National Gallery, and down Pall Mall. Grand buildings tower on either side, windows adorned with stonework flowers, garlands and faces, some with vast Corinthian columns that prop buildings up like wedding-cake tiers.

Nestled between two stone buildings is the red-brick gallery, as tall but narrower, with a triangular gable. It reminds me of Amsterdam, and ironically also, the cockerel plinth, standing out against the spectacular but uniform architecture all around it. The gallery itself is a work of art.

Inside, we find an immaculate white curved desk, and sitting behind it, a guy, urban cool personified. Sharp-suited and big-haired, he greets us with a well-rehearsed smile. His wild Afro jiggles as he talks, dancing like those toy sunflowers that react to noise. He talks, it boogies.

"Hello," says Boogie-Barnet.

"Hi," Isaac says. "Two for Disjointed Realities, please."

"That's twenty-four pounds." Isaac puts his card in the reader. "Enter your pin."

"God, that's loads," I say. "I'll buy the next coffees. They'll be half the size of a Starbucks and twice as expensive."

"Plan."

Behind the grand facade, the lobby is cool and clinical, with original features like the cornices painted a stark white, but through a set of double doors, the atmosphere changes. It's all wooden floorboards and shabby sofas, warm, inviting, but totally ostentatious. Oh-so-arty types mill about, gesturing at piles of burnt paper plates with the vivacity of kittens with a ball of string. On a blood-red chaise longue with lion-paw feet, a girl sits sketching, her vintage brogues on the velvet seat, but no one's bothered. French jazz pumps from the walls.

It's a big room, like the hall of a great manor, but roughed up, like squatters have moved in. Sculptures are dotted about like alien objects on sterile white plinths.

We pause in front of a doll with guitar strings emerging from its belly button. The caption reads: *Umbilical Chord.* Another plinth has a coil of severed electrical wire sitting on top of it. A stack of twenty-year-old newspapers sits in a glass box.

I wonder about this kind of art. What does it even mean?

But Isaac's forked out big time for the tickets and it was *my* idea…

"This is interesting," Isaac says, pointing to a solitary lipstick-stained wine glass on a white plinth, which could be:

1. a work of art
2. a bad work of art
3. not cleared away after the private view.

"Do you think it's meant to be here?" I ask.

"Maybe that's the point of it? What's real? What's not?"

"Deep," I joke. "Maybe I'm going about my project all wrong. I could do *this*, easy," I say, checking the other side of the plinth to make sure I'm not missing something wildly meaningful, but it's just a dirty glass on a plinth.

"Is it me? – I mean, no offence, maybe you get all this – or is it … absolute shit?" Isaac asks.

"Perhaps that's what they should have called the exhibition. *Absolute Shit: A Retrospective.*"

"Probably wouldn't pull in many punters."

"Maybe not."

"So what sort of art do you like?"

"I guess, I'm looking for something beautiful, well-crafted, with technique *and* meaning."

"What about your art? Does it have both?"

"I hope so. Well, I try. Means something to *me*, at least."

"Bet it's got aesthetics to match."

I shrug. "That'll be for the exam board to judge." My stomach rumbles. "Is it coffee time yet?"

"Definitely time for a caffeine boost."

In the cafe, I pick a corner where the light splices through an enormous window, like a spotlight. You know how seasons can affect health – seasonal affective disorder and all that – well, light can affect your mood too. I read about an experiment where they exposed lab rats to two extra hours of daylight daily, and they became much perkier, running about and searching for food. People must have been *seriously* depressed before electricity was discovered.

I plonk onto a green leather sofa.

Isaac's filled out lately, not in a chunky way, just toned up a bit… His T-shirt has a cool print of a man with his head drawn in lines and squiggles.

"Nice tee," I say.

"Limited edition. Got it online."

"Get you." *When did he get so cool?*

"I believe you were in charge of coffees," he says, stretching his arms along the back of the sofa.

"So I was." I buy two lattes and a £4 pecan chocolate brownie because, why not?

"Extravagant," Isaac muses as I sit back down beside him.

"Skipped breakfast. My stomach feels the size of an acorn."

"Tasty, nutritional lunch then?"

"Something like that. We can share though." I cut the

brownie with the edge of a plastic fork. Isaac picks up half and eats it in one go. "You're weird," I say.

"Hungry. Need to up my calorific intake." He munches. "Been doing a lot of running. Clears my head."

"I do the same with gym. I taught Finn how to cartwh—"

I stop short. A silence expands between us like a huge inflatable pink elephant. I have to stop myself tumbling into the memory, so I look around for a distraction. There are flyers on the table. A gig at the gallery in a few weeks. Poetry slam on Sundays. Screen-printing workshops in the basement on Saturday afternoons.

"Hey, you should enter this." Isaac thrusts a leaflet into my hand. It reads: *Maggie Penn Art Prize. Submissions by 20 August. Win £250 worth of materials and art-course funding. Plasma Gallery supports local talent.*

"No way. I'm so not good enough. It'll be a miracle if I pass."

"Do it."

"No time to make anything new. All I have is a tatty notebook full of half-baked ideas."

"Get it in the oven and bake it then. You've got weeks before the closing date."

"You mean like the flaming paper plates over there?"

"Ha. No. You know what I mean. Something 'beautiful, well-crafted', like you said."

"I don't think so," I say, then try to change the subject. "You know what's baked to perfection? This brownie. Mmm, totally worth it," I say, then sip my coffee.

"OK, ignore me if you like but I still think you should enter."

"You've got brownie on your chin."

"Where?" Isaac asks. I point to the crumb.

"Right there."

He struggles but finally wipes the brown blob from his face.

"All better?" Isaac asks, smiling, his gaze lingering a little too long. An uncomfortable feeling bubbles in my stomach. It's not the brownie. *Does he still like me that way?*

"Better," I confirm.

"Do you want to meet up after school tomorrow?"

"Um, I don't know... Got buckets of work to do. In revision sessions till half three. Biology's killing me. Applications of genetic engineering." I pause. "Or as it's commonly known, Gibberish Theory. I try to understand it but it's like reading Greek or binary or whatever."

"Applications of Gene-berish?"

"Something like that."

"We could revise together. You can say no if you want."

I *should* say no. Definitely no. Because my head's still full of Finn and the what-went-wrongs and what-a-fool-I-ams and how-am-I-gonna-get-throughs. I'm wrestling with too many regrets already. The thing is... Right now, I feel so at ease with Isaac. And actually, the negative thoughts seem to stop shouting when I'm with him. I feel ... *calm*. Why is that?

"Well... Maybe you can quiz me or show me some flashcards or something," I say.

"OK. See you in the park by the bandstand at quarter to four."

CHAPTER 40

In the park, the high sun lays glitter on the damp grass. I spread my jacket on the ground and sit down. Isaac's on his way. He's stopped to buy coffees. I look at my trembling hands and shake them out. Makes no difference. I've been uber-tense all day. A jack-in-the-box-wound-up-tight-stressed-out spring about to explode or suffer an aneurism or burst out of my skin. Exams, Finn, Isaac… Unless I chill out my eyes may pop out in cartoon fashion. After I got home last night, all my thoughts began to tangle themselves into knots. At the gallery with Isaac, I'd felt like I was standing still, like the ride had finally stopped. But away from him, the world began to spin again.

Suddenly the sky turns dark. "You're in my light," I say.

Isaac hands me an extra-sugary latte. "Here you go. The Carla Special: clogs your arteries with one sip." He sits down beside me and nudges my shoulder with his.

I sip my strong, sweet coffee. "Just because you're on a health drive doesn't mean we all have to conform."

I notice his black Converse, mostly hidden by his dark

jeans, navy T-shirt, plain and old, with a patch of murky white on the collar.

"Did you used to bleach your hair?"

"Finn's idea of a joke. He bleached my fringe when I was sleeping. It looked supremely awful. Like a human cockatoo."

"Ha. That's classic. Gold."

"Well, blond, technically..."

I feel the softness of his midnight-black hair as I stroke it with my eyes. It's never sticky with product. Stubble creeps evenly across his face. And then I think: *Fuck, why am I staring at Isaac?*

Over his shoulder, I see a group of figures heading towards us like a herd of livestock, moving as one. "Do you know them?" I ask.

Isaac stretches out on the grass, casual and unconcerned. "They look vaguely familiar, but no."

I sip my latte and flick through the pages of his current book, *Ham on Rye* by Charles Bukowski. The herd edges closer, definitely on course to trample us. Pretending to read, I watch them approach. Then we are under a cold blanket of shadow, looking up at them.

Six lads circle us, no longer cattle but hunting dogs. Wolves.

"You selling weed?" a guy with big brown eyes and cropped hair asks, his skin pale pink like an uncooked sausage.

"Nah, mate," Isaac answers.

"Come on. Course you are."

"I said no. I don't have any."

"Not what I heard." The boy grabs Isaac's collar, yanking him upwards.

Panic rises in my throat, hot and suffocating. I sit upright, scanning the group. I *do* recognize them. They're in Year 11. Not menacing individually, but as a group…

"Thing is, mate, we fancy a smoke. And a reliable source tells me you're the guy."

Wrong brother. But for some reason neither of us can get the words out.

Isaac stands up, tall and unflinching. "I don't want to fight you. You'll have to look elsewhere," he insists.

"We'll take your wallet then." The pale-skinned guy looks at the others, communicating a secret command with his eyes. He moves close to Isaac, nose to nose.

Instantly, the boy flicks his leg behind Isaac as if dancing an Argentine Tango, hooks Isaac's legs and pulls. Isaac falls backwards.

"Shit!" he cries. "Bastard."

Back on his feet, Isaac grabs his attacker's collar, sending them both falling to the ground. The boy rips at Isaac's hair, his clothes. *Stop it, stop it!* In a flash, they're all on him, thrashing, scuffling for his back pocket. I don't know what to do! *What can I do?*

A boy with dirty-looking stubble and a bad haircut pins Isaac's arms back. Isaac whips his head around and gnashes his teeth at the boy like a hungry dog. Twisting his body at the hips, he kicks at the twelve grappling hands and twelve stamping feet, but under a mass of muscle and flailing limbs, he's like the ball in a rugby scrum.

"Stop it!" I yell. "Get off him!"

With supernatural strength surprising even me, I grab the ringleader by the waist and yank him backwards. The boy gasps like I've given him the Heimlich and releases

Isaac, a few strands of Isaac's hair left in his palm. I suppress a wave of nausea.

Isaac lies on the ground, bruised and bloody-nosed. He could have beaten the shit out of one of them, but six? No chance.

The boy edges towards me, brow down, eyes narrowed. I stand frozen momentarily, a deer in headlights. I turn to run but he catches my arm, digging his nails into my wrist. My arm is almost wrenched from its socket and I shriek with pain. At this, Isaac is roused and jerks upright.

The boy squares up to me and pulls his fist back like a catapult. We stand motionless, staring at each other.

"If you touch her I'll pull your balls through your mouth," Isaac spits.

The others go to pin Isaac to the ground, but despite the battering, he's too quick. He lunges between the leader and me, getting a chinful of fist. He drops to his knees. I catch him as he falls backwards.

"You should've just given me your wallet," the ringleader says.

Isaac scrambles to his feet and grabs him by the collar and crotch. The boy howls while his mates look on, wincing.

"I suggest you shut up if you plan on having children any time in the future. And if you so much as breathe in her direction, you'll be sucking food through a straw for the rest of your miserable little life," Isaac's voice thunders. *Wow,* I think. *Where did he come from?*

"Aaaarrggh, all right."

Isaac releases him. The boy crumples like a Coke can crushed underfoot.

I hook Isaac under the arms and pull him upright.

"Tossers," he mumbles under his breath, wiping his bloody nose with the murky patch on his collar.

We stagger to the park toilets, ignoring gawping passers-by. He rests against the vile green concrete wall while I go into the ladies and grab a handful of damp pink toilet paper. *Ugh*.

"Here," I say, tilting his head upwards, "for your nose."

"Thanks."

I go and run some more paper under the tap. The water's Arctic cold. Back with Isaac, I dab the wet tissue under his eye. He recoils, grimacing.

"It's not that bad," I say, trying to be positive. "Are you OK?"

"Just a scratch. Surface wounds."

"They've scratched you all over; we'd better win the jackpot." I check him top to toe. "Nope, two bells and a cherry. Not our day."

"How's your arm?"

"Bit sore. Nothing to worry about," I say. "You knew they wanted Finn."

"Yeah. But he's my brother," Isaac says.

He stumbles, then steadies himself, holding my shoulder and leaning in. Not on purpose, but still, he's here. Close enough to…

My pulse quickens. Magnets depolarize and I want to pull him so close…

Thump, thump, thump…

I'm scared. Not ready.

Thump, thump, thump…

I try to look away but I'm drawn into his eyes, falling, falling, falling into the abyss… But … he has the same dark eyes, *Finn's* eyes… *I can't do this.*

The moment passes and all I'm left with is disappointment pinching at my stomach.

CHAPTER 41

On Saturday I board the coach heading to Sal's in Wales. Somehow I've made it through post-break-up-hell week, but now on half-term, I feel anything but free.

I'm noticing things about Isaac I never saw before. I thought he hated me. Now, he makes a little joke, or looks at me with a twinkle and I see something else in him. Something exciting. I want to grab those moments by the bull horns and hang on. Do I like Isaac? I mean, *like* like? No, I can't, must be residual Finn-feelings. I'm projecting. Anyway, it's not as if I've got time to explore the possibility. Hello? EXAMS COMETH.

My shoulder aches from the fight as I lift my bag into the overhead compartment.

I'm looking forwards to seeing Sal and hearing about her adventures down under: wallabies, boomerangs, all that stuff. My knowledge of Oz is limited to watching *Neighbours* and *Muriel's Wedding.* It needs some updating.

The air con's set to cryogenic.

I stare out of the window at the traffic, people shopping

on Oxford Street, the park blurring by, until we're out of the city and onto the M4. I put on some music and try to fade away. This break will be good. I've got to get my head straight. I'll be away from Finn, Isaac, drugs. That's good, I guess.

Three hours and a huge bag of Maltesers later, I remove my earphones to hear an announcement scratch out of the coach speakers: "Next stop, Cardiff."

I'm greeted with an enormous bear hug from a very tanned Sal.

"Good to see you, kid," she says, voice muffled in the fuzz of my unbrushed hair.

"You too. Welcome home," I say. "I've been banished."

"So they sent you to the naughty corner, AKA, the Welsh countryside," Sal says, in what sounds like an Aussie twang.

We walk to where she's parked.

"Hop in the awesomobile!" She opens the boot and chucks my bags in.

I'd forgotten how amazing Sal's car is. A '72 Ford Maverick Grabber with a not-so-classy brown and yellow paint job and furry seat covers. *Zoom, zoom. Hello, retro.*

"I love this car. I want to pet the seats like puppies. And what is that?" I point to the stereo. "An eight-track player?"

"Sure is. How do you even know what an eight-track is? You're, like, *eight* years old."

"I like vintage."

Sal steers the awesomobile like a guided missile out of Cardiff and into the sticks. It doesn't take long for the questions to start tumbling out.

"So tell me about your trip," I say. "Did you have fun with Toadie and Dr Karl?"

"Screw that, Carla! What's happened to get you exiled to the valleys?"

"Oh. Nothing. Mum and Dad whipping up a shit storm over nothing as usual."

From the car window, jagged limestone outcrops burst from murky green hills.

"If you say so," Sal says, "but either you're going to spill it now or I'm going to hassle you for the next week. I'll use my Jedi mind powers if I have to." Sal wobbles a hand towards me. "Use the Force."

"Watch the road, Sal."

"Ooh, tetchy. Fine." Sal huffs. "But I'm a good listener, you know. And I can tell something's up. You're white as a sheet and getting really skinny."

I pinch my stomach. "Am not." But I'm secretly pleased she's noticed. Not that I've changed my diet much; stress, drugs and dancing have a slimming effect.

Sal shrugs. "You totally are."

Sal hammers the awesomobile around a few more hairy bends up the country lanes. My bum flies off the seat several times, and then we're here.

Janice and Sal live in a house that smells of sawdust and old board games. The floorboards squeak. It's homey. Warm. The sofas are scarlet and there are hand-sewn throws and crocheted cushions everywhere.

There's a big leather armchair that can eat you whole. I love it. This is my first visit in years. We spent holidays here when I was little, and it's all coming back to me now: the sunlit conservatory where we left our muddy wellies and the kitchen that reminds me of those individual variety pack cereals we only ever had on holiday. The big back garden with pear trees and a rope swing. I remember Dad giving me a sparkler there one Guy Fawkes night. We ate hotdogs and sat on the patio steps and he told me about the stars. There was no light pollution, and we could see the whole band of the Milky Way.

"Earth to Carla." Sal taps me on the noggin. "Hellloooo?"

"Sorry, miles away."

"Mum's here."

Aunt Janice smooshes my face against her in a tight, borderline awkward hug. "Your dad says you need a break."

"I suppose," I say, nodding.

She's wearing jeans and a knitted jumper with an oh-so-bad-it's-good blue diamond pattern, and I can't work out whether it's intentionally retro or just a coincidence. Her wavy blonde hair's pulled back in a ponytail. I wonder whether she'd look like Mum if her hair was neat and her clothes, designer. Probably. If Mum chilled out and let herself get scruffy once in a while, would she be more like Janice?

I move to take my stuff upstairs.

"Don't unpack, Carla. Had an idea on the way home." Sal turns from me to Janice. "Mum, we're going to take the awesomobile and go camping out at the Rock. Think of it as a vision quest. We're young and going off to find ourselves in the wilderness."

"That's a bit sudden, love."

"Carla's in need of spiritual guidance. The kind you can

only get by being at one with nature. Also, it's sunny. In Wales. We'd better make the most of it."

"Well, if that's what you want to do… I'll pack you some food."

"Your mum's so nice," I whisper.

The Rock is actually a pile of rocks on a hill. Below it is a group of oak trees.

"How about that thicket over there?" I ask.

"Thicket?" Sal mocks. "Right-o, jolly good. Looks like a spiffing spot!"

In a clearing among the trees, a couple of logs lie on the ground beside a blackened patch for fires.

Sal takes a large disc from the boot of the car and unzips its edge. She throws it in the air and a tent magically appears. "Help me peg, will you?" she asks.

I take a metal rod from the peg bag. "This isn't a peg. It's a barbecue skewer."

"Oh, yeah," Sal chuckles. "Tino and I had a peg incident camping in the Bush in Oz. Wine plus hammer equals bent pegs. I was lucky to escape with all my toes. Not an example I want you to follow, by the way."

"I see." I smile at Sal then roll my eyes. I hammer in the last improvised peg. "That's got to be record time for setting up camp."

"I like to keep things simple. Besides. Let's not waste time. Tell me what's been going on, CC. I'm worried about you. You look ill."

"Cheers, mate!"

"Well, you do. Your pasty complexion offends me. You

look like an anaemic ghost."

"Compared to you, maybe. Ronseal's not good for your skin, you know."

"Ha bloody ha."

The temperature drops a few degrees and I pull on a hoodie. After gathering some wood, we light a fire. The moon looks chalky in the grey-blue sky but brightens as night falls. Sal twists a marshmallow on a stick over the flames. It starts to bubble and she pulls it out, blowing furiously on the gooey pink blob which slides off the stick and onto the ground.

"Oops." She shrugs and spikes another one. This time she manages to get it toasted *and* to her mouth. "Spill it, then."

I shake my head, pull my hood up, and try to hide.

"No story, no marshmallows."

So I tell Sal all about Finn and Violet, the drugs, the dealing, the lies, Isaac, the almost-kiss…

She listens and nods, without judgement.

"Shit." Sal moves to sit beside me on the log. I stick out my hands to warm them by the fire. She puts her arm around me and I rest my head on her shoulder. I can't believe I didn't talk to her earlier.

I pull out a pack of tobacco and roll a cigarette. Sal gawks.

"Yeah, and now I feel like I need to smoke," I say, disappointed in myself. "Hangover from doing it all the time with Finn. I want to stop, but it's hard."

She lets me light up.

"You've changed so much. What happened to the studious kid? You never said anything in your messages. I thought it was just the usual teen-angst stuff. But the drugs. You've *got* to give those up." Sal squeezes my arm. She doesn't sound preachy.

"I haven't done them for ages."

"Good."

We talk until the sun appears over the distant hills, painting a pink pastel crown on their heads.

I tuck into my sleeping bag, wrapping it tight to my ears. My eyelids are heavy as lead and I fall quickly into a sweet, dreamless sleep. The best I've had in months.

CHAPTER 42

We spend the next day lazing and talking rubbish, until Sal cracks the whip. She spots my rucksack, chocka with revision books, and drags it over to where I'm sitting on one of the logs, my head in my phone, replying to a message from Georgia… I've got a lot of respect for Georgia. There's more to her behind the red lipstick, and she hasn't stopped talking to me like some of the others – Slinky, Mike, Greg… I think they're all under the Violet Brody spell, but not Georgia. She does as she pleases.

"Glad to see you brought your bag of bricks. Never know when they might come in handy," Sal says.

"Please remove that sack of evil from my vicinity."

"Nope. Come on, Carla. You don't have to do it alone. Let me help you. I'm a *great* teacher. I taught a koala to wink."

I roll my eyes. "Course, that's *exactly* the same as teaching someone." I open the Psychology textbook to a random page, and read, "about *the main features of the sympatho-medullary pathway.*"

"Totally. Although fair play, the koala had been hit by a car and perhaps suffered some kind of facial deformity as a result, or brain injury or something."

"You're really filling me with confidence in your teaching skills."

"You want the help or not?"

"All right, all right. Please help me, oh wise koala whisperer. But I can already wink." I throw my best Fonz impression at Sal.

"Atta girl. Now, let's fill that brain of yours with the good stuff. When we're finished you'll be the Einstein of sympo–sympa–homo–meadow–ways..."

"Sympathomedullary pathways," I say.

"That's what I said." Sal pulls a notebook out of the bag and hands it to me, along with a pen. "Now, less talkie-talkie, more learnie-learnie."

Sal and I spend another day at the Rock, by which time I'm so grimy and gagging for a shower – and to charge my phone – that I practically beg to go back to her house and be reunited with technology, hot water and a meal that doesn't include:

1. baked beans
2. packet noodles or
3. today's lunchtime treat, cremated sausages.

It'll take a hell of a lot of ketchup to make *these* palatable.

"Shrivelled devil fingers," I say, stabbing one with my fork and examining its wrinkles.

Sal grabs one from her plate. "Pokey, pokey," she says, jabbing me in the arm with it. "Eat me, Carla," she says, in a voice for the sausage. "You need fattening up. Skinny cow. Eaaaaat meeeee!"

I grimace and lean back on the log. "Stay back, I have a mug of cold beans and I'm not afraid to use them."

"Eaaaaat meeeee!" Sal moves forwards, brandishing the sausage.

"Quit harrassing me!" I start to laugh and fall back on the log, the beans ejecting from the mug and all down my front. Sal breaks into hysterics.

"OK," I say, "enough wilderness exploration. Time to re-enter society … where they have showers … internet … food *not* possessed by demons."

"Right you are, CC," Sal says, still grinning from ear to freaking ear.

I love that girl.

Back at the house I'm fed and watered and feeling human again. To tell the truth, Janice is a bit of a feeder. Homemade pumpkin bread. Cheese. Blueberry muffins. Like, every hour, the hostess trolley comes by with a selection of snacks. First class.

I sit in the giant armchair, cosy, but not content, rereading the Emily Dickinson poems for the sixty-millionth time.

"Brain food," Janice says, handing me a packet of Brazil nuts.

But however many goji berries and spinach leaves I eat, I doubt my brain will be ready for what's coming…

I thought I would be ecstatic to be heading back to the Big Smoke, but I'm not.

Things I'm categorically *not* looking forwards to facing when I get back, in no particular order:

1. EXAMS
2. DAD'S RUBBISH COOKING
3. STAYING UP ALL NIGHT (CRAMMING, NOT BECAUSE I'M ON DRUGS)
4. VIOLET'S STUPID FACE.

Sal rounds the awesomobile into the coach station. "Call me any time," she says.

I smile my best brave smile, but I'm sad to leave. I drag my ass from the front seat and my loaded bag from the back seat. Janice has filled any gaps with snacks.

A box of fresh-baked cookies falls to the ground.

"Your mum's amazing," I say. "It's a wonder you don't have to be airlifted out of the house."

"Blessed with a fast metabolism. Dad was a hummingbird."

"You're so weird. But I love you for it."

Sal gets out of the car and comes around to my side.

"Enough soppy stuff, little one. Here," she says, handing me the rucksack, "don't forget your bag of bricks."

"How could I forget?" I gear up for the goodbye. "Thanks for—"

"No worries." Sal attempts a frankly abysmal wink, her whole face scrunching.

"And you say you taught a koala to wink? You look like you're in pain. Please refrain from winkage in the future. For your own safety."

Sal drowns me in a hug. "I'll miss you, kid. See you soon, all right?"

"Yeah," I say.

"You'll be fine, CC."

I head to the coach that will take me not only home, but back to reality, and I think about what Sal said. *I will be fine. I have to be.*

On the journey, I realize that this *punishment*, this *banishment*, has been a blessing. I haven't smoked, except for a couple of rollies while we were camping. I guess Sal provided a lot of distraction. I haven't had a drink. I haven't done any drugs or even thought about them. I've got on with my schoolwork. I feel like the good Carla but without the shyness. Without the fear.

The thing is – and this bothers me, confuses me – I don't miss Finn … but I do miss Isaac. Not once did I wonder what Finn was doing, where he was and who with… But Isaac? I thought about him, just a little. Arrrgh. *Begone, thoughts*. For now, it's got to be all about my Pre-Raphaelites critical study. No room for *that*.

I open my laptop, its cursor flashing expectantly…

Pre-Raphaelites were taught the traditional way to paint, but went off and did their own thing. They were rebels who stood out from the rest.

I think about everything that's happened. If going out with Finn and everything that came with it was my way of standing out, then was it worth it? Have I emerged from the chrysalis a winged beauty? Um, no. I need to *be someone*, to remove my invisibility cloak, but God knows how. Sometimes I feel I'm right back at the start, a nobody, unreflected in the mirror.

I try to put those thoughts aside and concentrate. It's easier with Art because it's a subject I have a handle on. I get lost in it. I'm in the zone, my synapses firing, creative juices flowing, when Facebook Messenger pops up.

Hey

Hey, yourself. How's life in the real world?

All right. Spent some time with my dad which is pretty cool. Bonding. Talking about man stuff.

Like boobs and power tools?

And football.

You still black 'n' blue?

I look badass with my black eye. How's exile in leek and sheep country?

It's worked out pretty well.

How so?

Fresh air, fresh perspective. You doing OK?

So-so. I've got some blues I'm trying to quash.

Deep. Any luck?

A little.

(The cursor pulsates.)

What's up? Do tell.

Really? It's pretty heavy stuff.

I'm all ears.

If you're sure.

Say it already!

OK. I've been having these thoughts.

The same thoughts I've had this whole time about you. And then – at the park

(Pulsate, pulsate, pulsate…)

you were about to kiss me. I think it means something.

I think you like me too but you're afraid to say.

(Flash, flash, flash…)

Seeing it committed to type flicks a switch in me. I like Isaac. Oh, God. I think I really do. I understand him. The twist of the gut when you see someone, joy and pain all merged into one super-charged turbo-emotion.

There it goes, the memory, on repeat: *Look at me. I think you're amazing.*

I might like you. A little bit.

It's a start.

The journey's gone by in a blur. Isaac's encouraged me about my art, and told me about the books he's reading, about the films he likes and that he would love to be a writer like Jonathan Safran Foer or Jonathan Franzen or Jonathan Coe, and I tell him that maybe he should change his name to Jonathan then. I tell him I hope to be an artist and travel the world and ride an elephant and maybe one day, just one day, feel free, like I don't have to pretend to be someone else to fit in... By which time I must have written the thousand words – an essay – just not on nineteenth-century painters. *Shit.*

CHAPTER 43

When I arrive home, Mum's out. Big surprise. But Dad's happy to see me and orders Chinese for dinner. Win.

DAD'S RUBBISH COOKING: AVOIDED.

I spend the evening procrastin-eating, then have a major *yikes* moment. Just one little, miniscule, barely-worth-bothering-with, teeny-tiny thing to finish: MY SCULPTURE.

I'm in Such. Deep. Crap.

My Art portfolio deadline looms and I've still got a gazillion tiny butterfly scales to paint. Oh … I've known about this date all term, all half-term break, all evening, yet it seemed a better use of time to dip mini spring rolls in sweet chilli sauce and watch *Can You Dance?* with Dad. I'm next to be voted off, for sure.

In my room, I flatten some cardboard boxes to protect the carpet. Lying on the floor, I set to work with my brush and inks on all those delicate butterfly wings.

I lose track of time. It was dark outside when I started;

now it's light, the birds are singing their cheery song. Half-dead and in pain, with crippled claw fingers from painting, I'm *so* not feeling chirpy.

I scan the colossal mess around me. The makeshift floor's an Impressionist landscape – a Monet with purple streaks and puddles of yellow seeping into cracked, dried-up rivers of aquamarine.

The intense colours have kindled life; she practically hovers above the inky landscape, luminous, incandescent, ablaze. Two pairs of wings, frozen in graceful flight. Each wing covered in tiny scales, and hinged to her slender body.

I can't believe I made it: *Ornithoptera alexandrae*, all hail the Queen of the Butterflies.

I did it. I am so freaking want-to-kill-myself-tired. But I. Did. It.

It's got to be worth it. It has to be.

I might pass one AS-level at least.

Dad gives me a lift to school, to save me having to carry my sculpture. I arrive ridiculously early. Havelock's not even in yet, so I head to the common room to wait.

I swallow a mouthful of purple tea that tastes of purple, with a purple aftertaste. It's supposed to have a reviving effect. So far all it's produced is the red-wine-lip-effect. At nine in the morning this is *not* a good look and I sit in the common room, resembling the corpse of Dita Von Teese: pale face, scarlet clown lips, bit scrawny. The sum of my AS-level Art portfolio sits in my lap: sketchbook, sculpture, studies. I yawn. My eyes well up.

I pick at my paint-stained nails. Jiggle my foot. Try to

slow my breathing. If I don't pass Art, then what have I got? I'll be good at nothing. Good *for* nothing.

The radio is on. I hear: *I could draw you under, let you drown in my depths. Fill your lungs with me, drink me in and never leave.*

I pretend to read *Closer* magazine. I slouch, attempting to disappear. I used to be good at disappearing, but not any more. Not since I famously dated, then dumped, the hottest guy in school.

Someone finds me.

"Hey," Isaac says, sitting down. "All right? I was hoping to see you today. Welcome back."

"I'd like to say it's good to be back but I managed to postpone finishing my coursework until last night. Rookie mistake."

"That explains the dark circles under your eyes."

"Oi!" I whack him on the arm.

"You got exams today?" he asks.

"No, just came to hand this in," I say, pointing to the cardboard box on the table with *kitchen cupboard* scribbled on it in black marker.

"Are they low on condiments in the cafeteria or is this modern art? You didn't seem too keen on that at the gallery."

"No, silly, it's *in* the box. The sculpture for Havelock's class. It's pretty much the best work I've done all year. Mainly because I've finished it, unlike my Psych, Chem, Biology or English Lit coursework. Hope it's good enough, because it's all I can do."

"Let me see."

"No!" I fend off his grasping hands.

"Come on!"

"No way," I say, but Isaac gives me a look and then somehow I'm smiling and bending back the cardboard flaps and letting him peer in.

"Ohmygod. It's amazing," he blurts.

"Shut up."

"You made this? Did you paint all those by hand?"

"No, I got my robot servant to do it. Of course I did it myself! I hear they frown upon cheating around here."

"I don't think you'll have a problem passing Art."

"We'll see. Not sure about my other exams though." I check my phone: 8.43 a.m.

"You'll be fine. Come on. You're the cleverest girl I know. You'll ace your exams. Deep breath, Carla. Go show Havelock what you're made of."

I push open the door to A2, set down my portfolio and box in my usual place and carefully lift the sculpture out.

All the other sculptures look so professional – well, so arty, abstract, trying to say something more. Mine is so delicate. I fill in the form. Name. Candidate number…

"This is good, Carla. Really good. And just in time." Havelock, clad in tan like a desert explorer, shuffles around, surveying my sculpture from all angles. He nods with satisfaction, or maybe relief, that I've *actually* turned in some coursework.

"Can I go now?" I ask.

Havelock gestures to the door. I take my bag and leave, catching myself wishing Isaac was standing outside waiting for me. He always seems to believe in me.

CHAPTER 44

The fact that Violet and I have to sit next to each other during some exams is a hardship I hadn't anticipated. A punishment even. The curse of the alphabetical seating plan: Violet Brody, Carla Carroll. I go to my exams. I do my best, but … the cramming is all too late, the questions foreign. Still, I try…

After a morning studying in my room, I need a break so crank up the volume of my sound dock and try to stop thinking altogether. Half an hour later I'm ready to return to reality. I turn it down a notch.

My phone vibrates. It's Isaac. "Can I come over?" he asks.

"If you like."

"Good. I've been standing outside your house for twenty minutes already and I'm sure your neighbour thinks I'm about to crowbar your window and steal your parents' sweet forty-two-inch flat screen."

"Sorry, I was drowning out the world with feisty chick music. Didn't hear the bell. Two secs."

I change from jogging bottoms into a short skirt made from an old pair of Levi's, leggings and a blue T-shirt. I twist my hair into a rough plait, elusive strands straying across my face. I've got some colour back in the last few weeks.

I rush to the front door and let him in.

"I brought you a Kinder Egg," he says.

"Thanks. Is chocolate part of your diet plan, then?"

"You eat the chocolate. I'll make the toy."

"Deal," I agree.

Since we're on study leave, I haven't seen Finn, save for our agonizing *fifteen-hour* Art exam and the Chemistry and Psychology papers. But I'm beginning to feel numb about Finn. I just switch off, shut him out. Trouble is, I can't seem to get the power back on for exams. It's like I'm running on autopilot, minimal output, back-up generators only. It used to be eat-sleep-rave-repeat, now it's eat-sleep-revise-EXCRUCIATING EXAM-repeat. I was a study whore; now I'm just a study zombie.

I'm sure Finn wouldn't be over the moon if he knew Isaac and I were hanging out – but as soon as I think it, I reject it. I don't allow him into my thoughts. At least, I try not to.

Isaac and I talk a lot. I wrap myself up with him like a child's safety blanket. He's not like Finn. I feel safe, in a world of two, where I can say anything, *be me*, like when I do gym: a place to escape.

There's been no repeat of the almost-kiss. Apart from the Finn complexity there's too much going on with exams. *The friendzone beckons.*

We head upstairs to my room. Isaac perches on the bed.

The music blares; all electric guitar and screaming.

I search through desk junk for the dock remote, then turn the volume down.

"You've been keeping something from me," he says.

I look at him, no clue what he's talking about.

He reaches into his jeans pocket for a small black box.

"Bit soon for proposals, isn't it?" I ask.

"Very funny. Open it."

I lift the lid. Sitting on lilac tissue paper is a butterfly on a silver chain, a silhouette in purple acrylic. With it, a note. I don't read it yet.

"Your Facebook wall is full of happy birthday messages. You kept that quiet."

"Wow, it's ... um..." I struggle to find words. It's so me, so thoughtful, so perfect.

"You don't like it?" Isaac says, confused by my inability to articulate.

"No, I love it," I say. Isaac unhooks the clasp and puts the necklace on me. "Really, thanks. I guess, I'm just... You took me by surprise. It's really kind of you. Thank you." And while I'm talking, I'm thinking, *All I ever got from your brother was a crushed donut and a drug habit.*

Isaac shrugs like it's no big deal, modest as ever, and the contrast between him and Finn is even bolder; he's the fourth plinth in Trafalgar Square.

"You're welcome," he says.

My eyes stray from Isaac's neck, to the tips of his hair, to the light jerking between the slats of the blind, to my toes, to his floppy hair, back to the blinds. I observe the barcode of light on the carpet. A car rumbles past. The lines of light vibrate like white guitar strings.

"This is just Part One of your present."

"There's more?"

Isaac nods.

"What is it?"

"Ah, time will tell, Carla Carroll. All will be revealed, but when you least expect it."

"How very cryptic."

"Got to go now. Keep your phone handy. Don't switch it off."

After Isaac leaves I unfold the note.

This seemed kind of, you know, you. I x

I think I like him a little bit more every time I see him.

Ten minutes pass. My phone rings.

"I've got a surprise for you. A birthday present," he says.

"You were just here."

"You see, you weren't expecting it."

"You're such a dork. Where did you go?"

"Your front garden." I move to the window and look out. Roll my eyes. "Seriously, your neighbour thinks I'm a stalker or something. I can see her picking up the phone. Quick. You really should come let me in."

Back in my room, Isaac perches on the corner of the bed. I swing round on my chair to face him. "So?" I ask, intrigued.

"It wouldn't be a surprise if I told you, would it?" He stretches his arms and leans back onto the duvet, eyes closed and smiling. I glimpse a sliver of lean tummy. All that running must be paying off.

"Suppose not," I say.

He looks pleased with himself. Bursting with energy. He jumps up and leans over to grab the pink heart-shaped Post-it notes on the desk behind me and I can smell his scent, lemons and coconut. "Have you got exams tomorrow?" he says.

"Nope. Why?" I ask but he doesn't reply.

I watch him scribble away and I'm too eager to wait for him to finish, so move next to him on the bed. I read aloud as he writes:

"Meet me at the river at midday tomorrow. Bring goggles (supplied)," I say, in my best secret-agent voice, before adding my own contribution: "Come alone. Wait for my signal. The rabbit is in the burrow. The eagle has landed. Project Birthday is a go. I repeat, Project Birthday is a go."

"It doesn't say that," he says, then draws a map. "Meet me here." An arrow points to the riverbank, by the picnic area in the park. He adds a stickman doodle of himself with a speech bubble saying, "Please come."

"I never knew you were an artist," I say. "It's realistic. You've really captured your crude wavy lines."

Isaac reaches into his rucksack and pulls out a pair of goggles like the ones in the school Chemistry lab.

"What are the goggles for? You loco now?" I ask.

"Patience, Carla."

"Sounds ominous. I mean, will I be walking into a *Shallow Grave* situation here? Should I bring my shovel?"

"Just come!"

The next morning is bright and clear, but my thoughts are clouded. What's Isaac planned? Why the goggles?

I texted him a few times last night but he wouldn't give up any details. *Patience*, he said, and, *This is going to be so good.* Annoyingly cryptic and painfully tantalizing in equal measure. It's 11.34 a.m. I'm ready to go, perched on the edge of my bed, excited. It's silly but I feel like a kid going to the zoo for the first time, or to the pet shop to get my first hamster. Something awesome is about to happen, I know it. I grab my bag, shove the goggles in and head out. I'm barely aware of the streets and trees melting by. My racing mind drives me forwards, feet moving of their own accord. Nearing the river, I notice something amazing, phenomenal. This, fuck, this is *something else.*

I can't believe my eyes.

Hundreds of butterflies form a sea of white on the muddy ground, their wings illuminated by the bright sun. The creatures line the footpath so densely, I can't see how to get past. This is *mental.* I shout for Isaac but hear only the low hum of multiple insects, closely packed and clambering over one another. Their long antennae twist and jerk, tiny rods receiving signals like TV aerials – but what transmission has drawn them here?

I edge towards the water, careful not to crush the pearly ocean underfoot. So exhilarated by the fantastical sight, I almost forget I'm looking for Isaac. It's really beautiful. I mean freaking, stuff-of-dreams-magical-realm-epic-movie-scene beautiful. *Did he do all this? No. How could he?*

"Do you like it?"

I look around but I can't see him anywhere. "Where are you?"

"Answer the question!"

"I love it!"

A tap on the shoulder makes me jump. I turn to see Isaac dangling upside down, legs hooked over a thick tree branch.

"Hello," he says.

"How did you do this?"

Isaac hoists himself up, slowly lowers his legs and swings carefully to the ground, so as to miss the butterflies. Dust puffs up where he lands and a few fly off into the treetops.

"Fireworks," he says.

"I don't understand."

Isaac just grins and takes my hand, leading me away from the butterflies.

"Where are we going?"

"We'll come back. I need to show you something."

Further down the riverbank, he stops. "When I was doing Chemistry GCSE, we came here to do an experiment. Not strictly school-endorsed."

He puts on a pair of safety gloves, then takes a small white pot from his pocket.

"Look, Isaac, I'm done with drugs."

He smiles. "It's not a rock of coke. It's sodium. Better put on your goggles."

I do as I'm told. Isaac takes out a pair of tweezers and grips the sodium.

"Stand back."

Chemistry lessons have taught me that sodium is a soft, waxy, silver-white, metallic element. Highly reactive. Oxidizes rapidly when exposed to air. Reacts violently with water. Bloody punch-drunk violently. A smallish bomb.

"Isn't this dangerous?"

"Maybe a little. But what's life without a little risk? Ready?"

Isaac's eyes widen with a mock look of terror.

"Dun-duuun-duuuuuuun!" He throws the rock into the river and it spits and glows white before exploding. Sparkles rain down.

"That's very cool. But I don't get what it has to do with the butterflies."

"Elementary, my dear Carla. A bunch of us stole thirty grams from school and threw it in the river one night. It was pretty awesome. It was only when I went back the next day that I noticed all the butterflies. When it exploded it left salt on the riverbank."

The salt called the butterflies down from the sky. What a birthday present.

I may be about to fail Biology, but I know about butterflies. I know they're champion drinkers. They can drink and void continuously for hours. They do it for the nutrients. The males use the dissolved salts and minerals to make pheromones. They crave sodium like pregnant women crave ice-cream and gherkins. They fill up and move on. And it doesn't hurt them at all. They do it in spectacular fashion, often consuming hundreds of times their body mass. To keep up, a human would have to drink about twelve thousand gallons a second. This isn't eating a handful of peanuts at a bar, this is a tankerful of seawater hooked directly to your veins. I like butterflies because they are pretty and graceful and remind me of the sycamore seeds floating down. I like them for the way they look, but you have to respect the science behind that. *Twelve thousand gallons a second.*

"So you did it again last night? How come you didn't get caught? People get jumpy these days when they hear loud noises."

"I just used some sea salt from Dad's business. Sprinkled it around. I've given up my life of crime and don't fancy losing an arm in a big bang. Plus last time we all got three weeks' detention for nicking from the lab. Think we'd have been expelled if Dad hadn't been catering for a school fund-raiser that same month."

"What about that bit you threw in the river?"

"Internet."

He walks me back towards the butterflies.

"I'm chuffed that it actually worked," he says. "I thought I might be bringing you out here to see, well, nothing, except a slightly salty mud patch."

A low branch curves out over the water. Isaac takes my hand as I climb onto it.

"You should be helping me keep *my* balance, gymnast girl."

The butterflies dance around us.

"Happy birthday," he says.

And I think, *This is a perfect moment.*

CHAPTER 45

After exams finish, summer officially starts. Free from school, I hardly see Finn. I get lost in London, which is so big you could go months without seeing the same face twice if you avoid certain haunts: the park, the cinema, the clubs. I feel like … I'm resting. Finally, I'm getting my breath back. The weeks melt away until suddenly results day approaches like a train rounding a bend in the track. I can see its headlights growing larger. I'm waiting on the platform but secretly hoping this particular train *doesn't stop here.* Whichever way you look at it, tomorrow is going to be a momentously craptacular day. Judgement Day: Apocalypse. Fire and brimstone. There's no avoiding it.

I haven't seriously considered going with Georgia and the others to the big-results-day-blow-out in Brighton because I can't think of a single plus point to the excursion. But when Isaac brings it up I feel the balance begin to tip in its favour.

"I thought we could go together."

"Not your brightest idea ever."

"We don't have to hang around with those guys. We'll do our own thing, go to the beach, chill out. Celebrate."

"I might just have done enough to scrape through but I can't see a big fanfare being necessary."

"I'll buy you an ice-cream."

"With a flake?"

"And fudge sauce."

"Hot fudge sauce?"

"Course."

I grin. "Tempting, but … no. The last thing I want to do is watch Finn parade about with Miss Swish-Swish" – I flip my hair – "you know what I'm talking about. And then hang about with a bunch of people who haven't – apart from Georgia – said one word to me since I was ousted from the group. It would feel fake."

"*I've* talked to you."

"That's different. You're not like them. You're like … a stand-alone."

"A loner, you mean."

"No, someone who doesn't need all those others around to congratulate you on your awesomeness. You're just great the way you are."

"Is that a compliment, Miss Carroll? Because it sounds like it's trying to be one."

"It is what it is."

"Well, maybe I don't want to stand alone this time. I could do with the company."

"It'd be too weird." But then I think of all the lovely things Isaac has done for me recently, and all without hope or agenda. The butterflies, the encouragement, protecting me from those boys in the park. If he can do all that, maybe I can take a little weirdness for him. He deserves it. "OK, I'll come. But don't leave me on my own with them."

"Done."

CHAPTER 46

I pack a rucksack with a hoodie, a change of underwear and some make-up. I've given up styling my hair and reverted to my original barely contained frizzy blob. I'm done trying to be someone else. The plan is to spend the day at the beach, head to a club on the seafront in the evening, then back to the hostel. Isaac picks me up and we drive down to Brighton, me singing along to all the power ballads on Magic radio and him rolling his eyes. The car clunks and shudders a few times on the way and at times I think we won't make it. But we do.

"She's on her last legs. My beautiful car. Had her since I passed."

"So, one whole year."

"What can I say? Couldn't afford a Bugatti, had to make do."

"What's a Bugatti?"

"Oh, my dear Carla, you have so much to learn."

"Maybe you could teach me?"

"About cars?"

"No. To drive. When you're back from uni in the summer.

Then maybe I could come and visit you. Remember, I used to live in Nottingham. Could show you around."

Isaac has aced his exams and got into his first-choice uni. I'm glad for him, but kind of sad he'll be leaving soon.

We go to the beach first, before the hostel, because I want to see and smell the sea. The sun's high and people are milling about, swimming, lazing, content. But although the day is golden and I'm out of the shackles of school and home, I can't let myself be happy.

I picked up my results envelope from school this morning. All around me people cried and laughed and hugged and felt proud. I don't dare open my letter. It's in my back pocket, crumpled, hopefully vaporizing out of existence.

"Do you want me to open it?" Isaac asks.

"No."

"Well, then, are *you* going to open it?"

"Nope."

"You'll have to face them sometime."

"I won't. I'll just drop out, run away to South Africa, work at a butterfly sanctuary." I let my mind wander, let it fill with beautiful butterflies. I think about that perfect moment by the river on my birthday. The sodium rock that looked like coke. "Hey, Isaac, you're not doing any drugs tonight, are you?"

"No, I'm done with that."

"I wouldn't want to stop you having a good time."

"Honestly, I don't need to, *want* to. I think" – Isaac kicks a pebble – "they're overrated. Besides, who needs drugs on a day like this: sun shining, waves lapping, ice-creams, er … ice-creaming?"

Will I ever do drugs again? My mind runs through all the times I've done them before. Reliving the highs. Feeling loud, confident, pretty. Like a queen. My fifteen minutes of fame, on a coke high. On a pedestal. On top of the world. Pilled up and free. But the feeling never lasts. Sure, I could do it. I could use drugs to dissociate from reality and not face my results. The flaw in that plan is that tomorrow will always rear its ugly head and the results will still be there, unchanged. Like Isaac says, the drugs are just a hiding place. Pretty soon you have to come out into the light and face the day, whatever it may bring.

I think back over the weekends with Finn, lost to drugs.

Sometimes I wouldn't see a weekend at all. The blinds were always down.

I think about how I camped in my bedroom, under a duvet, worshipping artificial sunlight from my Sunday God: the television. All hail the romcoms. Bow to the chick-flicks. Raise your spliffs in praise of the Eighties robot-themed action movie. Comedown films must be like comedown food: easy to digest.

Adrenalin overload, zero sleep.

I'd get paranoid.

Feel sick.

Look like a ghost.

Why would I want to go through that agony again?

I watch the sea sloshing against the wooden legs of the pier, an enormous neon centipede standing in the water. The smell of popcorn fills the air as we edge closer to the sound of clinking coins and arcade games. I beat Isaac on the dance machine; he trounces me at *Street Racer.* He says he hasn't played in ages, but evidently, fingers never forget. Like it's a fair contest! I can't even drive.

We play a couple of rounds of air hockey, at which, by the way, I'm awesome. Well, usually I am, but Isaac seems to have some special puck-flicking technique apparently learned from a Jedi master, so I may have let a few goals in.

Isaac's phone buzzes.

"The others have arrived. They're on the beach."

"Oh."

"We don't have to go."

"We do. I need to make peace at least. We have a whole other year to spend together in the same classes."

The waves rush at the shore like a herd of wild horses, galloping and intent. In the distance I see Finn, Slinky, Greg and Georgia paddling in the shallows. Greg picks up Georgia to throw her in the water but stops at the last second. She laughs, pushes him back and he splashes into the waves. Violet sits on the beach in a very teeny bikini, shades on, reading a magazine. She reminds me of an iguana basking in the sun, trying to get some sort of warmth into her stone-hearted, cold-blooded being.

Georgia sees Isaac and me and runs over to meet us.

"I hear congrats are in order," she says to Isaac. "You're off to Nottingham."

"Just barely."

"Modest much?" Georgia pokes Isaac playfully on the shoulder. "All *A*s says otherwise. Greg told me."

Isaac shrugs. "Yeah, well, it's not all about results. It

doesn't matter what you get, really." We all know that's not true but I appreciate him trying to make me feel better, and I don't say anything when he puts his arm around my waist to comfort me, even though I know for certain it will raise eyebrows.

"You're coming tonight, right?" Georgia asks.

"Not really in the mood."

"You have to come."

Finn starts to walk over, then stops, Violet tugging at his T-shirt, arms snaking around his chest and whispering in his ear. But something has changed in me and strangely, I don't feel jealous. I've taken off the rose-tinted specs. Finn abandons the plan to confront us and instead nods in our direction and steers clear.

I pick up a stone and throw it into the rolling waves. "I think I'm going to talk to him. Clear the air," I tell Isaac.

"You want me to come?"

"I'll be all right. Just … don't go far."

"There's an ice-cream truck up on the promenade. I'll get us some cones."

Finn sees me coming and gets to his feet. He looks as cute as ever in board shorts and flip-flops, hair wild and windswept.

Violet shoots me a stare loaded with all kinds of evil. She aims a similar glance at Finn but he takes no notice.

"Can we walk?" I ask Finn.

"Sure."

We leave the scowler flipping through the pages of *Glamour.*

"Where are you going?" she asks Finn. He waves her off.

"She's kind of dramatic," I say.

"She's not so bad, just has a mean streak."

"A crazy streak, if you ask me."

"What do you care who I see anyway?"

"You're seeing her?"

"No, nothing's changed. I get her stuff, that's all." Finn runs a hand through his hair. "What do you want, Carla?"

"I guess I just wanted to call a truce. We'll have to see each other next year so let's agree to get on."

"Fine. But, Carla, I never stopped getting along with you. I still *love* you."

"Don't say that."

"It's true."

"I don't believe you."

I thought it wasn't possible for Finn's eyes to darken any more, but just now they do. He grips me by the shoulder. "What are you doing with Isaac?"

Oh, so that's it. He's trying to manipulate me into not seeing his brother. If he can't have me, no one else can.

"We're friends, that's all."

A lump rises in my throat.

Finn grabs my wrist. "Doesn't look that way."

"Let go of me."

He releases my arm. "You'd better go. Your *friend* is waiting for you," he says.

I walk along the beach towards Isaac, not looking back. But I hear Finn calling after me, "He's the liar, Carla. He only wanted to take you from me. He doesn't care about you like I do. I know you. I know what you are. You're just like me."

I'm done with Finn Masterson.

* * *

As I walk back across the beach Violet sticks her foot out to trip me.

"Grow up."

"Well, which one is it, Carla? You can't have both. Isn't one enough for you?"

I try to ignore her.

"You're certainly working your way through the group. Slut."

She's really pushing my buttons.

"He doesn't want you any more. So just leave us alone. He only went out with you to make me jealous. Like that could work."

"Then why aren't you two back together? Go on." I point to where Finn is standing, looking out to sea. "There he is. Go get him."

Violet shrugs.

"You're full of shit," I say. "You and Finn may have had a thing once but now he's just your dealer. It's pretty sad when you think about it."

"Finn loves me, always has, always will," Violet says.

"Well, good luck with that. Look, there's no reason why I should try and help you, but I'll give you one nugget of advice: Finn doesn't love you any more than he loved me; forget about him and move on."

"Right, so you can swoop in and get him back? Never going to happen. Anyway he would never go for you now. You're just a little girl who couldn't handle playing with the big kids. You wish you were me. I can see it in your eyes. I saw it the day you started at Thorncroft."

Violet takes a baggie out of her bikini top and uses a key to scoop up a little mound of coke or *godknowswhat.*

"You couldn't be further from the truth right now. Yeah, go powder your nose with poison, darling. That'll make it all better."

"Why are you even here? Finn's moved on and you're still chasing after him. It's so sad."

"Er, hello. Look in a mirror, Violet. You've been groping him all year."

Violet shrugs and goes back to her magazine. "Go home, ho-bag. No one wants you here."

But when she says that, it has the opposite effect to what she intends. I know I deserve to be here as much as she does. I was invited. And I'll go out tonight and show her that.

I jog back to Isaac and he drops an arm around my shoulder. It feels natural and not at all weighted with expectation.

He hands me a Mr Whippy. "With hot fudge sauce. Just the way you like it."

"Thanks."

We walk down the beach towards the water, away from the group. I carry my flip-flops so I can feel the sand between my toes. Isaac does the same. The beach is mostly pebbles but there's sand nearer the water.

"Saw you talking to Vi. You OK?" Isaac asks.

"Yeah. Wicked Witch of the West was just spitting her usual caustic diatribe," I say, dipping a toe in the cool seawater. "I'm fine though. She's delusional. I kind of feel sorry for her."

I tell him it didn't go so well with Finn either. "He said

he still loves me, but he's full of it."

Isaac looks concerned and I try to reassure him.

"Don't worry, I'm over it," I say, and mean it.

CHAPTER 47

Before we know it, the crystal-clear day has turned into a clammy night and we're still talking on the beach. A curtain of stars has drawn over the blue; but dark stains of cloud are beginning to seep into the fabric of the sky and the intense heat promises a downpour later.

"We better go check into the hostel."

After a spit and a hiss and a *crunk* the little Micra clatters to a halt on a roundabout.

"Not good." Isaac bites his lip and ruffles his hair. "Erm, you may have to help push us to the side of the road."

After a lot of huffing and puffing – and *how much does this thing weigh?* – we manage to get the car to relative safety, hazard lights flashing into the night.

"How bad is it?"

"Clutch has gone. We're basically screwed. I'll call the AA."

"What can I do?"

"You could take the bags to the hostel. It's getting late and they might think we're not coming. It's not far, just on the corner over there, by the chippy."

"So near, yet so far!"

"I'll meet you in the club, if you don't mind hanging with Georgia for a while. Shouldn't be more than an hour."

I'm really starting to think Georgia's OK. She and Greg came to join us on the beach earlier and she admitted she didn't like the divide in the group. We actually have a lot in common. Her dad works away quite often; even though her parents have millions, it just makes him work harder to keep them. He puts money into start-ups and is very hands-on with his investments. I can sympathize with her about missing having him around.

I tell Isaac of course that's fine and I buy him some chips to keep him going, before heading to the hostel to get ready to go out.

I've just about finished doing my eyeliner when there's a knock on the door. Georgia's hair explodes in red tendrils from the top of her head like a mad octopus. She's wearing one of those mini top hats. She's a gentrified Mr Tickle.

"That's an interesting hair development since I saw you this afternoon."

"You likey?"

"Beautiful."

"Come on, let's go. It's only a fiver to get in before ten. Finn and the others have already left. You can stay with me and Greg, if you want to. Must be awkward."

"A little. Loads actually."

"Stick with me, Miss C."

* * *

The door to the club, curved in the brickwork, opens like a black hole. Like the wide, dark jaw of a crocodile, about to swallow me up. Georgia and I got to reminiscing about nights out on the way over here and I'd be lying if I said I don't have a pang of longing to do drugs, but it's quickly quashed. I never want to go back there again.

A female bouncer pads me down and checks through my bag. I pay a girl wearing a top that's too small for her and too brightly coloured for *anyone* and she stamps my hand with a smiley face.

It isn't long before a man sidles up to me, dressed in jeans and a T-shirt: just a normal bloke, but his eyes are wide and dart around the room. The green lasers bounce off his irises.

"Any pills? Tenner each. It's good stuff. A high like old-school pills. Lasts all night." He flashes me a baggie full of blue pills. "B2Ms. They're new."

"Betamax?"

"So new you could coin that as its street name... Look, I dropped one hours ago and I'm still rushing. They're well worth the cash."

"No thanks."

I check my phone, partly because I want to look busy so this guy goes away and partly because I'm willing it to buzz so I know Isaac will be here soon. But there are no new messages. Maybe I should have stayed with him.

The man gets the hint and leaves.

"There's Greg, crazy coke eyes at four o'clock." Georgia gestures a bangle-laden arm towards a makeshift bar under a hot-pink awning that says AUDIO FRICTION! ELECTRO AND BREAKS 10 P.M. – 7 A.M. EVERY FRIDAY @ FUNCT.

He's wide-eyed, wallet between his teeth, attempting to carry two beer bottles in each hand.

He acknowledges me with a nod and strides over, on a mission. Greg gives Georgia two bottles and takes the wallet from his mouth.

"Hey, baby." She greets him with a big lip smacker.

"Queue's fucking ridiculous. Got two beers each for us, but here you go." He hands me a bottle. "Thought you weren't coming."

"Changed my mind. Where's Slinky?" I ask.

"Dancing like a nutter. Some dude gave him something. ABCs or JCBs?"

"B2Ms?" I ask.

"Yeah, that's it. Fuck knows what they are but he's off his head and he only did half. Hope he doesn't do a Leah Betts."

"She drank too much water. It wasn't the E," Georgia interjects. "I've got some if you want – B2Ms."

Greg gulps from his bottle. "Not sure I want to do something I know nothing about," he says. "Could be bloody rat poison."

"The dealer wouldn't get many return customers if it was dodgy," Georgia says.

"True." He shrugs. "Carla, you want?"

"No, not doing it any more. Have you seen Isaac?"

"Not since this afternoon on the beach."

"Maybe I'll do a recce. Back in a minute," I say.

On the dance floor Finn is snogging Violet. It was going to happen sometime and although it makes my heart ache, it's not jealousy, it's over what we could have been. If he'd told the truth. If he'd been real. But it was all my own fantasy.

Violet breaks away from Finn and strides over, an expert stilt-walker on six-inch heels. I just know she's coming to rub it in.

"I told you Finn and I were solid."

"Whatever. Fine. I concede. Lucky you."

"Look, let's not argue. I actually… I wanted to apologize for, you know, being a bitch before. I was out of order," Violet says.

"You're apologizing to me? You must've had a skinful."

"Take it or leave it, I'm offering an olive branch here." She flicks her hair. "Let me buy you a drink."

"Um, thanks, I guess."

I'm wary of this new Violet, but perhaps now she's snagged her man she's got no reason to be pissed at me. And I could do with an easy life next year at school, so I let her do what she's got to do. At the bar she gets me a beer.

"No hard feelings, OK?" she says.

"Sure. Thanks."

"Cheers!" she says, and we clink bottles and drink.

I don't mean them to, but my eyes wander the room, the sea of people, searching for a lifeboat. I don't want to be left alone with Violet, even if she has turned a leaf.

"Do you want to come dance?" she asks. With her and Finn? *Is she totally mental?*

I can hardly say no since I'm Billy No Mates… But luck shines upon me and Georgia sidles up, and let me tell you, I've never been happier to see anyone in my life, *ever.*

"Hey. Eyeliner emergency. Need your expert drawing arm," she says.

"OK."

I follow Georgia to the toilets, where Greg's waiting.

"Your eyes look fine," I say.

"I know. Cheeky line time," she says.

I definitely *won't* be partaking though.

We pile into the cubicle, Georgia and Greg making more noise trying to shush each other than we would if we were carrying on a normal conversation. Boundaries, limits, the concept of volume, time and morality all disappear when you're wasted. So, loud as you like, we're bashing about in the cubicle like marbles in a pinball machine.

"Oi!" booms a voice. A fist thumps, rattling the door hinges. "Oi! One at a time."

Bash, bash, bash…

"Shit." Greg frantically tries to push the powder back into the baggie with his bank card. "Shh*iiii*t!"

Another aggressive shout resonates. "Open up. Now."

Bash, bash, bash…

Georgia and I exchange petrified glances, then hear laughter.

"It's only me, numbnuts. Open the door," the voice says.

"It's Slinky. Fucking hell." Georgia unbolts the door and lets him squash in, compressing us to sardines.

"Fuck's sake, Slinky," Greg says. "You scared the life out of me. What if I'd flushed the lot?"

"Ssshhhh! Someone will hear," Georgia and I warn in unison.

"You having a good night?" Greg asks Slinky.

"Fan-bloody-tastic. I dropped half a pill and I'm bouncing off the walls. You all look like angels. You girls are utterly, totally, completely one-hundred-per-cent *gorgeous*. Have I told you that before?"

"Good work, Slink," Greg says. "What about me?" he jokes.

"You, son, are a prince among men. The best of men."

"Was it a pill you had, or magic beans?"

"Who the hell cares? I'm high as a kite."

Greg's licking the coke from the edge of his bank card. He turns to me.

"Are you medicine or medic-out?" he asks.

"Out."

"Ooh, laa-de-dah. Miss Sensible."

"That's me."

Back on the dance floor, I feel a sudden rush, a jolt like a stalling car. *Vrrooom. Thud. Restart.* Cruise along at a new fast pace, straight down the motorway approaching ninety, rapidly gaining speed.

"Whoa. Something's wrong," I say, gripping Georgia's arm. Everything's spinning. Chemicals go BOOM ALERT AWAKE in my body, my brain, my jaw. *But I haven't done any drugs.*

I start to shake. My heart thuds in my ears, Grand National gallop.

"I need to get out of here," I say, tugging on a tassel of Georgia's oh-so-vintage Twenties red-fringed flapper dress.

"She OK?" Greg asks.

"Not sure. I'll take her outside. Find Isaac."

Leaving Greg and Slinky to swim in the sea of wreck-heads, we go to the smoking area. Georgia kicks the fag butts aside and we sit on the ground, backs against the wall, careful to avoid patches of sticky spilled beer. Georgia lights a Marlboro, staining the butt with her ra-ra rouge lipstick. Even though I've quit, the urge to smoke is overwhelming, so I ask Georgia for one. Hands trembling, I try to light it but I keep missing. She does it for me.

I taste the tinniness of blood on my tongue, mingling with smoke and beer. *I'm grinding my teeth* … biting the inside of my cheeks, shredding my lip. *Stop it. Please stop it.* Sick and panic rise.

"You don't look so hot. What have you taken?" asks Georgia.

"Nothing. I haven't done any."

"Mate, you're chewing your face off. You must have dropped something." A burly bouncer heads our way, ready to cattle-prod us inside, or worse, kick us out. "Better go back."

Stumbling back in, the people around and in front of me seem to move in slow motion. I see a boy moving faster than everyone, a blur sliding past. He slows from a wave of colour and solidifies in to a recognizable human shape.

"Carla?" Isaac says, pulling me to the edge of the corridor and whipping me around to face him, his hands gripping my shoulders. "You all right?" he asks, his eyes two dark bullets fired from a double-barrelled stare.

"She's wrecked, mate." Georgia pats Isaac on the arm and heads back in. "Stay with her. I'll get some water."

"I'll take her to the toilets," Isaac says.

In the cubicle, he fiddles with my belt loop, twisting it around his fingers. I grab him by the waist. His eyes gleam in the bright artificial light. Isaac looks at me, confused, and shakes his head.

"You took something," he says. "Your pupils are massive."

"I didn't, I swear. I don't know what's happening."

What the fuck is happeningwhatthefuckishappeningingingi...

"I was right from the start. Finn's still managed to mess you up. God! I would've taken care of you." In that moment I see him give up on me. My stomach freefalls. Isaac slams his fist on the door, angry like he was with Finn at the start of Georgia's birthday party. Fuming like he was at school.

"I swear ... I don't ... can't..." It's difficult to concentrate. My thoughts are disjointed, angular. I don't know how else to describe it. In my head I see adrenalin release, like an explanatory film on a biology programme, like the "here comes the science" bit on a shampoo ad, or the close-up of a bullet-into-brain on *CSI*. In my body I feel the rushes. Fight or flight.

He stares at me, eyebrows raised and patronizing, his tongue shooting daggers. I don't dodge them, I swallow them like a circus performer. *I don't want to fight.*

"What have you done?" he asks.

"Nothing! You said you wouldn't leave me!"

"The car broke down. You were *with me.* I had to get it fixed."

"I don't remember."

"Took longer than I thought. I texted you to say I was

late… Probably no signal in here." He swallows, his Adam's apple bobbing. Rubs his forehead. "I leave you with them for five minutes and you go and do this. You promised you were off it. You lied to me. You're just as bad as Finn. You two deserve each other."

Isaac's face screws up and I can see hurt in his eyes and I want to cry out that he's the one I want and that I didn't touch any drugs but I can't get my mouth to move because I feel so wrecked and sick and confused and I snap into another personality, into the girl I wanted to be way back when I started at Thorncroft. I can't help it. *The drugs are taking over.* They're running the show now, whether I like it or not.

"Come on, let's go. You're wasted. You must've been dropping pills like the fucking cookie monster."

"I'm a monster, raaa! Raaa! You know what? I'm a fucking tiger! I'm a tiger! I'm Finn's tiger. Raaa!"

"I'm taking you home."

"No!" I scream. "Not with you!" My face contorts. I throw my bottle to the wall. It smashes. Beer glugs onto the floor. I wish it were me crashing against that concrete and my head shattering into a million little pieces.

"I can't deal with this." Isaac waves me away. "You totally lied to me," he says, his temper well and truly frayed.

I slide down the wall, to the gross, tacky floor of the cubicle, my head in my hands. He steps over my legs, unbolts the door and leaves.

"Sort it out, Carla!" he spits, and lets the door slam back on its hinges.

* * *

I seal myself in, unzip my bag and take out my eyeliner.

On the cubicle wall I draw pictures of Finn, Isaac's face, Greg's hand – all those contours lit up like a map and the *X* – the pill on it, waiting for me to find it and change into the confident girl.

I try to tidy myself up. I wipe the black from around my eyes and try to smile into my compact mirror, but I look like a china doll, pale, dead. My face, a moment of *déjà vu* that I'm familiar with, fades to non-existence in the same instance. *Who are you?*

I recognize hints of emotions, flickers of smiles, remnants of lust and anger and joy and excitement, but they vanish, evaporating like water in heat. I try and draw it on the wall. I sketch outlines of my features, unable to fill them in.

I've caught myself drawing on the wall with crayons…

I pack up and swim through the crowds towards the exit. It's getting light. I exit the sweaty box without saying goodbye, just leave through the mouth of the crocodile and walk to the pier. I sit, hugging my knees for warmth. *What's happened to me?*

I let my legs swing to and fro over the edge.

I take my results letter from my back pocket.

Now seems as good a time as any. I rip open the envelope and unfold the paper. It's hard to focus my eyes on the jumble of letters and numbers, but I manage it with great effort.

Art – A
Biology – U

Chemistry – E
English Literature – C
Psychology – U

I feel a hand on my shoulder.
As I lift my head I see him.

CHAPTER 48

"Fuck me, it's cold."

Finn looks at his watch, then pulls the sleeves of his hoodie over his hands, clasping them in place with his thumbs, forming fists. The birds tell us it's morning. Daylight is beginning to draw the shapes of the big wheel, the rollercoaster, the carousel. The water is shaded in, waves edged with silver highlights. The roads are pencilled in, rough lines sketched by the dusky light. The street begins to animate again.

"You OK?"

He waves, his hands like dancing puppets against a backdrop of painted sky. The sunrise is a wash of inky colour, intensifying rapidly with the haste of day, but gunmetal clouds are gathering.

"Hello? Carla?"

Finn unwraps his fingers and knots them with mine. "You're freezing."

"It was her. She spiked me."

He sits down on the bridge, his legs dangling over the

edge. He's smoking. A silhouetted chimney. He leans in and I feel a cold shiver as his breath tickles my ear.

"You'll never be able to prove it."

"Time to let go," I whisper. I close my eyes. When I open them again, he's gone. Back to the party.

Adjusting my chemically widened pupils to the daylight I wonder if my mind's been playing tricks. Have I made the last year up? Have I been playing games with myself because I've been so mind-fuckingly desperate to be noticed … so desperate for love? Was my Brainy Plain Girl invisibility *so* painful that this, *this* semi-crazed confusion was better?

The streetlights click off and another day begins.

But not for me.

I stare up at the sky with its brewing clouds. I see the drop. The first drop of the rainfall. I see it linger for a second on the edge of the world, and then fall, fall, fall to meet me. Dark crushes in on every side. Blackness shrinks my vision to a pinpoint of light, a single drop, and the world ends.

CHAPTER 49

I'm floating in black nothing.

Am I dead? No, if I'm thinking, I can't be. Am I dreaming?

Out of nothing comes *something.*

A man.

Colours seep in, an unfinished sketch.

A desk.

I know what to say.

I ask him if he thinks I'm crazy. He asks me, "Do *you* think you're crazy?" Instinctively I assume that no, I'm not. But I'm here, after all. By force or not, something brought me here, to this room, to this point in time where everything converges to a single point. At this moment, I'm being urged to describe in no small detail every relevant and irrelevant moment of my existence thus far. All there is in the universe is this room where I have to explain myself. And the only words I can summon are not my own, but the ravings of some lunatic I've morphed into, and all I can think about is where I can get an impressive *chaise longue* for my room like this one I'm lying on.

I feel powerfully unknown.

So today, who shall I be for the doctor? Shall I be a tree, a goat, a burlesque dancer, a cabbie, a sock? The invisible girl? *Someone?* Shall I tell him about the brothers? The butterflies? The sodium?

"Are you unhappy?" he throws at me.

"No, I'm happy."

"Are you happy because you're happy, or happy because the stereotype says you should be?"

"What stereotype is that?"

"Young, healthy, able to feed and clothe yourself, a warm bed to sleep in at night." *Dull, dull, dull.*

"I'm not too pleased about some things."

"So you're unhappy."

"No. Yes. About some things."

"What things make you feel this way?" Now, the ceiling begins to crack, splitting from cornice to cornice and widening like clamped ribs, prepped for surgery. Snow begins to fall through the gap, pouring in and settling gently on the oversized, file-scattered desk, the worn green leather chair and the couch where I'm lying. I have a good view from here. I extend my tongue to catch a flake, but it doesn't taste like snow. It's salt dusting this room. Sodium.

"Don't ask me that..."

"Shall we explore this further?" His voice booms louder.

"Am I dead? Am I dreaming? Am I crazy?"

"Shall we explore this further? Hmmm?" Again and again, louder and louder. He looks over his half-moon glasses and stares, wide-eyed and menacing. "Shall we explore this further? Shall we explore this further? Shall we explore this further?"

"Answer me!" I yell.

I cry into the steady streams of white flakes. And then they come. Drawn to the salt. "Oh no," the psychiatrist continues, "now this is not good, no, no indeed, very interesting, very interesting…" He starts to scribble intently in his notepad. He shakes his head, tuts and continues to mutter to himself. I can no longer hear what he's saying and I no longer care. The butterflies swoop and dart and scratch, so many that collectively they are able to lift me, twirl me. *So many butterflies.* They've got me.

I'm not scared.

I'm not scared.

I'm not scared.

They drop me.

Am I really schizing out?

Then nothing. Darkness snares me again. Loneliness hooks me.

Whirr

Flutter

Whirr

Flutter

Gently, gracefully, a butterfly floats down and comes to rest on my stomach. The Queen of the Butterflies. The largest in the world, a wingspan of thirty centimetres. Green and yellow and red, she's magnificent. She's *perfect.* I can hear her in my head. I'm Doctor fucking Dolittle.

"My God, Carla. Look at you," she says. I try to speak but no sound comes out. I'm paralyzed. "What have you done to yourself?"

An Adonis Blue, with brilliant sapphire wings, flies in from the darkness, swooping and darting before landing on my hand. "Carla, can you hear me? Squeeze my hand if you can hear me."

I can't. I want to but I can't.

"I'm going to get a coffee."

The Adonis Blue flies out of sight.

I hear crying.

"It's Mum. Can you hear me?"

I can hear you, I say in my head, the words unable to escape to the audible world.

"I'm sorry. Look at you." The butterfly tickles my forehead. "I'm so sorry."

It's OK, Mum. The words echo, unreleased.

"I've really screwed things up for you."

No, I screwed things up for me.

"I failed Biology," I croak. "And Psychology."

"Oh, Carla. Thank God." She wraps her arms around me. I can hardly move; my eyes feel full of sand. I try to open them. Through the blur I see Mum, a smudge of pale pink and brown, her diamond earrings white and twinkling.

"She's awake. Nurse! She's awake!" she calls.

CHAPTER 50

Time is ticking again. Hour follows hour. Minute follows minute. Thought follows thought. My thoughts are no longer crazy. I'm not drugged-up, I'm just me. No DVD extras.

I walk to Bus Stop E. Tower blocks gaze lazily at the September sun. Sugary golden rays, like fingertips, massage their concrete skin. He's waiting for me. He's early. I feel a pang of excitement. Not an epic drum solo, more a short sharp tap on the snare. It's life-piercing. I haven't seen him since I came out of hospital.

He's dressed in jeans and a T-shirt that says, *I quite like music.* His hair flaps like a black flag, an unintentional Eighties throw-back.

"Loving the George Michael Wham-era look," I say.

"Accidental, I promise." He hugs me tight.

I wave my hand and the red bus crawls to a halt. We climb to the top deck.

The trees zoom past. They're about to start losing their leaves. The houses rush past, and then the skyscrapers.

Twenty silent minutes go by, not a peep from either of

us. Nothing said, but so much hanging there between us.

Stop. Stop. Stop. Fourth stop. A hand grasps the yellow pole at the top of the stairs and pulls a cracked face and weathered body upwards. She's wearing a poncho and a fishing hat. The hands, though, are what fascinate me. Not because I like to draw hands, or because her nails are long and bright red with paint, which they are, but because they are wrapped in those cloudy, thin plastic bags used for packing loose fruit and veg at the supermarket. Carrots. Mushrooms. Auber-fucking-gines.

If it's a plastic fetish, surely she could get some Marigolds? Penchant for gloves, sweaty hands? Old lady bag hands: she's a fruitcake. I could have been her. That might have been my future.

"Look, I'm—" I begin to say to Isaac.

"Don't say anything." He looks me in the eye. "Not yet. Let's just enjoy the ride."

This is becoming one ride I want to stay on.

At Trafalgar Square, we jump off the bus, heading for the gallery on Pall Mall, but Isaac stops when we get to the steps just past the fountain on the Square. He sits me down on a step and kneels in front of me. "Bit soon for proposals," I say, remembering when he gave me the butterfly necklace.

"I thought you were going to do a Heath Ledger on me," he says.

"I didn't mean to… It wasn't intentional or anything."

Isaac furrows his brow, and then relaxes into a smile.

"Textbook cry for help! You do Psychology!"

"Yes, I *do* Psychology. Note that? I failed and so I still *do* Psychology. I'm resitting in January."

"If only you'd known you were going to go loco. Would've made a great coursework topic."

"This has all been an elaborate AS-level Psychology experiment. Didn't you know?" I joke. "You know I didn't do it. Violet crushed a load of those blue pills into my drink."

I think about all that's gone on, and wonder if it wasn't the first time I'd been set up...

"I know. I'm sorry about the stuff I said. I was really harsh on you. I flipped. I should've trusted you," Isaac says.

"I'm sorry, too. I said some weird stuff when I was out of it."

"I'm just... It's good to see you... I'm glad you're all right."

"So am I."

"How are you feeling?"

"Inside out. But on the mend. I'm seeing someone, a counsellor. Thought it might help."

"That's great. Good idea."

"Oh, no, I don't mean seeing him professionally. He's just great in bed."

"Oh, yeah?" He smiles.

"I'm kidding." I shrug. But he already knew that.

"Want to share some uberly overpriced but totally delicious brownie?"

"Yeah. I really do."

We amble to the gallery, the red-brick building among all the white stone, and inside, Boogie-Barnet greets us with that practised smile. Isaac doesn't reach for my hand, but somehow, knowing he's only a few inches away is more exciting, and holding back is … right, for now.

We do one of those unnecessarily slow gallery walks, stopping at each piece and pretending to look interested.

"So, what do you want to be when you grow up?" Isaac asks.

"Oh, druggie, whore, general trashbag, the usual," I reply.

"Excellent career opportunities there."

"Yeah, I thought so. That, or plumbing. I hear women plumbers make a mint." We pause to muse on a sculpture of a stuffed mouse moving electronically around a maze. I roll my eyes.

"I think you should stick to what you know. You could be the next great artist. All you need is some flaming paper plates, right? A dirty glass or two?"

"It's not art! But thanks. You can be my muse. I'll be a regular little Edie Sedgwick, Mr Warhol. Or would that make you Sedgwick?"

A familiar figure approaches.

"What's he doing here?" I ask.

Havelock, in his brown shoes, jeans and a red-and-white chequered shirt, glides over, propelled by his own calm breeze, one smooth continuous movement. He blows a dark lock of hair out of his eyes.

"Hello," he says.

"Um, hi."

"What are yo—?"

"Have you seen the gallery guide?"

"No, missed them at the door."

He hands me a glossy brochure. "Have a look."

Flicking the pages, I scan the text.

Ohmygod. Bottom of page 2. *Me.*

Special congratulations to Carla Carroll, who is this year's recipient of the Maggie Penn Art Prize and receives funding for an art course of her choice and £250 towards materials.

"How did…? When did this happen? Did you do this?" I scan Havelock's face for answers.

"I can't take credit, I'm afraid. It was Mr Masterson here. He told me you'd agreed to let him collect your sculpture, and I let him have it. He called me yesterday and told me he'd entered it in this competition and now here we are. Carla Carroll, prizewinner."

Isaac's grinning cheekily.

"Why didn't you tell me?"

"You said you weren't interested in submitting. I thought you could win. What was the harm?"

"No, it's great, thank you. But … I just can't believe I *won*."

"I told you, you have talent." The corners of Havelock's mouth turn upwards. "You're good at this, Carla. Why not pursue it? You have the skills. Now you've got the tools."

"Yeah, maybe."

"Retakes in January, though." He snaps back into teacher mode.

"I know," I say, nodding.

Havelock raises his eyebrows in a distinctly dad-like fashion, then turns to continue walking around the exhibition.

"Shall we go bask in the glory of your success?" Isaac asks. "It's on display. Prime position, on a very fetching plinth … next to some flaming paper plates."

"Are you joking?"

"Yeah, about the plates anyway."

"You mean the sculpture is here? In public? For people to see?"

"Yeah, you're practically famous."

We walk to the opposite end of the gallery, and there she is, glinting in a shaft of gold under a skylight: MY BUTTERFLY!

I look to Isaac, his floppy hair and face full of sincerity, and realize it's been the same face all along, not always the arc of a smile upon it, but always the truth. I hug him, moist-eyed and lost for words.

Last year might have been a thousand years or one short second. Like taking that first pill, it was over so quickly. Misjudgements strew the months like litter on a festival field. But for the pain, I wonder if it ever happened at all. I entered some inky-lit club, got lost in the dark and emerged at sunrise. I thought I lost my soul that night in Brighton, but it seems that's when I got it back. Like getting laid for the first time, it's never how you picture it. They say the darkest hour is just before the dawn. I feel myself returning to reality, a new reality. Soft edges are sharpening; light is intensifying. Daybreak.

I'm not naive. I'm going to need help and it'll take time. Do I even have the strength and determination? I don't know. But I've made a start and I'm making changes.

Smoke less.

Draw more.

Pass retakes.

Take one step at a time.

I look back over the year and see my own metamorphosis. Back then I was desperate to fit in. I trusted the drugs and Finn to give me confidence to remodel myself. *Not your most intelligent decision.*

What if I was already a butterfly?

Maybe I just couldn't see it.

But Isaac saw it from the beginning.

I twist the purple butterfly necklace between my fingers and smile.

I cartwheel across the park, turning my world upside down: a complete revolution.

Somehow, after all, I've landed on my feet.

ACKNOWLEDGEMENTS

There's no word big enough to express the thanks I owe my editor, Mara Bergman, for glimpsing potential in my writing and helping me at every stage to unlock it; and my agent, Jo Unwin, for all her hard work and unwavering encouragement.

I'm so grateful to Maria Soler Cantón for the stunning cover design, and to all the other lovely folks at Walker Books.

Juliet Foster, you always believed in me: thank you for convincing me to show my first draft to Mara. *Kuliet for ever!*, even when we're old.

To my mum, Lynda, who caught me when I was falling; my dad, Roger, ever the calm at the eye of the storm; and my enormous family, for hugs, dinners, cheerleading and general awesomeness – thank you.

And finally, to my wonderful Sean... I promise to thank you in the next book too if you throw out that jumper I hate. The material's scratchy and it's a horrible colour.